Micah

THE BRASH BROTHERS BOOK TWO

JENNA MYLES

THE BRASH BROTHERS
READING ORDER

Book 1: Kade
Book 2: Micah
Book 3: Colton
Book 4: Declan
Book 5: Zach
Book 6: Jonas

More to come!

So many thanks to
Joanne, Tammy, Chloe, Melissa
The absolute best alpha readers an
author could hope for.

AUTHORS NOTE

This story's heroine has lived through severe domestic violence. This book includes many triggers, including pregnancy loss, violence, sexual violence. All of the violence happens before this book, but she as she processes she will share details of what happened to her.

My characters make prolific use of swears, and there is graphic representation of sex. If this isn't your cup of tea, then RUN!

Our hero, Micah, suffers from Asphasia. I have taken some liberties with the depiction of this disorder. He uses both speech and American Sign Language. You will notice some paragraphs that he will speak and then continue in ASL, indicated by italics within the quotation marks. It will look like this: "Nope," he mutters, *I don't want anything to do with it.*"

If you spot any typos, or want to reach out to me for any other reason, please email me: jenna@authorjennamyles.com

PROLOGUE
HOLLY

Sometimes I think the day I met Becca is the day I became the new me. Or at least started the process.

Before walking into her self-defense class, I lived in a perpetual state of fear. It was with me when I woke up in the morning, while I brushed my teeth, while I rode the bus to my job, and even when I crawled into bed at night. Looking around corners, scanning crowds, checking behind me every few seconds...it was exhausting, both mentally and physically. It wasn't just fear of him finding me, but fear of the unknown.

After seven years in an abusive marriage, I didn't know how to decide for myself anymore. A trip to the grocery store would be simple for most people.

Not for me.

First was the checking and rechecking of my door to make sure it's locked, then putting a tiny piece of tape at the bottom, so I could see if someone was in my apartment while I was gone. Then the walk to the bus, searching for signs of someone following me, while trying to avoid eye contact with every man I pass. Then the bus ride, trying desperately to get a seat at the back so I could see what was coming.

The grocery store itself was a whole other set of problems. Do I buy the brand of spaghetti sauce my husband likes? Because that was all that mattered in the past, that *he* liked it. My taste, my preferences, my wants, were irrelevant to him. I didn't even know what I liked anymore, so when I finally got out of the shelter and into my own place, I stuck with what I knew.

I wore dark clothes, because he told me they were slimming, because God forbid anyone see I was fat. I ate the same food because it was easier than trying to learn what I liked. And at night I sat in fear in my cheap apartment, worrying about what would happen when he found me.

When, not if.

So when I overheard a girl at work talking about going to the class, my first thought was *no way*. But I couldn't get it out of my mind. It felt like something outside of me was pushing me to go, even though it was wildly outside of my comfort zone.

I stayed in my box. I didn't deviate.

Ever.

So why was I dressed in shabby workout clothes riding a bus towards the industrial area?

I stood outside for twenty minutes, talking myself into, and then out of, going in. But then a tall, strong, curvy, beautiful woman passed me, spinning to walk backwards. "You coming inside sunshine? I'm teaching self-defense tonight. I'll teach you how to make a grown man cry." She said with a bright smile and laughing eyes.

Yes. Yes, I am, I thought. But I only nodded and followed that magnetic woman inside. During that class, I fell a little bit in love. She seemed to focus on me, and I swear I felt bigger than five-foot-one in her presence, like her energy and confidence seeped into me. She treated me so kindly, and cheered me on so loudly, that I collapsed in my bed that night and sobbed.

Sobbed, because for the first time, I felt like someone truly saw me. She knew, somehow, how damaged I was, but she saw through that to me, to the person I didn't even know was inside. The person who yelled when she punched the bag, imagining it was Brent's face. The person who leaned forward each time Becca demonstrated a strike to the groin. Who mentally practiced that move the whole bus ride home.

Somehow, I was changed. On the outside, everything was the same. Brent was still out there looking for me. He wouldn't ever stop. I knew that for sure. But I didn't check the door as many times that morning. I didn't check behind me as often, and when my disgusting, handsy boss tried to corner me the next day, I didn't freeze. Those might be little things to other people, but to me, they felt monumental.

Somehow, in a matter of weeks, she became my best friend. And right after that, we were working together. She was leaving her job at a garage to work full time teaching martial arts and self-defense and needed someone to take over for her.

It felt...heaven sent.

I was so excited for my first day that I went to the thrift store and found a beautiful bright dress that made me feel lighter just looking at it. I didn't want to wear those dark clothes for my fresh start.

As Becca introduced me around, I kept reminding myself that this was my fresh start, and no way would Becca ever let anyone hurt me here. She had a 'low tolerance for bullshit' as she put it, and wouldn't tolerate working for men who were unkind or...other things. So I smiled, even if it was a little forced, and while I avoided shaking hands, no one seemed to mind.

Then she took me to meet Micah.

She'd warned me he didn't talk much. And so my smile felt less forced as we approached. He sounded like a kind, quiet, gentle soul. We would get along great.

He was crouched down next to a half restored car, and I felt my cheeks heat when our eyes met. His beautiful brown eyes widened, and something like appreciation swept over his face as he gazed at me.

"Hi...Woah." He breathed, making me blush and my smile widen. Something about him just drew me in, whether it was the kindness on his face or his obvious appreciation of me. Something made me put out my hand to shake his.

That's where everything went wrong.

He rose, reaching for my hand, and I startled. I could tell he was quite a powerful man from the width of his shoulders, but as he stood, the sheer size of him overwhelmed me. He must have been at least six-and-a-half feet tall. I backed up in my surprise, tripping on something behind me, and suddenly Micah was there, his arms wrapped around me.

I panicked, memories of Brent's restraining arms flashing through my brain.

I barely remember the next few minutes, other than Becca helping me calm down, and my quick apology to Micah. He was apologizing to me in sign, sorry he scared me. I do remember his surprise when he realized I understood ASL. I hoped I had smoothed my freak out over, and that we could pretend it never happened.

But instead, it seemed to have turned him against me. Every time he saw me, he would scowl, as if I'd personally offended him. It terrified me at first, then only scared me, and eventually it made me angry.

I loved everything about my new job. I loved how kind the guys in the garage were. I loved the customers. The only dark spot was Micah. A few times I felt like quitting, but that was the old me talking. The new me wasn't going to let this scowling man chase me away.

Then Brent found me.

Walking into that office, seeing Brent holding a knife on

Becca was one of the worst days of my life, and there had been a lot of bad ones.

As soon as I saw what was happening, I tried to go to him, hoping that he would just take me and go. That no one would be hurt because of me. But Micah pulled me behind him, seeming to not notice my efforts to get to Becca. Trapped behind his immense wall of muscle, I missed a lot of what happened, but I heard Brent screaming in a way that made the hairs on my arm stand up.

The pain in those screams made me so...happy.

Becca had completely overpowered my monster of a husband.

I was afraid that I would go back to that weak, cowering woman. The woman who couldn't stand up for herself. And some days, the guilt of bringing my problems into my friend's life was crippling.

But knowing that Brent was in jail, the easing of that worry was...transformational. And when he pled guilty, instead of fighting it like I was sure he would, it felt like a gift from God. A true chance to start my new life. So I promised myself I would work to be the new me. To stand up for myself.

Micah gave me more practice at that than I would like. His scowls and anger didn't seem to abate, though he wouldn't tolerate anyone else being mean to me. He scared more than one customer into apologizing to me for their bad temper. I don't know how he always knew I was dealing with someone difficult, but he did.

The first few times he stood up for me, I stood back and let him handle it. But when he blazed in one day, ready to intimidate the man in front of me arguing about the labor charge on his bill, I lost my cool.

From the stool I stand on at the front desk, I turned on him, waving my finger in his face. "Did I ask for your help, Micah?" Not waiting for a reply, I barrelled on. "I am fully capable of running this office and handling customer complaints." I pointed to the door into the garage bays. "Go back to your job, and let me do mine, thank you very much."

I let myself savor his wide eyes, and watched him turn away, so I didn't miss the glare he shot the customer. But I let it pass. Turning back to my now subdued customer, I asked him pleasantly. "Your bill is fair and final. How would you like to pay?"

It was honestly one of the best moments of my life. I felt in charge and ready to step into my new life.

Until the fire happened.

1

HOLLY

"Are you sure you don't want me to go in with you?" Becca's voice is so achingly kind, it brings tears to my eyes. I want her to come with me desperately. But it would only make things worse. The second Brent got a look at her, he would lose his mind. For a man like him, one who relishes his role as the breaker of bones, seeing the woman who broke his would send him over the edge. I reach over the console to grip her hand, holding tightly, drawing strength from her sure grip.

"Yes. I have to do this on my own. I have to face him, Becca."

"You really don't Holly. You don't have to do a damn thing. Your piece of shit husband doesn't deserve any more of your time." She's not even trying to disguise her disgust. If she ever knew how much that disgust hurts me, she would be horrified. That's why I don't let her see it. She's too good to be exposed to that illness.

Intellectually I get it. Nothing my husband has done, to me or anyone else, is my fault. The doctors told me that. So did the trauma counselors and the women at the shelter.

Some days I believe it.

But they don't know. They don't understand. The shame of what he did to me is so big. So overwhelming that intellect doesn't come into play. Sometimes it feels like every blow, every broken rib, every split lip spread his poison in me. It's there, through the skin, past the muscle, all the way to my bones.

It's melded to me. The sickness, so much a part of me I'll never be free of it. Somehow, knowing he tried to hurt Becca is worse than all the times he actually hurt me. I'm sure a therapist would have a field day with that, but there it is.

I grip the envelope in my right hand tighter, so tightly my knuckles turn white, then squeeze Becca's hand one more time before letting go. "Just wait here. Please." She studies me, looking for me to fall apart, I imagine, before grudgingly nodding her head, her reddish brown waves moving lightly.

I can't quite bring myself to actually get out of the car. My heart is racing, and I take a deep breath, consciously trying to control it. I focus on the tower in the corner of the yard, trying to figure how many feet from the ground to the guard at the top. He's wearing dark aviators, his uniform snug and unwrinkled. His arms seem relaxed, holding that big gun, but I can tell that he's aware of everything around him. His head constantly sweeping the yard below him. The gun looks like one Brent owned. My hands start to shake, remembering the way he would pull his guns out and clean them in front of me, telling me how big a hole each one could blow in me.

"Holly," the soft voice sounds like it's coming from the other end of a tunnel. "Holly. Breathe, honey. You're ok. Everything is ok. You're safe. Breathe with me."

I don't have enough air to feel embarrassed at how often she's had to do this for me. Help me breathe. I'm too busy being grateful she's here. I follow her instructions; she's the only thing real right now. In. Out. In. Out. The pattern of it is soothing. Something to hold on to as I wait for the black spots dancing in front of my eyes to recede. Thank God for her. Thank God.

"You got it Hol." Her hand is back on mine, stroking my knuckles. I focus on her kind touch, soaking it in the way parched, dry ground soaks up the rain. How is it that such a gentle caress is still painful? Still makes my nerves hum and twitch? It's like I've been so conditioned to pain that all touch hurts.

I sit, soaking in her comfort, until I've pulled myself together. Becca's ocean blue eyes are steady. That's the only reason I can look at her. So many people have looked at me with pity or morbid curiosity. But not her. Never her. She somehow always makes me feel like she's in the trenches with me. Ready and waiting to help me climb out. I've never had that before. From anyone. Someone who looked at me and saw me as capable, as whole.

"I'm sorry," I murmur, knowing she won't like the apology, but unable to not apologize. Apologizing is what I do. It's what I was trained to do. Sorry you bumped into me. Sorry for not making the right dinner. Sorry for getting fat. Sorry for making you beat me. Sorry, sorry, sorry.

As expected, Becca blows a raspberry in my direction, not caring that she's spitting all over her car. Despite how anxious I am, I can't help but giggle at her.

"You keep apologizing to me and I'll...pinch you in the tit." She nods, satisfied with her plan. It's a little weird that the woman teaching me to protect myself is also threatening bodily harm, but I shake my head and chalk it up to all the weird that is Becca. I wouldn't want to change her, not even a little bit. "Holly...you know there's no way he can touch you in here, right? Kade and Ransom made sure of it. He'll be chained to the table. And remember, you can definitely outrun him!"

The giggle snort explodes from my body, and she joins me. We have a tendency to dissolve into a giggle snort spiral, so I try to compose myself. But she's right. Considering she absolutely shattered his knee a couple of months ago, I can definitely outrun him.

A sick satisfaction comes over me at that idea. I like that he's hurt. That she caused him pain. And I'm jealous that she did it so easily. I spent seven years in that hellish marriage, and nearly two hiding from him. And somehow, in a matter of minutes, Becca had him shattered and bleeding on the floor.

I push away my bitterness, knowing it has no place here with my friend. My best friend since Robyn. Evie came close, but my lies, my hiding, kept us from ever truly knowing each other. But in the end, when it truly mattered, she was there for me. The thought of the strong women who've helped me get here today puts some steel into my spine. I take one last deep breath, pull away from Becca, and exit the car.

The landscaping around the front of the building is colorful, a riot of flowers and bushes. It somehow seems out of place against the barbed wire fences and armed guards beyond it. I wonder if the prisoners take care of it? Maybe there's a prison equivalent of a garden club?

Imagining a group of hardened men discussing flowers and soil conditions gets me through security and the pat down without freaking out, but it's not enough to distract me when they lead Brent into the room.

He's complaining as he's wheeled into the room, his arm and leg in heavy plaster casts. He's wearing a dull beige uniform, the waistband of the pants rolled at his waist. They must have had to give him a large pair to fit over the cast, and it makes him look like a kid wearing his older brother's hand-me-downs. His normally tanned skin is sallow, his hair thin and oily. The strong controlling man I lived with is diminished, made smaller somehow.

The guard handcuffs his good hand to the table, then settles against the wall as requested. I'm grateful again that

Kade and his friend Ransom butted in and arranged everything with the prison. I never want to be in a room alone with Brent again.

Never.

He shifts uncomfortably in the chair as his eyes travel around the room, widening as they land on me tucked in the corner. I could have sat down when they brought me in, but the instinct to protect my back was too strong. I needed this safe corner to settle myself while I waited.

Brent's mouth curls up in a sneer. "Well, if it isn't my fat little wife." He snickers, running his eyes up and down my body. I hold in the shudder and settle my features into an aloof mask, determined not to let him see how much his presence affects me. "You've been hitting the wagon wheels pretty hard, haven't you, Hannah? Humm?"

Somehow, the familiarity of this put down grounds me. I don't correct him when he calls me Hannah. That's who I'll always be to him. I don't want his lips touching my new name. The one I picked after I ran.

Somehow, the put down hurts less when he's calling me by my old name. As soon as I started putting on weight, it became his favorite thing to criticize about me. I used to give him the satisfaction of cringing or crying when he did it, but this time, I smile.

He never caught on when I put on a show.

I didn't do it on purpose, at first. I started eating because I was isolated and bored. Brent made me quit school, and other than volunteering at the hospital and grocery shopping, I wasn't allowed to leave the house. So food became a big focus in my life.

But the weight saved me in two ways. First it redirected Brent's vitriol from how stupid and useless I am. Somehow, having him criticize my body was easier to take than having him pick away at my intelligence, at the core of who I am. It also had the benefit of cushioning me from his fists. Sure, it still hurt, but the bone deep bruises that lasted for a month happened less often. So I let him think he hurt me worse than he did. I love that layer of fat. I love how it protects me. I'm not sure I'll ever give it up.

Brent's face twitches in confusion, his smirk slowly falling off his face. His eyes shift between me and the guard. I have to laugh again. He wanted me to cry and cower. To make himself look like the big man in front of the guard. But he's going to have to try harder than that.

He will.

And he'll hit the bullseye before I leave this room, I'm sure of it. But for now, I'll pretend I'm in control.

"Brent," I say as I walk slowly towards him, "sign these." I take the papers out of the envelope, tossing them onto the table in front of him.

I don't sit. No way will I get that close to him. I kinda like standing here, forcing him to look up at me. It makes me feel…not powerful, but a little less like his victim. He scowls and uses one finger to push the papers around on the table.

"What the fuck is this?"

I raise my eyebrow at his outrage. "Did you really think I'd stay married to you?" He had to know this was coming. By some miracle, he pleaded guilty to all of his charges, and he's going to be in here a good long time. I don't have to go through the trauma of a trial. I can finally be free of him. And in twenty years when he gets out? Well, I have to hope that I'm strong enough to protect myself by then.

"You stupid cunt. No fucking way am I signing those papers. You fucking made vows, bitch. Till death, remember?" His words lash at me, the spit flying with his angry words. I swallow and take a few more breaths.

"Yes Brent. I remember. You promised to love and protect me. Turns out you were the thing I needed protection from. No way does God expect me to stay married to you." I'm proud of how level my voice is. My heart's pounding like I'm running a sprint, but he can't tell. "Sign the papers."

"No fucking way. I will sign those over my dead fucking body." His face is flushed red, the vein over his eye throbbing. I take a step back despite myself, and a sick smile comes over his face. He's satisfied he scared me. He thinks he has the upper hand.

"Hannah. Stupid fat pathetic Hannah. You can't get away from me. You're nothing without me. You know your place, wife. You're my little cum bucket. And I can't wait to make you scream under me again. You'll see Hannah. I'll be out of this fucking place before you know it."

I swallow hard against the bile rising in my throat, and widen my eyes to dry the moisture there. I can't bear to let him see how much his words sicken me. How the flashbacks and memories of screaming and begging him to stop are clouding my mind.

I wish I hadn't worn heels. I thought they would make me seem more confident facing him, but instead I'm wobbly. I lock my knees and twine my fingers behind my back.

"Sign them or don't. I'm done with you." I let my eyes travel his body, before finally locking on his. I let him see it then. How much he disgusts me. And I should win an academy award for the show I put on then, as I say the words I've practiced for days. "Maybe you can find yourself a boyfriend in here. I'm sure you'll make a lovely bottom."

I smile, then spin on my heels and press the button to exit, leaving him without a backward glance. His curses and screaming only stopped by the heavy metal door. I push back through security, then I have to press my hand to my mouth to hold in the vomit as I slam into the bathroom down the hall and into a stall. I fall to my knees in front of the toilet, heaving and crying.

The heaving continues for several minutes after I empty my stomach. My body is completely out of control, and I have to grip the sides of the toilet to ground myself. My throat and nose are stinging, my eyes aching. My entire face is wet.

Thank God no one else is in here.

I use some toilet paper to wipe little spots of vomit off the seat, then flush and make my way on shaky legs to the sink to rinse my face and mouth. I avoid looking at my reflection, not wanting to know what I look like right now. I can pretend everything's ok, as long as I don't look. I pull out the travel sized toothbrush and toothpaste from the little side pocket of my purse, grateful I remembered to bring them, and scrub away the taste of bile.

Finally, when I stop shaking, when my breathing evens out, I look. There are red splotches, burst blood vessels, around my left eye, stark against the blue of my iris. Huh. I haven't seen that since I lived with Brent. Though this is the first time it's ever happened from puking. I smooth down my blonde waves and pull my sunglasses out of my purse, sliding them on my face before heading out to Becca's old car.

We sit side by side in silence, before she finally asks quietly. "Are you ok?" I think about lying. I could put on another act, tell her I'm good, and convince her to drop me at home. But I just can't. I can't go home to the silence, the memories his words brought up.

"No," I tell her. "I'm really not." She nods, reaching over to squeeze my arm. Her crappy car starts with a purr, the benefits of living with a billionaire mechanic I guess, and we hit the highway back to the city.

"Kade and Micah are waiting for us. I think they're going to cook." She laughs and glances over at me. "It should be a shit show." I smile, because she's right. From what I can tell, neither of them are capable of making anything edible.

I ignore the flutter of nervousness in my stomach, knowing Micah is there. I'm not sure I can handle his glaring eyes today. But the alternative? Today, I'll take his anger over the silence of my apartment.

2

MICAH

"Kade...fire." I say, pointing to the flames licking up the side of the BBQ. We just spent the last hour putting the fucking thing together. And did he buy the small one? No, he bought the 300 pound six-burner Cadillac of BBQs. Carting that beast up here was no fucking joke.

I laugh as he bolts through the open patio doors, slapping at the dials on the front and cursing. The fucks are flying fast and furious from his mouth. We all swear, but he's the worst of us by far. To be fair, if I could speak more than a few words at a time, I'd probably swear just as much. But when I have to struggle just to get the few words I do say out? Well, wasting them on fuck seems stupid. When I sign though? I can swear with the best of them.

I grab a beer from the fridge, then wander towards the patio, dodging Becca's shoes as I step out. The dumbfuck is still playing with the knobs so the flames are shooting higher. I shake my head and lean down to turn off the gas valve on the wall. Kade's swearing runs out of steam, and I join him, staring at the charred steaks on the grill. I slap him on the arm to get his attention.

"Way to go, genius, you burned it. Why did you think you could cook?" I sign.

He shoves his hands through his hair, gripping the back of his neck. "I don't fucking know, man. I watched that fucking cooking guy. You know, the one with the fucking mouth on him?" I laugh, knowing exactly which chef he's talking about. Of course, Kade would watch that guy.

"And you thought that a fucking video was going to turn you into a chef?"

"Fuck you, man. You could have helped!"

I raise my eyebrows. *"Really? What exactly did you think I could do? You've known me my whole life. When was the last time I cooked a fucking steak?"*

Kade groans and pokes at the steak with his shiny new BBQ fork. "I thought it would be easier." He runs all of our garages without breaking a sweat, but somehow this is about to send him over the edge.

"Why...care?" I ask. *"You're fucking rich. Just get something delivered. You can afford it. Why are you pushing this cooking thing?"*

Kade exhales, looking away as he answers. "I...now that Becca's here, I just...want to do things for her. She's always doing the cooking. I...want to take care of her, too."

Well, if that doesn't just hit me in the chest.

Watching the way he's been with Becca the last couple of months has been eye opening. I haven't seen this version of Kade before. He always dated fucked up women. So him wanting to take care of them was the norm. But it usually took the form of making sure they didn't OD. Or paying for the damage because of a bar fight they'd started.

This Kade, though? He's floundering, being with someone so capable. Becca has her shit together, and it's forcing him to up his game. It's really fucking fun to watch.

I take pity on him. "Yo," I say, then sign when he looks at me. *"You have any more steaks?"*

"Yeah," he says, waving at the fridge. "I bought ten."

Laughing, I ask *"Knew you were going to fuck up, didn't you?"*

"Fuck off, Micah," is his brilliant reply.

Still laughing, I head to the fridge, grabbing the extra packages of steak. I carry it all back to the outdoor kitchen built around the BBQ. Ransom insisted we all have them, but Kade's the first to actually put in a BBQ.

None of us have ever bothered to cook. I guess we never had a reason to. It's just as easy to make a sandwich when you're young. And now that we're really fucking rich? It's easy to text one of my brothers and head out to eat. Before Becca, I would usually text Kade. Kade's shiny new relationship has fucked with my life. But I'm not bitter.

Maybe a bit jealous, though.

I really fucking like Becca. She's an ass kicker, and she keeps Kade in line. She's great for him. He's finally looking healthy. Most of that has to do with getting a full eight hours every night, since, thanks to Becca and now Holly, he doesn't have to work in the garage office at night.

Now, he's at our head office most days doing his real job, running all the Brash Auto Group's garages. The nine of us grew up with nothing. Less than nothing, actually, in foster care. But together, we built a fucking empire and became a family. I have eight brothers, tighter than blood, and every one of them live right here, at the top of our castle...a forty-story high rise. Way better than a fucking castle. But until Becca, it's just been us brothers.

It's good he has her. I just fucking miss him. I've gone from seeing him every day to only catching him at our weekly family dinners and the occasional weekend. Becca invites me over all the time, but it's awkward as hell, sitting next to them while they rub up on each other on the couch 'cuddling'.

But today, I said yes to hanging out. I told myself it's

because Kade needed help carting up the BBQ, but that's a lie. It has nothing to do with the fact that *she* will be here. Another lie. And no, I have absolutely no interest in making her mine. Might as well go for the lie trifecta while I'm at it.

I stand back and watch Kade frantically season the steaks, muttering the whole time. I almost wish I knew how to cook so I could help. So I could cook Holly's steak.

Maybe I do understand why he's cooking.

Fuck. She's not mine so that thought is messed up. I shouldn't have come. But I can't not be here. Holly's going to see that fucker today and I hate it. She shouldn't ever have to lay eyes on him again. Just the idea of her husband makes the rage course through my body. I wish for the thousandth time that I could have been the one to put him down. To make him bleed. Becca was too damn efficient. I would have dragged it out. Made him whimper. But his time will come. I'll make sure of it. I won't be satisfied until he has to spend the rest of his life being hand fed and shitting himself.

The idea of him putting his hands on Holly. Making her hurt, making her bleed. It guts me. Nothing I do — or have done — to him is going to be enough to make up for what he did.

She's so fucking tiny. She looks like a fairytale princess. The top of her head only comes up to my chest. And those fucking curves. She is so round and soft and perfect. I can still feel the slight weight of her in my arms when I stopped her from tripping when we met. How soft her skin was. She was perfect. It was perfect.

At least, I thought it was. My ears heat thinking about her reaction. The way she froze. No way would I have let her fall, but I shouldn't have grabbed her. Now every time I look at her, I think about her panicked breaths and wide eyes, and all the things that happened to her to make her react that way.

I'm a big guy. I know that. But I would never hurt her. Never. And I hate that she thinks I will. Every time I try to talk to her, she backs up or looks away. Then I get frustrated and get the fuck out. It's all kinds of fucked up.

Kade finally pulls out his phone, and I knock my shoulder into his to get him to shove over. We stand there together watching that fucking chef teach us idiots how to grill a steak. I don't know what the hell I'm doing, but I don't want the poor guy to fail again. He already looks like he's on the edge. One more burnt steak may leave him babbling in the corner.

"Too...long." I say as I turn back to the BBQ. Idiot left it on high for twenty minutes at least. I flick them all to the off position before turning the gas back on. Slowly, I spin the dials to high and close the lid. We stand, watching the temperature gauge tick up, both lost in thought. I can't stop thinking about Holly, and I know for sure he's thinking about Becca. He always is. He finally breaks the silence.

"Would it be weird to ask Becca to marry me?"

My eyes widen. "Yes."

"Yes, it would be weird, or yes, I should ask her to marry me?"

I put down my beer. That's the downside of signing. I always have to have a place to put my beer when I'm having a conversation. *"It would be really fucking weird to ask her to marry you. You've only known her a few months, man!"* Is he seriously considering it? Holy shit.

Kade's nodding, but he doesn't look like he agrees. "But... she's it for me, man. I have no doubts about that. Why shouldn't I propose?"

This dense motherfucker. "Why?" I ask. *"Why do you want to propose?"*

He shrugs, and rubs the back of his neck, then mumbles, "So she'll stay with me."

God. I shake my head and plant my ass on the concrete countertop. *"So you think, if you put a ring on it, that Becca will stay? Is it a fucking ball and chain? Is it going to be so heavy she can't walk out the door with it on?"*

"Fuck you, man," he mutters, hiding behind his beer.

I stare at him until he looks at me again, giving him time to settle. *"You can't make her stay with you. You know that, right?"*

"Yeah," he says grudgingly.

"So a ring won't change that. But it sure as fuck could chase her away."

Kade's beer sloshes when he slams it down next to the BBQ. "What the fuck do you mean?"

Does he really not understand how desperate it is? *"Brother, you've got to settle the fuck down. You want to keep her? Asking her to marry you out of desperation is not going to do it. You need to chill. Fucking enjoy her, Kade. Be with her instead of worrying about her leaving. Show up every day, make her life better in any way you can, and love her. It's not that complicated."*

He's scowling at me like I took away his favorite toy. Or like I dropped a truth bomb on him. But I'm right about this. "Did you get that out of one of your fancy books, man?"

This asshole. *"Seriously? Just because I read doesn't mean they're fancy books, dickwad. They're just books. And if you're smart, you'll read a couple of relationship books before you fuck up."*

He looks intrigued at that. "You have relationship books?"

"Why are you so surprised? I have books about everything. There's a few I could lend you." I make the offer, but I doubt he'll take me up on it. Kade and reading don't really go together. He can't seem to sit still long enough to read a book.

He's gazing off over the city, and I can almost see his gears grinding. Finally, he nods "Yeah man. Maybe you can lend me one."

My mouth drops open. Maybe I don't know him as well as I thought I did. I smile at him. "Good," I say. *"I'll give you a couple, and you read the one that interests you the most. I'll go grab them."* I don't want to wait and give him time to change his mind. I suck back the rest of my beer, then head through

Kade's apartment across the little elevator entryway, into mine.

Ransom didn't want to waste any square footage outside the apartments, so the elevator lobby is half the size of our entryways. Kade's and my condo's layouts are mirror images of each other. Hell, all eight of our apartments are the same. The large entryways open into large great rooms. Big chefs kitchens, huge living rooms and a dining room fill the space, with a large terrace complete with outdoor kitchens just outside the floor to ceiling windows. The patio doors all fold in on themselves, so inside and outside blend. In the four years we've lived here, I've never gone on the patio. Kade hadn't used his until today, either. The only outdoor space we ever used was up in Ransom's penthouse.

Off to one side is a short hallway with two guest rooms, one that's furnished that I sleep in and the other is empty. On the opposite side are the main bedroom and the bathroom. That room is way too big, bigger than any room I've ever slept in. I tried for a few nights, but gave up and ended up in the smaller room. It just felt too open. I like the closed-in space better.

I have to stop for a quick minute to run my fingers down Minnie's back. If I don't, she'll just keep winding around me until I give in. Once she's satisfied I've paid her enough attention, she climbs back up the seven-foot cat tree in front of the windows to continue her nap. Then I head over to my books.

The shelves take up the entire wall, extending all the way to the nine-foot ceiling, on either side of the fireplace and TV. Even with my massive wingspan, I still can't reach the books at the top. I've been thinking about getting one of those cool rolling ladders installed, but for now the ugly step ladder that lives right next to the shelves works fine.

I grab the ladder and pull a couple of books off the top shelf, stopping to admire my collection for a minute. I run my finger over the spines of some of my favorites, passages flashing through my mind. Thousands of books fill these shelves, and I've read every page.

I don't really think about being rich most of the time. I wear coveralls over jeans most days, rarely go to fancy restaurants, and drive a mint car I fixed up myself. But walking into a bookstore, knowing I can afford anything I want? Well, that's where I feel truly rich.

There's something about seeing a wall full of books in my space that makes me feel settled. At home. I wonder if Holly reads? My fiction section has a couple of really great romances in it. Maybe she'd like those? Colton made fun of me when I bought them, but I got the fucker hooked, too. Nobody would make fun of her for reading them, though. I'd make sure of it.

Spotting the books I want, I tuck them under my arm and head back over to Kade's, using my palm print to unlock his door. Declan insisted on high-tech security, but we're all programmed into each other's door. We're supposed to set our system to privacy mode to lock everyone out, but we don't use it very often. I've walked in to see some of my brothers doing shit that scarred me for life.

I hear Becca's voice as soon as the door opens, and my hands go clammy. They're back. Holly's here.

3

HOLLY

I'm always a little intimidated walking into this apartment. It's so far removed from where I live, even where I used to live, that I'm afraid to touch anything. Kade and Becca have never made me feel that way, but I can't help calculating how much everything must have cost. That couch? Twenty grand, easy. The six burner range in the kitchen? Fifteen grand. The list goes on. Everything is top of the line for Kade.

You'd never know it from looking at him. I mean, he drives a nice truck and wears nice clothes, but he just seems so comfortable, you know? Like he can be anywhere and not judge. It looks like a home, though. Touches of Becca in the cozy blankets on the couch, the photo albums on the table and frames on the walls. She's turning it into their home. Though from what I can tell, she could paint the whole place glittery pink and Kade wouldn't care. As long as she's with him, he's happy. And so is she.

Becca's laughter rings out from the deck. She's wrapped up in Kade's arms, holding…a big lump of coal? That can't be right. I pad closer in my bare feet, stopping at the outside threshold.

"Aw baby. It's ok," she says, teasing, "You don't have to be embarrassed. Not everyone can be a master chef." It's not a lump of coal. It's a charred steak. There are three more of them sitting beside the Barbecue. I cover my mouth to hide my smile. Becca was right. Shit-show. He's laughing and whispers something in her ear but he sees me and straightens.

"Holly," he says, moving towards me. "How are you, honey?" As always, he opens his arms, then drops them to his side when I step back a little. I see the understanding on his face, and he rolls on as if it never happened. I haven't been able to accept his hug, any hug really except Becca's, in years. Kade is just too big. Too male. Maybe if he were small like me, it would be easier? I don't know. "Ok?" he asks softly, trying to peer at me through my sunglasses. I still have them on, covering my red eye.

I curl my lip up to give him a small smile. "I'm ok. It could have been worse." He doesn't look like he believes me, but he doesn't push, which I appreciate. I don't want to share what happened in that room. Not with anyone.

"Did he sign the papers?" Kade asks. I'm sure he already knows the answer. Why is he going to make me say it? The little spurt of frustration dies. I can't keep it alive when he's looking at me with such concern. Not that I'd ever show him I'm angry. I learned that lesson long ago. Anger only makes things worse, makes me bleed.

"No, he didn't sign them. His exact words were 'over my dead body'." The loud growl behind me stops my heart. I jump, instinctively backing up to the corner of the windows.

It's him. Micah. The bane of my existence. He's scowling again, and it immediately shoots my blood pressure up. I spent almost two years away from Brent, but I still can't shake the programming. When Micah scowls at me, I end up in a spiral of fear, worrying about what I've done wrong and what he might do. I don't think he'd hurt me, but I didn't think

Brent would either when I married him. I was very, very wrong.

My judgment is crap.

Micah's deep voice seems to fill the room. "Arrange... that." He doesn't stutter. He never does. Instead, he pauses between the words until he's sure they'll come out clear and strong. I've watched him do it over and over again the two months I've worked at the garage. Somehow he always gets his point across to the guys at the garage, to the customer, to me. But this time I'm confused. Arrange what? I look up at him, but his eyes are fixed on Kade. When I swing my gaze to Kade, he's smiling.

"Fuck yeah! I like the way you think. We've waited too long already. He held a fucking knife on my girl." He says with a snarl.

"Oh no," Becca scolds, her hands on her hips. "You're not killing him. How would you even do that? He's in jail already, nimrods."

I don't know where to look. They want to kill Brent? Can they do that? Would they get caught? Is it wrong that I like the idea of him dead?

Micah's laugh is dark. The sound raises goosebumps on my arms, and I press my back a little harder into the wall. He's wearing a simple pair of sweats and a t-shirt, but somehow looks as dangerous as someone wearing full combat gear. "Easy," he says before continuing in sign, *"Everyone in this town owes us. And we know guys inside. One phone call and he'll be bleeding out by morning."*

My face blanches at the casual way he signs that. Like it's no big deal. Like it would be simple. I can't imagine a world Brent didn't exist in. The shadow he casts over my life is so big, so dark, even from prison, that it seems impossible to escape it.

"Can you really do that?" Crap. I didn't mean to ask that

out loud. Micah and Kade swing to face me. Kade's features soften. Micah's scowl deepens and it steals my breath.

"We're not respectable, Holly." Kade says slowly. "We may not look like it now, but we're thugs at our core. So yeah, hypothetically, a phone call to the right person and a bag full of cash is all it would take."

They're all studying me, waiting for…what? Do they want me to ask them to do it? I can't do that. Thou shalt not kill. I can't knowingly hurt someone. God may have abandoned me a long time ago, but I can't cross that line. It's not right.

"He…he's in jail." I stammer. "He can't hurt anyone now."

Becca nods reassuringly, but Kade and Micah don't look convinced. They're both still studying me, faces serious. Finally, Kade turns to Micah and nods. Micah's lips tighten and he nods back. I don't like it. I shouldn't ask. I shouldn't question. It's not my place. But I steel myself and do it anyway. "What was that? Kade? What was that nod?"

Kade raises his eyebrows. "Nothing you need to worry about, Holly. You don't need to worry at all anymore."

"How can I not worry? It looks an awful lot like you and Micah just agreed on something. You're not hurting Brent. You can't do that."

That dark smile is back on Micah's face. "We…won't."

I push off the wall, stepping closer to him. He's so tall, I have to stop a few feet away to maintain eye contact without hurting my neck. "You won't do anything. You won't make a phone call. You won't pay anyone. You won't hurt Brent. Say it Micah."

Micah's lips twist, and his eyes cloud over. The smile is long gone. He lowers his face, stepping closer to me. Close enough that I can feel the heat radiating off his body.

"No." He says, his voice like ice. *"Why are you protecting that worthless piece of shit? Why Holly?"*

I raise my chin, wrapping the fabric of my skirt in my hands to hide the trembling. "I'm not protecting him." I'm not. I don't care if Brent dies. I hope he does, truth be told. But I can't allow anyone to dirty their hands on my behalf. He's not worth it. I'm not worth it.

"Liar," Micah spits. *"You should want him dead more than anyone. You had to live with him. I've seen the medical reports, Holly. He hurt you."* Micah's chest is heaving, his glare heavier than ever. I feel myself wilting under the weight of his anger.

I'm so tired of bearing the weight of everyone else's emotions. I rub my eyes, pushing my sunglasses to the top of my head in frustration. I need to not be here. I want my tiny apartment. I want the thin walls and the sounds of families going about their day. I want my threadbare sofa and lumpy bed. I want to not exist for just a little while, just until I can smooth out the rough edges of today.

I drop my hands, the rubbing having irritated my eyes further. I ease back a couple of steps, away from Micah's overwhelming presence, glancing briefly over at Kade and Becca. "He's not worth it," I breathe. "Don't dirty your hands, please."

I jump when big hands close over my shoulders. Micah's grip is powerful and my hands automatically come up to press against his chest, eyes locking on his light brown ones. The blazing anger there steals my breath. The trembling starts in my legs, moving up my body.

He's angry. Very angry. It's going to be so much worse than Brent. He's so much bigger. Stronger. I finally manage to draw in a tiny breath, but I can't fill my lungs completely.

Gasping, I manage to yell "No," as I shove him. I didn't expect it to work. Brent always just dug his fingers in harder, pulled me in tighter. It was the preamble to more pain. So I'm surprised when Micah's hands release immediately.

I don't spare him a glance, instead backing up to the wall again. My legs feel like they're going to give out, but I lock them and focus on the breathing Becca always does with me. Long, deep inhale, slow exhale for a count of five. My gaze is on the ground, shifting between the three sets of feet facing me. They're all immobile.

I keep breathing as I study them. Becca's bare feet, long and strong, toes painted with bright red polish. Kade's in black Vans. I've never seen him wear anything but work boots or dress shoes. Finally, Micah's. They're bigger than Kade's, but not by much. He's wearing a pair of battered running shoes, the toes scuffed. Maybe he drags his feet when he walks? I stay focused on those scuffed toes until my head feels less floaty.

Reluctantly, I raise my head, knowing what I'll see on their faces. Becca's is full of empathy, as expected. I manage a small smile for her, and thankfully, she smiles back. Kade's eyes are tight. He's trying to mask it, but I can still see the pity. I hate that he looks at me that way, but I'm not even a little bit surprised. I am pitiful.

Finally, when I can't stand the silence anymore, I slide my eyes to Micah and my heart stutters at the tears filling his eyes.

I don't understand.

Anger, frustration, disgust. Any of those would make sense, but tears? He looks shattered. He stares at me, his throat bobbing, before carefully backing up. He places some books gently on the kitchen counter before turning and walking away. I'm left wondering, as the front door closes behind him, what hurt him? Who were those tears for? No way they're for me. And why does the idea that he's hurting make me so sad?

4

HOLLY

"I need to go," I whisper. I can't process anything more right now.

"I'll take you," Becca says, moving towards her purse.

"No. I'll take the bus. Stay. Enjoy your Saturday." I can't lean on her forever. And she deserves to have some time with her guy. I can't call him her boyfriend. There's nothing boy about him.

"Not a chance, Hol. I'm taking you, or Kade is. You pick."

I feel that anger rising again, but push it down. She's trying to help. I know that. But she's treating me like a child. I know how to take the bus, for heaven's sake. I've been doing it since I've been on my own. Normally, I wouldn't mind skipping the bus, especially since summer's here. A hot summer day means the air in the bus will be an awful body odor soup.

It's gross, but I'd rather be on a bus with sweaty, hard-working people than married to Brent and driving a car. The bus means freedom to go where I want, when I want. Usually anyway. As I meet her gaze, I realize she won't let this go, and

I don't have the energy to fight. I nod yes, and say a quick apology to Kade, then move to wait by the door.

I watch from the corner of my eye as Becca hugs and kisses Kade goodbye. They look good together. Both tall and strong, his large frame complementing her curvy body. She looks completely at home in his arms, and he looks like he never wants to let her go. I'm more likely to discover a Unicorn than find a relationship like that. From everything I've seen, they're rare, only for special people like Becca and Kade.

As we wait for the elevator, I have to twist my fingers together to stop myself from knocking on Micah's door. My need to check on him is strong, but it's not my place. He can barely stand me, and honestly, until today, I avoided him as much as possible. It's hard to be around someone who seems to actively dislike you. Add in the six-and-a-half feet of pure muscle, and there's no way I can bring myself to approach him.

It didn't start out that way. The day I met him, I thought his eyes were so warm, his smile so welcoming. I wanted to poke my finger in his dimples, for God's sake. Then I tripped and freaked out, and he got grumpy. Any chance we had at being friendly was gone in seconds.

Besides, he's too big. Or I'm too small. Either way, just standing near him makes goosebumps break out on my arms. I've never felt anything like it before. It must be my gut's early warning system or something.

The ride down to the parkade is silent. I hide my smile when I see Becca's old car parked next to Kade's huge, shiny truck. I wonder when she'll cave and let him buy her a new one. He's been alternating between begging and ordering her to let him buy her something safer.

Beyond it is Micah's black car. The rest of the vehicles in this secured section of the parkade must all belong to the rest of Kade and Micah's brothers. There's everything from a yellow hummer to a fancy sports car. I have no idea what kind of car it might be, but it looks like it's worth more than some of the other vehicles combined. The only other car that really doesn't look like it fits is a shiny blue minivan. I have to know, "Which of the guys drives a minivan? Do they have kids?"

Becca glances over at the van and snorts. "Jonas drives the van. He doesn't have kids, but he says it's one of the safest vehicles on the road, so he bought one." She snickers a bit. "He's usually the DD when they go out, and all the guys rave about the push button sliding doors."

"That's...nice." I say.

It's weird.

They're all a little weird, honestly. Becca snorts some more and waves me into the car.

"Jonas is an odd duck. A very loveable one, though." It's clear by the warmth in her voice that she likes him and it makes me want to meet him. I like the idea that I could be connected to other people through Becca. That the guys could be more than my bosses. Like, maybe we can wave hello to each other. Maybe chat about the weather. I like the idea of being seen by them. I've spent so much of my life invisible that the idea of other people caring about me, even just a bit, is tantalizing.

Becca's running chatter fills the silence on the way home. I respond when necessary, but she seems to be able to carry on the conversation by herself. My mind is occupied with thoughts of Micah. What actually happened today? He's a puzzle I'm missing pieces to. Micah didn't act the way I expected him to, and I feel off balance. It's safer when I can put people in a box. Today, Micah escaped the *grumpy guy I need to avoid* box and I need to figure out how to stuff him back in.

"Why was Micah crying?" I ask suddenly. Becca's words

stutter to a stop. I'm worried she won't answer, but she glances at me out of the side of her eye.

Her words are soft, and I lean towards her so I don't miss a word. "You burst a blood vessel in your eye...how did that happen?"

Shifting in my seat, I focus on the taillights of the car stopped in front of us. "I threw up after I saw Brent."

She nods, her lips tight. "Micah is having a hard time with..." she trails off and gives me a guilty look.

"Me," I clear my throat. "He's having a hard time with me." I knew he didn't like me, but I didn't realize it went this deep.

Becca bites her lip and props one elbow on the door. "I... it's not really my place to say, but..." she sighs heavily. "Fuck it." She leans her head on her fist. "Micah's dad beat his mom, and him, pretty badly. It went on for a long while." I suck a breath in, my eyes tearing up. He's so stable and solid, I never would have known. "I think he's struggling," she continues, "with the way you panicked when you met...then again today."

My hackles rise and my tears dry up. "He's been glaring at me the entire time I've worked at the garage." It's not fair. Most things in life aren't fair, at least in my experience, but I thought working at the garage was going to be better than my old job. In a lot of ways, it is. No one hits on me or corners me there. But having Micah not like me is...embarrassing.

Becca talked so much about how great he was, and then he meets me and hates me. It makes me feel...worthless. That's a feeling I've been trying very hard to expel from my body, but its teeth have sunk deep. I promised myself that when I left Brent, I wouldn't let anyone treat me like I was less than. I learned pretty quickly that I couldn't keep that promise and stay employed. Turns out most bosses think their office staff are less than. At least all the bosses I've had to think that way. And now Micah, too.

"He's not angry with you Holly," she finally says, turning onto my street. "He's just struggling with a few things."

"Right. And he only struggles around me? That's bull crap, Becca. He smiles and acts normal with everyone else in the garage. It's just me. I'm the one making him grumpy."

My breath is speeding up. I'm going to have to get a new job. While technically Kade is my boss, Micah's part owner of the garage. If he wants me gone, I'm gone. Tears prick my eyes at the precariousness of my situation. I am so alone. And If I lose this job, I don't know what I'll do. Living in the city is way more expensive than back home, so I haven't been able to save anything. Brent never let me work, instead giving me a strict allowance, so saving money was impossible. If it wasn't for Evie, I wouldn't have had anything when I ran. I have less than $200 in my bank account now. My financial safety net is non-existent.

Becca's voice halts my spiraling thoughts. "You need to talk to him, Holly. There's a lot going on with him you don't understand. I'm not even certain he realizes what he's doing at work. Just...talk to him. I think the way he's reacting to you is because he's upset you were hurt."

I slowly shake my head. "That doesn't make sense. If he's upset that I was hurt, why would he look at me with such anger? You're wrong." There's no way she's right. Maybe she's used to seeing the good in people. Maybe she just wants to see Micah in the best light. I don't know. Either way, it's clear her judgment is clouded.

We are very different people. She has the strength and skills to handle a bad judgment call. Me? Well, I made one bad decision, and I ended up in hell for seven years. I can't afford to give anyone, but especially Micah, the benefit of the doubt.

As she pulls up to my building, I quickly unfasten my belt and hop out. "Thank you for driving me. I'll see you next week at class."

"Wait!" she calls. I debate pretending I didn't hear her, but she'll just chase me down. I turn around and raise an eyebrow. "Talk to Micah." She urges. "I see you stewing, Hol. Promise me you'll talk to him before you make any rash decisions." She's done this before. Tried to push me to make a promise. I value her friendship too much to lie, so I settle for a shake of my head. "I don't have a plan to leave."

"That's not a promise."

"No, but it's the best you're going to get. Now skedaddle. Get back home to your guy." I shoo her away and paste a fake smile on my face. I stand there, smiling until she's left the parking lot, then let it fall, exhaling heavily.

My whole body is tired, from my feet to my eyelids. I turn and drag myself into the rickety building, walking up to the third floor and letting myself into my small studio. I was so excited to move in here. After a year at the shelter, this felt like a palace. But every time I come home from Kade's, my place seems smaller and dingier. It's one small room, really, with a tiny bathroom tucked off the kitchen. I have a twin bed tucked in the little alcove near the bathroom and a minuscule living room beyond that. One small window facing the parking lot lets in light.

Thank goodness I didn't let Micah come in when he drove me home after the night Brent attacked Becca. I don't think I could bear his judgment. His scorn if he saw it. He may have grown up in a place like this, but he is so far removed from this kind of life now that I know that he'd see it as a hovel. He would look at my flowerpots and instead of thinking they're pretty like I do, he'd think they were mismatched and ugly. Instead of seeing the love that I put into the crocheted blankets on the couch, he'd judge the threadbare cushions underneath. No, Micah doesn't feel bad. It's just that we are from such different worlds, we might as well be different species.

5

MICAH

I've been expecting the knock on the door. I'm surprised it took him this long, actually. I slide my bookmark into my new Reacher novel and put it carefully on the coffee table, then slowly open the door.

"Kade," I say, waving him in. His print is still coded in my door. He knows he doesn't need to wait to come in. He only started knocking when Becca moved into his place. Before that? He'd just walk the fuck in. Maybe now that he's bumping uglies on the regular, he's discovered boundaries? Who the fuck knows.

He moves to my large brown sectional and flops down with a sigh, waiting for me to join him before speaking. I detour to the fridge for a few beers. I think we're going to need it for this conversation.

"Are you ok?" he asks quietly. And yep, we're talking about feelings. Apparently, that's something we do now. I'd blame it on us maturing, but honestly, Becca coming into the mix has a lot more to do with it.

I take a long pull on my beer before setting it down to answer. *"Not really. Watching her flinch away from me fucking guts me. I shouldn't have touched her."*

He leans forward on the couch, his beer dangling between his legs. "But you want to though, don't you?"

I study him before answering, seeing only acceptance on his face. "Yes," I admit. *"More than I've wanted anything in my life."* I want her more than I want my next breath. *"But it's not gonna happen man. I know that. It's better for her if I keep my distance."*

"Is that what you're doing? Keeping your fucking distance?"

"What…mean?" I ask him.

"When you're looking at her like you wish she'd just fucking disappear, man."

I don't understand what the fuck we're talking about. *"She's the best part of my day. I never want her to go. Just seeing her, seeing that she's ok makes everything better."*

Kade's shaking his head at me. "You dumbfuck." He says on a heavy breath. "If you want to keep her around, then why the hell are you mean mugging at her all the time? You're doing it at work. You just did it in my fucking apartment. Why, man?"

I honestly don't know what to say. I don't think it's been that bad, so I just shrug my shoulders and drink my beer. BB (Before Becca) the conversation would end here. But not anymore. Not since Kade caught fucking feelings.

The corner of his eyes narrow. His disappointment in me clear to see."When you're near her at work, what are you thinking? I mean, about her specifically."

My ears are hot. *"That she's so small and beautiful. That I hate she was hurt by fuckwad Brent. That I'm too big and mean to be anywhere near her."*

Kade whistles through his teeth and settles back into the couch. "Jesus, man, you're fucked. Lemme get this straight. You think she's beautiful, you want her, and you don't think you deserve her."

"I wouldn't use those words, but…yeah."

He shakes his head and rubs his hand over the back of his head. "This is my fucking fault, man. I'm sorry."

I cock my eyebrow at him. "Sorry?"

"Yeah. Sorry. Becca pointed out to me that you and I needed to have a conversation months ago, and I dropped the fucking ball." His leg bounces, heel tapping against the floor. "When we were kids...you were so angry. About everything. You were like a live grenade and I never knew when the fuck you were going to go off."

I nod, because it's true. *"I had fucking brain damage, man. My piece-of-shit father took away my words."*

"I know, man," he says softly. "It made it so fucking hard for you. But you popping off? It gave you a pretty wicked rep. You were unpredictable, and violent as hell. Honestly, we made it work for all of us. Did you know Ransom brought you to meetings just to intimidate people?

I have to laugh. *"I guess. I mean, I knew I wasn't there to fucking negotiate. All I could do was stand there and be intimidating."*

"Exactly man. Just your rep, and your mean mug put people on edge. It was a killer tactic, honestly. But that's not who you are anymore."

"What?" I say in exasperation, throwing my hands up. *"Where are we going with this?"*

Kade's leg finally stops bouncing when he laughs. "When was the last time you beat anyone up?"

I have to think for a minute. "Nick. Last...week." I smile, thinking of that fight.

Kade snorts. "Wrestling with our brother over the last piece of cake doesn't count, man. I mean, really lost your temper and used your fists to solve a problem?"

I sit back, thinking. Then thinking some more before finally shaking my head. "Years."

"Right, because that's not who you are anymore. You're the top custom guy on this side of the country. You have a years-long waiting list. You're a master. And you're a fucking billionaire. You're not the brawler, because you don't need to be anymore." His smug smile is getting on my nerves.

"And," I prompt. There's a little tingle of...something in my gut.

"You thinking you're too big and mean to be with Holly is bullshit."

I shake my head, rising to my feet, unable to sit still for this. "Not."

"Yeah it is. Would you ever raise a hand to her?"

My stomach churns at the idea of hurting her, even accidentally "N...Never."

"Of course you wouldn't. Because you're a good fucking man." He rises, stopping next to me, putting his heavy hand on my shoulder. "You're the best man I know. Holly would be so fucking lucky to have you." His voice is so sincere. He truly believes it. For a minute, I imagine it's true. That I could deserve Holly. That we could be together. But I don't get far in my imaginings.

"She's afraid of me. Anytime I'm around her, she backs away. She doesn't feel the same."

"I don't know how she feels, but Becca shared something you need to know."

I lean forward, wanting any bit of insight he can give me.

"Holly thinks you hate her," he says, hand tightening on my shoulder. "You've been glaring, staring, and generally acting like a grumpy ass around her. She's taking it personally."

I close my eyes. "Fuck." The word comes from deep in my chest, from a pit of self-disgust I've never felt before. *"I didn't realize. My face...I didn't know."* I would never look at her like that on purpose. Never.

"I know that," he says, nodding. "That's not who you are. I think maybe it's just leftover from the old you? Or a habit?"

"Maybe...both." I admit.

"You can fix it, man." He says, smiling at me."There's still time." His smile drops as he continues, "But don't wait. You have to talk to her soon. Don't let her keep misunderstanding you...I don't want her to bolt."

"She can't go," I sign. *"I need her to stay."*

He takes his hand from my shoulder, moving it to rub the back of his head again. "Listen, I made a lot of mistakes with Becca."

"No shit sherlock. You had your head up your ass." I say, dodging the fist he aims at my gut.

"Why am I even trying to help you, man? I should just let you rot here with your books." There's no heat in his words. We've been there for each other through all sorts of shit, this conversation won't break us. Though we may have a rough time looking at each other for a while because...feelings.

"Tell," I prompt him.

He exhales and drops back on the couch. "I almost lost her, man, because I couldn't believe I deserved her. I didn't think I was good enough. Now I get it."

"You...deserve?" I ask, arching my brow.

He snorts, rubbing a hand over his face. "Nah. I don't deserve her. She's way too good for me. But she chose me, so everyday I wake up and try to be the man she deserves. It's work, brother. But the best fucking work I've ever done." He stops to wiggle his eyebrows. "Trust me, really fucking great work. I mean, first class."

Laughing with him, the possibility that he might be right settles in me, makes me...well not hopeful, but less pessimistic. Maybe I'm not the monster I thought I was, but she's still a wounded bird.

"Kade," I say to draw his eyes back to me. *"She's still broken. She's been so hurt by that bastard. She might never be able to..."* I drop my hands, unable to finish that thought. Never be able to love me. To let someone love her.

His jaw clenches and releases, making the muscles in his

cheek pop. "I know, man. You're right. She might not. But that doesn't stop you from being her fucking friend." His eyes are locked on mine so firmly I can't look away. "You know how to do that. Just be you."

I drop back to the couch and lean back, contemplating the ceiling. Can I do that? Be her friend? In the deepest part of the night, when I'm most honest with myself, I know my feelings don't have much to do with friendship. This fucking obsession with a woman is unfamiliar territory for me. Maybe I'll always be too much for her to ever be her boyfriend. But maybe she'll let me be her friend, let me bear some of her burden.

"Micah," Kade says. I roll my head towards him, giving him my full attention. "I still don't like that Brent's breathing, man. But it's not my fucking place to make that decision. He's hurt Holly the most, and since she's yours…I'll leave you to handle him." I don't bother denying it. Even if she walked away from me tomorrow, she'd somehow always be mine.

"Agreed" I say. I'll handle it. With pleasure.

"Ok, good talk!" He says, rising from the couch. "I gotta go wrestle around with my girl now. Be good. Come up with a good fucking apology. You can practice it on me tomorrow." He calls over his shoulder.

I raise my middle finger to his retreating back. "Fuck… You." His manic laugh echoes through the room until the door closes softly behind him. Those soft close doors really ruin his dramatic exits.

I'll never admit it to him, but maybe Kade has a point. Because I can't fucking find the right words to apologize to Holly with. Somehow, *I'm sorry I was wearing my mean face around you, I'll put it away.* Doesn't cut it. But do I really want to just…lay it all out there? Tell her exactly how I feel about her? No fucking way. If she wasn't planning to run before, guaranteed she'll run after that.

No, my smartest option seems to be telling her part of it.

That I hate that she was hurt, and I've let my anger at Brent show on my face. And maybe that I think she's absolutely perfect in every way. Or maybe not. Fuck, will that scare her away?

I'm going out of my Goddamn mind. I need to work this out in the gym. I pull out my phone and hit up our family text. As usual, the replies come fast and furious. We may ignore other texts, but never the family chat.

Me: Hitting the gym. Anyone coming?

Declan: Gaming man. Can't

Colt: Going out soon.

Jonas: Be there soon. Just finishing up a puzzle.

Ransom: Early business dinner.

Colt: Puzzle - You fuckin promised!!!! You finished without me asshole?

Declan: Where you eating Ran?

Mavrick: I'll be down in 10

Zach: Colt he's doing the dogs playing poker one. Not the windmill dude. Chill.

Kade: Busy with my ladaaaayyyyy!

Nick: Fuck off Kade. Heading down now Micah.

Ransom: Castillos

Declan: Bring me Enchiladas. Please!

Ransom: Order it your fucking self.

Declan: Fine. Be that way. I'll hit up Gino's later and U can't have any!

Nick: Spicy Sausage Man.

Jonas: You should make a healthier choice, Declan. Try a salad.

Zach: Spicy Sausage!

Declan: You're a thundercunt Jonas. Fuck Salads.

Me: Spicy sausage. Get a few.

I toss my phone on the counter, dinging with repeated

texts while I change into my workout gear. I check the thread quickly, chuckling at the idiocy, then head down to the gym to meet Jonas, Mav and Nick. We better get our pump on cause apparently pizzas are gonna be here in an hour. It's just enough time to get my head out of my ass and settle my thoughts.

After a workout and a large pizza of my own, I've managed to convince myself that everything will go to plan on Monday morning. I'll apologize, Holly will forgive me, and we'll be friends.

Easy.

6

HOLLY

I tuck away my conversation with Becca, putting it in the corner of my mind, unwilling to examine it too closely. Somehow the idea that Micah's thinking about Brent and the way he hurt me every time he looks at me feels worse than him just not liking me.

I spend the rest of my day puttering around my small apartment, doing chores and making myself a quick, cold supper. Brash Auto pays well, so I'm hopeful I can ditch the ham sandwiches and peanut butter soon. If I'm very careful, I can build up my nest egg and still afford a little higher grocery bill. I watch a couple of cooking videos on my secondhand laptop, tapping into my neighbor's Wi-Fi, then head to bed early.

Sunday's laundry day, so I boil water to make tea, pulling back with a squeal when I unplug the kettle. Those stupid outlets spark every time I use them, but the building manager doesn't seem to care. I pour the water over the tea bag in my *I Heart Cats* travel mug, $1.99 at the thrift shop, and tuck it carefully down the side of my laundry basket along with a dog eared paperback. Then I pull a small knife out of the drawer and wrap it in a napkin, stuffing it down next to my tea.

I do heart cats. I've never actually had a pet, but I think I'm a cat person. I would spend as much time as I could with my friends' pets when I was little. Momma said animals were soulless and didn't belong in the house. That didn't make sense to me even then, but pushing her on it would have ended up with me on my knees for hours, praying to cleanse my sinful heart.

From everything I've learned in my twenty-nine years on this earth, people are the soulless ones. I've never met an animal that wanted to hurt someone just because they could. Animals are born pure and are corrupted by bad owners. Maybe that's what happens to people too? Maybe we're all born pure, but we're slowly diminished by the people around us. I hope that's not true, because if it is, then there's really no good left in me either.

It takes me way too long to get my basket down to the laundry room. I know I should get smaller baskets, or break the loads up, but I just don't ever seem to do it. Instead, I wait until I have nothing clean left, then pack down the basket as tightly as I can to try and fit everything in it. Dragging it down behind me, one slow step at a time. When I lived with Brent, I thought it was such a hassle to take the laundry out to the garage. Only now, after hauling everything down four flights to the basement every week, do I appreciate what I had.

I can't help the little spurt of pride in my chest when I look at my full basket. It's filled with items that I chose. Sure, they're mainly thrift store clothes, but after years of wearing only dark colors my husband approved of, my heart thrills at the bright colors and cheerful patterns. The vibrant clothing somehow makes me feel stronger than I actually am. Like a better version of me. Maybe their vibrancy, their color, will slowly leach into me, turning me into someone bright and vibrant too. I smile as I imagine my skin swirling with bright patterns and shapes.

I'm lucky today. The laundry room isn't busy this morning, the only occupants a few harried women. I'll be able to leave the knife tucked away for now. I started carrying it after being cornered in here by a man. I got lucky that day. Someone else came in and he took off, but I won't ever make the mistake of being unprotected again. I spend the morning reading and watching the door to the room carefully. It's not until I'm tucked back into my apartment though, with the locks all secured, that I take a full breath.

Crawling into bed that night, I pull out yesterday's conversation with Becca, unraveling it in my mind. Wondering if she might be right. That Micah doesn't hate me. Wishing it were true won't make it so, but a tiny swirl of interest floats in among the anxiety I feel about seeing him tomorrow.

Working with someone who hates you is hard. Working with someone who pities you would be harder, I think. The smart move would be to avoid the whole subject, just put my head down and work. But this thread of curiosity doesn't feel like it's going away. At a minimum, I should apologize to him for yesterday.

I treated him unfairly, I know that. He's never shown a hint of violence, and I shouldn't have reacted like he had. I wish it was as simple as snapping my fingers and poof, the panic I feel around men would disappear. It's not, I've tried. But for Micah, for peace at work, I'll try.

I fall into a restless sleep, unable to escape the memories of Brent. Images of our past mixing in with our present. Screaming. So much screaming.

I wake disoriented, and it takes me a minute to realize the screaming is real, and it's coming from outside. Slowly, the smell of smoke fills my nose. My whole body breaks into a sweat as the cries become clearer.

Fire.

As I sit up, I get a big lungful of smoke. Coughing and choking, I drop to the floor. My thoughts are a swirling mess, but one thought rises above the others.

Get out. Get out now.

I crawl on my hands and knees to the door, pressing my hand against it. My entire third-grade class practiced this. I remember firefighters bringing a miniature house to our school. We all crawled inside, and when we smelled the strawberry scented smoke, we crawled out to safety. There were popsicles and firetruck rides for us when we got out. It was fun, most of us giggling as we crawled out.

I'm not giggling now.

This smoke is black, choking, and even down on the floor I can barely breathe. The door isn't hot, so I swing it open and crawl towards the stairs. Most of the screams are below me, and when I look back, I see an orange glow pushing me to move faster. I slide down the first set of stairs on my stomach, then the second, sobbing when I reach the second floor landing. Almost there. I don't expect the heavy weight dropping onto me, or the tumble down the stairs. And I don't feel the scraping and banging of my body as it rattles down the stairs. I just...drift away.

7

MICAH

She's late. She's never late and I'm spinning the fuck out. I got in at 7:45 as usual, rehearsing my apology the whole drive in, and no Holly. She's usually here right at 7:30 and has the coffee going by now. But today everything was still locked up and dark. Where the hell is she?

I spend fifteen minutes opening up, giving curt nods to the other guys as they trickle in, keeping watch at the front door. Something is very wrong. She's had a rough go of it, but that woman has a backbone of steel. No way would she just take off. I pull out my phone and text Becca.

Me: Holly's not here. What's her address?

I'm kicking myself. The day Holly's piece of shit ex pulled a knife on us, I actually got to drive her home. But I was freaking the fuck out, because I just realized seeing Holly every day lights up my fucking life. The idea of her hurt just gutted me. So when I drove her home that night, it was with wild thoughts spinning in my head. Thoughts about what she dealt with during her marriage. How she might have been hurt. I followed her whispered directions *left, right, right, left*, and by the time I made it back home that night, I had no idea where I'd been.

I wait a minute, but when I don't get a response from Becca, I pull up the group text with my brothers.

Me: 911. I need Holly's address.

The first set of dots appear right away. A moment of relief washes over me. I'm going to find her.

Declan: 2 minutes.

That's how 911 works. We may fuck around and annoy the shit out of each other, but 911 means drop everything. And we do. Doesn't matter why. If a brother texts 911, it means it's important to him. I might not have said anything, but we gossip worse than a group of teenage girls, so I'm sure they all know I'm obsessed with her. Plus, she's one of ours. We take care of our own.

Ransom: What's wrong?
Maverick: Is she ok?
Declan: Fuck no she's not.

My heart fucking stops when I click the link he sends through. It's a news article about an early morning apartment fire, the picture showing the blackened skeleton of a clearly shitty apartment building, firetrucks and ambulances in the foreground. Bile crawls up the back of my throat.

Me: Where is she? Tell me Dec.
Declan: Found her listed at Mercy. Head to Emerg.

I'm already running to my car, catching one last text before I pull out like a bat out of hell.

Ransom: I'll meet you there

THE WAITING ROOM IS PACKED WITH PEOPLE, A LOT OF THEM STILL in their pyjamas. Some are softly crying, others look shell-shocked. The smell of smoke is heavy in the air.

My eyes pick through the bodies, locking on every blonde head before moving on in disappointment. If she's not here, that means she's back there, where the people more badly injured would be.

My hands are shaking as I approach the front desk and the annoyed looking woman behind it. Her eyes widen as I walk up to her, taking in my enormous frame in my plain white t-shirt and jeans. I open up my mouth and say two words to her. The two words I practiced the whole way over. Because the way I'm feeling right now, if I don't, I might stutter or not be able to get them out at all. Not going to fucking happen. This is too important.

"Holly Clarke." I have to force the words out, but not because my brain is scrambling them, but because of the lump in my throat. The woman drops her eyes.

"Are you family?" She asks curtly. I knew that question was coming. And I practiced that too.

I nod, "Fiancé." I'm not even a tiny bit guilty for the lie. Holly has no one. No emergency contacts, no other friends but us. She needs me. So I'll say whatever I have to in order to get to her.

Suddenly the energy in the room shifts, voices dropping to a hush, and I take my first full breath since I got to the garage this morning and found it still dark. The heavy hand landing on my shoulder sends a wave of relief down my back.

Ransom's here.

My aphasia is a fucking pain in my ass most days, but when my emotions are high? When it's a fucking emergency? It can be a huge barrier. If I can't pull out my phone to type or find a paper and pen, I'm fucked.

It's worse if I'm the patient. People barking questions at me and not getting answers. I've been talked to like I'm stupid by more than one doctor. The last time it happened, over a decade ago, Ransom lost his shit. My brain damage doesn't affect my intelligence, just my ability to verbalize my thoughts. I can handle my shit as long as I'm given the opportunity. So Ransom insisted I wear the medic alert bracelet he had made for me. I run my fingers down the silver links; the action calms me. I haven't taken it off since the day he gave it to me. It's more familiar to me than anything else I've ever worn.

So having my brother here? Someone who would intimidate the most hardcore Navy General, is a welcome relief. "Ransom," I mutter, not taking my eyes off the top of the nurse's head. He squeezes my shoulder in response. Finally, she raises her head, eyes widening.

I know what she sees. Tall, hard, powerful men, loaded with muscle, dark hair, dark eyes. We look like blood brothers. But instead of the $100 outfit I'm wearing, he's got on a ten-thousand dollar suit. The damn cufflinks on the suit are worth double that. He wears it like it's his birthright, even though I know he'd rather be in sweats. But Ransom lives by a simple premise 'money is power', hence the power suits. They've opened more doors for us than I can even count, so none of us question them. I'm sure he just walked out of an important meeting, and did it without a second's thought. That's how we roll in our family.

"Holly Clarke," I prompt the woman again, frustrated that she's still staring at us. Ransom's face is stern. He raises an eyebrow at her and her face flushes.

"B...Bed twenty-three". I tap the desk in thanks and beeline for the security doors. "Only one visitor, sir—". I look back, a small grin crossing my face at the look Ransom gives her. She stutters to a stop, glancing between us then nodding at the security guard, who opens the door and lets us both through.

It's eerily calm in the back. The silence broken by beeping and the soft voices of the staff. My eyes dart to the signs, heading left towards bed twenty-three, the tap of Ransom's dress shoes joining the thud of my work boots. Most of the staff are moving quickly between beds with charts and medications, but a few watch us pass, whispering and giggling.

I ignore all of it, focused on getting to her. My heart feels like it's about to break out of my chest, and I slap a hand on it, as if that will keep it in place. The curtain around bed twenty-three is pulled closed. I reach out and wrap my fist around it, but can't bring myself to open it. *It can't be that bad*, I tell myself. The doctors would be with her right now if it was bad. But I still can't open the curtain.

"We'll deal with it, brother. Whatever we find, we'll deal with it." Ransom says quietly behind me. I nod before gently pulling the curtain back. And I can't stop the sound of agony that comes out of me at the sight of her.

8

MICAH

"Jesus fucking christ," Ransom breathes beside me.

I want to howl. I want to break something. I want to take it all away for her. It's bad. Everywhere I look, her skin is bruised. Butterfly bandages are holding together her eyebrow, her lip, the bridge of her nose and the cuts on her cheek. Her eyes look bruised. Even the one small hand outside the covers is scratched and battered. She's so small, lying in that bed, her feet still a foot away from the bottom.

"Doctor." I tell Ransom, not taking my eyes off of her. I can't leave her.

"On it," he says, voice thick.

There's a chair in the corner, and I move it right next to the bed. Sitting, I gently touch her, running my fingers lightly over her wrist, her jaw, her shoulder. There's so little undamaged skin. I swallow heavily, my breathing rapid. So much pain. Is she sleeping, or did they give her something? Is she unconscious? I need to know. Where is the fucking doctor?

Like I summoned him, Ransom appears in the doorway, his hand on the arm of a doctor. She looks frazzled and angry.

Not an uncommon reaction around him. Her eyes land on Holly, and her face softens before shifting to me. "I'm Dr. Fuentes," she says "and you are?"

I clear my throat "Micah...f...fiancé." The stutter a clear sign of my emotional state. *"Is she going to be ok? Please tell me."* I sign.

Ransom's eyes widen briefly. *"Fiance? Anything you need to tell me, brother?"* He signs back.

"I needed to make sure they let me in. She doesn't have anyone."

The Doctor's eyes are wide, moving from our faces to our hands and back. She fixes her gaze on Ransom when he speaks. "Is my brother's fiancé going to be ok? Give us the rundown...please"

I listen carefully as the doctor lists out Holly's injuries. I can't miss anything.

"From what the paramedics told us, the firefighters found her at the base of a stairwell. There was an elderly man found on top of her. I can only imagine in all the smoke that they tripped or fell down those stairs. Her injuries are consistent with that scenario, anyway. Until she wakes up, we won't know for sure."

She sighs heavily. "Miss Clarke is concussed and has multiple lacerations and bruising, but luckily, no broken bones, and no brain bleeds. Her left ankle is severely sprained. It's going to need to stay immobile for at least a week before physical therapy. She's going to be very tender and painful for a week or two, but she's...and I hate to use the word considering she's lost her home...lucky. It could have been so much worse."

Worse? It sounds fucking horrific already. "Unconscious?" I ask roughly.

"No. She was awake earlier. We've given her something for the pain. She was also quite upset, so we gave her medication to calm her."

"Home?" I ask.

Dr. Fuentes shakes her head. "We'd like to keep her overnight to ensure she's doing well. She's also dealing with smoke inhalation and, well…it's safer for her to stay and be monitored. We're just waiting for a bed for her in one of the wards upstairs."

Wards? No fucking way. I shoot a glance at Ransom, and he nods. "Get her transferred to a private room. Now." I can see the doctor's hackles rise at his tone, and despite the seriousness of the situation, Ransom's slow smile makes me cough out a laugh. He's in his fucking element, so I let him handle it. I reach out and gently stroke the back of Holly's hand as they speak.

"It's not really that easy Mr…"

"Kyle," he answers, his voice clipped. "Ransom Kyle."

I duck my head as she pauses, hiding my grin.

"Ransom Kyle…as in the new Kyle Cancer wing of the hospital. That's you?"

Ransom's laugh is low. "No…that's us." He says, pointing between us. I turn my head, nodding at her before turning my focus back to my Holly.

We insisted Ransom's name go on the building, but all nine of us wanted to make the donation. Good political capital, Ransom said. I don't know about that, but helping sick people sounded like a good use of money. And let's face it, we have more money than God at this point. Might as well spend it doing some good. Dr. Fuentes mutters a bit before backing away to make arrangements, leaving us alone with Holly.

"She's going to need care, Micah." He says quietly, reaching out to touch her foot through the covers. His hand covers it completely.

"I…know," I say roughly. There's no doubt in my mind that I'm going to be the one to take care of her. "*I know we were on rocky ground before this, but I will do whatever I have to, to smooth that over. I need her with me, Ransom. I'll take care of her."* I sign.

He nods, rubbing the top of Holly's foot, looking lost in thought. This is where Kade would jump in making assumptions, defending his right to care for her. His relationship with Ransom has always been more volatile. Me? I wait, holding Holly's hand.

"You ever wonder if Kade's right?" he asks. I raise my eyebrows at him, letting him see my confusion. "Last family dinner, he said something...about fate." I hum at him to continue. "First Becca. Her car dies right at the garage, so Kade meets her. She couldn't be more perfect for him. And then Holly?" My eyes are steady on his. I want to know where he's going with this. "It's been just us for so long, Micah. The nine of us. Sure, the odd woman came around. There's been fucking and fun, but nothing significant. Until now."

"Holly knows sign," I tell him.

He exhales heavily. "That's what Kade said...what do you think the odds are, brother? A woman who can sign showing up to Becca's class, them becoming friends and her taking the job at the garage? Jonas ran the numbers, and well, you're more likely to win the lottery."

I smile, thinking of Jonas sitting in his cardigan, running those calculations. *"We already have. Our lives are one big lottery win. The money, the family we built. The business. All of it."*

"Yeah," he says, fiddling with his cufflink. "So none of this feels like a fucking coincidence. Us. Becca. Now Holly. Maybe it's all...perfect."

I smile, liking that word. Our childhoods were far from perfect. My father beat me so badly I have permanent brain damage. But still, I can see the perfection, especially in Holly.

"She's so tiny," he says, a shadow in his eyes. She is. A touch over five feet with generous curves. Mainstream media would label her fat. Mainstream media can go fuck themselves. I think she's fucking delicious.

I can see the fire in Ran's eyes. The anger. Anger that she's hurt now, and anger that she's ever been hurt. He's already on her side, just because she's vulnerable. But the fact that I'm claiming her, even just to him, even if she's never truly mine, means she's ours. His. She doesn't know it yet, but she'll never have to worry again a day in her life. I've got her. We've got her. But she's strong. She's going to fight it, just like we did when Ransom first found us. She's going to test me, push me away. And just like Ransom, I'll hold steady. I'll be her fucking rock.

"You going to help me keep her?"

He smiles, his eyes shifting from me to Holly. "Yeah man. I can't think of anyone better. But she's going to put you through fucking fire man. You know that, right?"

"She's been controlled, beaten, and probably raped by her ex. She has a lot of fucking healing to do. Even if she heals, she'll be left with scars. So yeah, she's going to put me through fire. I'll walk through it, man. I'll do whatever it takes to help her feel whole again."

He nods, pulling his hand away from her foot to take his phone out. "Ok brother, let's get to work."

So we do.

With Ransom's help, it only takes a few calls and texts to arrange everything. By the time the orderlies come to move her upstairs, all my custom clients have been pushed back and I'm free to focus on her for the next few weeks. Ransom and I walk behind her stretcher, riding up to the private floor with her. We wait in the hallway while the nurses get her settled. They've been giving us looks on this floor too, but I don't care. If our money buys Holly a second more care or comfort, then good. They can gawk at us all they want.

"Do you want me to stick around?" Ransom asks. I want to say no, but I need to make sure the nurses up here know about me and are ready to communicate with me. It used to embarrass me, asking for help or support. But not anymore. I wish I didn't have the disability I do, but it's never going away, so there's no point fighting it.

"I'll need a notebook, or..." I drift off as a young nurse comes up to Ransom, a sparkly pink notebook in her hand. "Here, Mr. Kyle," she says shyly. "I'm sorry it's a little...pink."

I smile at her, taking them from his hands and tucking them under my arm, signing and saying "Thanks." She rushes away with a blush, and I turn to my brother. "Thanks...brother" I say, realizing he's already made sure every single person on this floor knows how to communicate with me. It's pretty typical of him, always smoothing our way if he can.

He smiles, the smile only his brothers get. The big one. The real one. He reaches out and grabs the back of my neck, pulling me in until our foreheads touch. "You text me, man. For anything either of you need. Anytime. Yeah?"

"Yeah," I agree, tugging him into a hug. He hugs me back, then raps me on the back twice before releasing me.

As he steps back, his *Ransom Kyle - Billionaire* mask slides back over his face. "I'll check in later, brother," he says, before turning and walking away. All the nurses watch him go, making me chuckle. Their eyes dart to me, most of them blushing and hurrying back to what they were doing. Except one older nurse who just winks at me.

"I'm not gonna lie honey, I'll be watching you walk away too while you're here. I've gotta get my thrills where I can."

I bark out a laugh. "Deal."

Just then, the nurses exit Holly's room. "You can go in now, Mr. James." I murmur my thanks, already heading into the room, my focus on getting back to Holly as quickly as I can. I need to be there when she wakes up. I need to see those pretty blue eyes. She needs to know she's not alone.

This room is much bigger than the little ER cubby. The

walls are rich paneled wood, and there's a private bathroom attached. I pull the big armchair near the bed closer so I can reach her hand, carefully tucking hers inside mine. As I sit in the peace of the room, the panic of the last couple of hours dissipates. She's here, she's breathing, and I'm right next to her. Nothing else matters. I rest my head back and close my eyes, content to wait for her to wake up.

9

HOLLY

The flaring pain in my body, and especially the throb in my ankle, pull me out of the blackness. Everything hurts.

Like I've done hundreds of times, I stay still, tuning into the room around me, listening for any sign Brent is still here. Too often I moved without thinking and he'd pick up where he left off, feeling like he hadn't properly punished me if I was still conscious. But I don't hear his heavy breaths or smell his heavy cologne. Though I do smell smoke.

The scent feels like it's wrapped around me. But past it I catch a whiff of Irish Spring soap, the fresh smell a welcome relief from the smoke. Feeling safer, I take a deep breath and immediately start coughing. The deep racking movement sends pain shuddering through my body. An arm slides behind me, lifting me against a warm chest. It doesn't feel like Brent. It feels bigger…safe.

"Shh, Shh," the voice whispers as the rim of a cup is pressed to my lips. I wrap my hands around the big one, holding the cup as I take a sip, then another. Slowly my coughing tapers off and I'm able to take a full breath. The arm around my back is gently rocking me now, and I calm as I listen to the warm voice near my ear. "Shh, Holly. Safe. Shh. Safe." The words are slow and deep, and they hum through my chest.

I turn my cheek into him, letting him comfort me. Because I know who this is. I know who owns that deep, rough voice. And for the first time in a decade, I'm comforted. I let myself float in the feeling, feeling tears drip from my sore eyes. A rough thumb comes up to wipe them away, again and again, with featherlight touches. And still, he rocks me. "Shh. Safe. Holly. Ok."

When my tears taper off, and I've tucked the pain away for a few moments, I open my eyes, blinking in the soft glow of the room. All I see are those rough hands, the soft white T-shirt under my cheek, and the line of Micah's jaw. My body's exhausted, and I can't seem to muster up any panic at being this close to a man. Brent never held me like this. Never tried to make me feel better. No one's ever held me, rocked me, soothed me.

I let myself soak it in for just a little while longer. I nearly drift off when memories of last night...this morning flash through my head. With a gasp, I push away from Micah. "Fire," I say, the word traveling through the shattered glass of my throat.

Micah lets me pull away, but his arm stays banded behind me. My eyes drift up his throat before meeting his eyes. His face is so warm, so caring, my tears well up again.

He reaches up to brush away my tears again, looking pained. "Shh. Ok Holly. Shh."

I take a few deep breaths, trying to control myself. I don't want to think about it, but I need the confirmation "Fire, Micah?" I manage to force out through the pain in my throat.

He nods slowly, seriously. "All...gone."

I firm my jaw, not wanting to let the sobs out. My clothes, my flowers. My blanket. Everything I've worked so hard for since I escaped Brent, is gone. I'm back to less than square one. At least when I left Brent, I had a small backpack of clothing. Now I have nothing, not even a pair of underwear.

Micah gently lowers me back to the bed, reaching to tuck the blanket up over me again. For the first time, I wonder where I am. The bed I'm in has railings like a hospital bed, but this room doesn't look like it belongs in any hospital I've been in. There's art on the walls, side tables and lamps, and the softest blanket I've ever felt covering me.

Micah steps back, calling my name. When I focus on him, he signs, *"The firefighters pulled you out. They found you unconscious at the bottom of the stairs. They think you and an old man fell down them together. You're really banged up and you have a concussion. They're going to keep you here overnight, then you'll be released tomorrow. All you have to focus on right now is healing."* I vaguely wonder if the old man survived, but I'm afraid to ask in case he didn't.

Micah reaches out and gently touches my throbbing ankle. "Sprain...hurt?" he asks. I nod. God, I'm in so much pain it's making my teeth throb. He frowns and stands, pushing a button on the side of the bed, then sits back down. He reaches out and starts stroking my arm, the movements slow and steady. I let him lull me into a peaceful detachment, riding the undulating waves of pain, until the door opens and a nurse walks in. Micah doesn't move, other than that slow, gentle rub.

I answer the nurse's questions as best I can, wincing every time I talk. After about the third time, I realize Micah's wincing too. I watch him out of the corner of my eye, and yep, he's only wincing when I do. Huh. If I didn't know he hated me, I'd almost think he was sympathetic. But he hasn't acted like he hates me at all in this room. And that's ... confusing. Him hating me is predictable, reliable. I need predictable.

Finally, the nurse presses a button, and a blessed relief comes over me. The painful throbbing dulling before fading away. I'm being pulled back into sleep, but before I do, I have a moment to wonder, "What am I going to do?"

I didn't realize I asked it out loud until a soft reply comes from Micah. "Home...with...me."

I ponder his words as I fall into sleep. They must not mean what I thought. He hates me, and I honestly can't imagine ever living with another man. It's too risky. Men are volatile, unpredictable, and dangerous. No, it must have been the drugs talking.

10

MICAH

"I 'm not going home with you. You can't make me." Holly crosses her arms over her chest, huffing in annoyance. I hide my smile, smart enough to realize that any sign of amusement is going to be taken the wrong way. But, God, I'm so glad she's feeling good enough to argue with me. She slept most of yesterday and all night, waking briefly for water or for pain management. I'm not sure she even realized it was me with her each time she woke. When I left her to meet Becca and Kade in the lobby this morning, she was still sleeping.

I press my lips into a firm line, and sign, *"You're right. I can't make you. And I won't. But coming home with me makes the most sense. You're still injured. You need looking after."*

She frowns at me, tightening her arms across her chest. The little line between her eyes is adorable. I want to kiss it, kiss her until it goes away. I can't resist dipping my eyes down to admire the way her crossed arms push her breasts up into her hospital gown. I doubt she realizes she's doing it, so I look away. I don't want her to stop.

"It doesn't make any sense at all. You don't even like me. Why on earth would you want me to stay with you?"

I exhale, relieved we can have this conversation now. It's been sitting like a weight on my chest. "Like...you" I say. She's not ready to know how much I do like her. If she knew, she'd probably decide living in a box under a bridge is preferable to coming home with me. *"Becca told Kade you think that. I'm so sorry. That's not how I feel at all."*

She studies me suspiciously, her arms dropping so she can pick at the soft blanket covering her. "Then why do you always look so angry with me? You smile at everyone else, then you see me and boom," she snaps her fingers, "you're looking grumpy." She's trying to hide it, but I can see the hurt on her face.

My neck gets hot. How on earth did I fuck this up so badly? I lean forward in my chair, resting my forearms on my knees. Discarding the list of excuses I've been practicing, I opt for the truth.

"The day we met...when you tripped. You remember?" She bites her lip and nods. *"Well, when I caught you and you panicked...I've seen that before. Felt that before."* I resist the urge to look away as I continue. *"My mom...I saw her react like that more than once. Fuck, I've frozen up like that too. My dad liked to use his fists...he liked to kick when we were down."*

I can't go on, closing my eyes and letting the memories wash through me, letting them have their way with me. I learned a long time ago that pushing them away only prolongs the pain. The hurt. Better to walk through them to the other side. My eyes fly open at the gentle press of fingers on my cheek. I freeze, afraid she'll pull away. Other than the day we met, it's the first time she's ever voluntarily touched me. Yes, she's pushed me away. But this touch, this comfort? I've waited my whole life for it.

"You were hurt too." Her voice is soft, sad.

I swallow thickly and whisper "Yes." She gently scratches the stubble on my cheek before drawing her hand back. I clench every muscle in my body to stop myself from snatching it back to press against my face.

"I still don't understand Micah."

I nod and finish my explanation, hoping she'll forgive my stupidity. "*You're so tiny. So delicate.*" Her eyebrows shoot up. "*Every time I saw you after that day, all I could think about was that someone hurt you. And it made me fucking insane. I have never hated you.*" I clear my throat. "Never," I say strongly. Praying she'll believe me.

I shift in my chair, uncomfortable with this next part. "*I am so sorry I made you afraid of me. You never have to fear me. I would slit my own throat before I ever raise a hand to you.*"

Holly's eyes shift away, her mouth tight. I wait, breathless for the verdict. "It's not just hands that hurt, Micah." She whispers. Her eyes jump back to me at the sound of pain I can't hold in.

"I...know," I say. She studies me while I sit there awaiting judgment. I will take any punishment she wants to dish out. She sighs heavily, leaning back on the raised head of the bed.

"I think we can move on from...all of that." She says carefully. "But I don't think staying with you is a good idea." She's wringing her hands together in her lap. "Maybe I can stay with Becca?" Her voice is so hopeful. I'm tempted to say yes.

"*Becca's taking over for you at the garage. Then she has her classes to teach too. Kade's at work all day, too. You can't stay alone.*"

"You'll be working too." She challenges.

I smile and shake my head. "Nope," I say. "*I pushed all my jobs back. I'm yours for three weeks.*"

Her eyes widen. "You...can you do that?"

I have to laugh. "*I have a three year waiting list Holly. If they can't give me three weeks, then they're free to go elsewhere.*"

"But the money...." She trails off in embarrassment.

"Brash Auto doesn't need their money. I don't need their money. I work because I enjoy taking something damaged and making it beautiful again. But if I never worked a day in my life, I'd still have more money than I could spend in a thousand lifetimes. Next objection?" I ask, raising my eyebrows at her. I know she's got more tucked up in that worried mind of hers.

"What if I need a shower or help...you know? I'm not comfortable with you..." Her face is beet red. I hate that she's embarrassed, but I fucking love the view.

"I have a nurse coming. She'll come twice a day. Morning and bedtime. I can help you to the bathroom during the day. I'll wait on the other side of the closed door. I promise I will respect your boundaries. I just want to take care of you." I swallow roughly, "Please...let...me," I beg. I'll get on my knees for her if she needs me to.

She's considering it. I hold my breath, waiting for her next objection, but she surprises me. "Ok," she mumbles. I manage to stop myself from yelling. But I can't hold back my smile. I don't give her any time to change her mind.

"The doctor will be in soon. He's going to discharge you, then we'll head home."

The doctor's entrance saves her from answering. He checks her over carefully, asking her about her pain levels and concussion symptoms. He gives us a big list of discharge instructions and then heads out to inform the nurses. The older flirty nurse, Mary, is with us in minutes, the benefits of being a VIP, and helps Holly into an air cast. I pay close attention to her instructions, committing them to memory.

"You can take it off to bathe, love. But don't you dare put any weight on this ankle for at least a week. At that point, you should see the rehab team so they can assess how it's healing. Ok?" Holly smiles and murmurs her agreement, looking a little overwhelmed by the Mom energy coming off the nurse. "Now let's get you into some going home clothes. I'm sure your handsome fiancé has something lovely for you."

Holly's eyes widen comically when Mary calls me her fiancé. I rush to explain, *"I told them we're engaged. They wouldn't let anyone in otherwise. They wouldn't have anyone to call, and I couldn't let you be alone here."*

Holly looks flustered, and her eyes narrow. I'm positive she's about to out me, but instead tugs at her gown. "I don't have—". She stops when I grab the bag next to the bed, placing the soft dress in her hands, the bra and panties tucked inside. "I...you?" She asks, her eyes glassy.

I stand, backing away from the bed. *"Becca did some shopping for you yesterday. You've got a whole wardrobe waiting for you at home. I'll give you some privacy."* The nurse is already tugging Holly's gown away, so I head into the adjoining bathroom to regroup.

She's coming. She will be in my home, under my roof. In my bed. That last one sends a bolt of lust through me. I eye the large shower, wondering if it would be inappropriate to take a quick cold one, but the nurse's call sends me spinning back into the room.

Holly and I scuffle a bit over me lifting her into the wheelchair, the nurse laughing at us, but I finally win. I insist on pushing the chair. The nurses all wave, watching us walk out. I turn and meet the older nurse's eyes, shaking my ass at her as we leave. Her laughter rings out brightly. Holly's hiding her face in embarrassment while I wave, saying, "Bye," to everyone. She's ok, and she's coming home, so I'm pretty damn chipper.

My car's waiting right out front thanks to the VIP hospital parking. I pull the wheelchair up to the door, setting the brakes the way the nurse showed me. I pull open the door, then reach down for her. I know better than to just scoop her up, instead coming in close, slowly sliding my arm under her knees, the other under her back. I lock eyes with her anxious ones. "Ok?" I ask, waiting for her nod. Finally, she nods and I stand slowly with her in my arms, taking a few seconds to appreciate her warm weight. I slide her into the car, buckling her up carefully, then closing the door. I run around the car to my side with a spring in my step. She's coming home, and I'm going to be so fucking good to her.

She'll never want to leave.

11

HOLLY

H e's smiling.

Ever since I agreed to stay with him, he hasn't stopped. And I haven't been able to take my eyes off of it. Micah's always been a compelling guy. I can admit that I've been drawn to him since the day I met him. But the scowling and glaring made it easy to stay removed.

Now though? With him looking at me like that? Well, that distance is getting harder and harder to find. Maybe it's an anomaly. He could go back to the grumpy guy any time. In my experience, most men are really excellent actors, but his true colors will shine through, eventually.

I pull my eyes from him, looking around his car instead. This is only the second time I've been in it. I was too upset to pay attention to any details the first time. Having your husband attack your friend with a knife right in front of you will do that. But now I can appreciate how soft the leather seat is, how comfortable. I've worked at the garage for just over two months, but I still don't know much about cars. But I can tell this one is old and beautifully restored.

"What kind of car is this?" I ask him. He glances over, smiling again.

"Dodge...Co.." He trails off, taking a deep breath. "Coronet".

"It looks like a car from the seventies." Wow Holly, brilliant observation.

"Yeah," He says, patting the dash. "Fixed...it." He slows to a crawl, taking a careful right. He's driving like an old woman.

The car is rumbling under me, the vibrations almost like a massage. Between the rumbles and how gently he's driving, I relax. I've been on the verge of a panic attack since we left the hospital. It's not just going home with Micah, though I'm not sure I want to think about that too hard right now. Better to compartmentalize that. It's that everything I've worked so hard for is gone.

"Ok?" Micah asks, his voice concerned.

"No," I say, frustrated by that question. I swear I've been asked it fifty times over the last two days, and I'm over it.

"Say...it," he rumbles.

"I've lost everything!" I yell, wincing in pain. My throat is still so sore. "I have nothing left. Nothing! Every time I try to build something for myself, it goes up in flames. Literally this time!" I'm such a failure.

Micah makes a sympathetic sound, lifting a hand from the steering wheel before dropping back to clench on the steering wheel. "Be...ok."

I snort and drop my tired head against the headrest. "Easy for you to say. You have no concept of what it's like to be my age and have no safety net. You'll never know. You've got a family that is always there for you."

He meets my eyes briefly, his lips pressed together tightly. "I...got...you." He says, voice strong and clear. It's a nice sentiment, but that's all it is. Sentiment. When push comes to shove, I'll be on my own.

This isn't my first rodeo.

I've lived this before. Someone coming to my rescue. It's

never free. There's always a price to pay, no matter what he says.

We finally pull into the guy's high rise. I crane my neck to look all the way to the top. It's still strange to me that the guy next to me, the guy who spends his day working on cars, lives in a multi-million dollar condo. He lives a life I honestly can't comprehend. They all do.

What would it be like to wake up and not have to worry about how you're going to buy food that week? Or keep a roof over your head?

Micah swings into the underground garage, looping down until he goes through the next security gate. He parks, exhaling heavily, and grabs his phone, sending a quick text, then turns to me. "Home."

I swallow tightly and nod, the easy way he says that word clattering through my body. For most of my life, home has not been an easy place for me. It's always been somewhere I had to make myself smaller, invisible, just to stay safe.

Micah swings my door open, crouching to release my belt. I look down at my bare toes again, wiggling them into the plush floor mat, before looking back at him. I slowly reach out, putting my hand on his shoulder. He smiles at me warmly before sliding his arm behind my back and under my knees.

As he stands, I'm bombarded by sensation. My back and legs are tingling where he's holding me. The warmth of his chest is radiating through me, warming me straight to my core.

I've been held before. Even with my extra padding, I'm still a small woman. Brent never hesitated to pick me up. But he never did it with the care and consideration Micah does. He's always checking in with me, checking that I'm ok. That I'm not freaking out. I really like that he does that, just as much as I hate that he needs to.

We stop in front of the private elevator servicing just the

top floors. It takes me a second to realize we're just standing there, Micah holding me casually, his stance relaxed. I'm about to tell him he can put me down when the doors swing open revealing Colton.

Despite my discomfort, my anxiety, I smile. There's just something about him that is so sweet. So approachable. It makes no sense. He's as tall as Micah, but wider. An absolute wall of muscle, tattoos winding up his arms into the sleeves of his t-shirt. His brown eyes are piercing and his dark beard should make him look scary, but somehow he's not.

"Hey sweet girl," he says with a smile, "your chariot awaits." He waves us into the elevator, gently bumping shoulders with Micah. We settle at the back of the elevator, Micah leaning against the wall as Colton enters his security code and scans his palm. He hits the button for Kade and Micah's floor, then turns to me with kind eyes. "You hanging in there?"

I bite the inside of my cheek, conscious of Micah's eyes on me too. "I'm alive," I say finally. "I guess that counts for something." I can't muster up any more enthusiasm than that, and I'm embarrassed. I should be more grateful. I know that. Life is precious, yada, yada. But I'm still in the throes of *why me*, so I'll need to wallow a bit longer before I get to grateful.

Colton glances at Micah before reaching out to pat my shoulder with his big hand. "It's ok to not be ok, sweets. We've got you for as long as you need us. Micah's going to take such good care of you, and we'll all come check on you so you don't get sick of his ugly mug."

My lips curl at the playful grumble coming from Micah's chest. The way these guys interact is pretty special. I haven't spent much time around them, but there's always a clear undercurrent of affection when they speak to each other.

I'm woman enough to admit that it hurts to see sometimes. The affection in their chosen family makes the absence of it in my family and my marriage glaring. No one's ever looked at me like they love me. I thought Brent did, at the beginning, but I'm coming to see it was just a pale shadow of the real thing. He didn't love me. Maybe he couldn't love me. Maybe it was me.

It feels like only seconds and the elevator doors open to the little foyer. Colton moves out first, pressing his palm to the scanner and unlocking Micah's door. As nervous as I am to be here, to be alone with him, I am also intensely curious to see how he lives. Kade's apartment is sleek and industrial. It suits him. Will Micah's be that way too? He seems to have such an appreciation for old things that I somehow can't picture him living with concrete and steel.

As the door swings open, my attention is immediately caught by frantic meowing. I'm a long way from the floor, but I strain to look down, catching quick peeks of a small cat winding around Micah's feet.

He. Has. A. Cat.

Suddenly, staying here doesn't seem like it'll be so bad.

"Minnie," Micah calls, making little kissing noises. My eyes widen and I stare at him, unable to process what I'm witnessing. Micah has a cat. She's tiny. Her freaking name is Minnie. And Micah's calling her like she's his baby.

He huffs out a laugh, shuffling slowly through the door so he doesn't trip on the cat. "Colt," he calls with a laugh.

"On it," Colt says as he reaches down to scoop her up. He presses her to his face, her little body so tiny in his hands, giving her little kisses. She doesn't look like a kitten, but she can't be full grown, can she? My hands flex, desperate to hold her. Colton's dancing eyes move from my hands to my face. Then he reaches out and drops that little ball of sweetness on my chest.

My hands come up reflexively. She's so incredibly soft. Her little body is rumbling with purrs. She lets me stroke her a few times before turning to climb up Micah's chest to his shoulder. She pushes her head against his jaw, and he turns his head to run his cheek over hers. When she seems satisfied with the attention, she settles against his neck, purring, looking perfectly at home. Micah's still smiling when he focuses back on me. "Bed...couch?" he asks.

I take a minute to check in with my body. I'm exhausted, but I feel like I've just entered an alternate universe. No way can I sleep yet. "Couch," I say quietly, briefly meeting his eyes before reaching up to scratch under Minnie's chin.

Micah strides through the entryway, moving to the living room and placing me gently on a big, brown sectional. The cushions cradle me, and some of the tension in my body releases. I'm not used to being so close to a man, any man, for so long and despite Micah being a perfect gentleman, I was still anxious. He pulls a red blanket off the back of the couch and carefully covers me, tucking it around my waist and under my feet. I just watch, dumbfounded, as he takes care of me. His cat doesn't move from her perch, just digging her nails in to hold on as he bends and twists.

Micah barely seems to notice she's there. The ease they both seem to have with the position tells me it's normal for him. I shake my head slowly, making Micah tilt his in confusion. "You have a cat," I say. Clearly I'm a sparkling conversationalist. But I'm having trouble wrapping my head around this version of Micah.

He smiles again, then signs, "*Yeah. I've had her a couple of years.*"

"And you named her Minnie? Like Minnie Mouse?"

"*The rescue named her. I didn't want to confuse her by changing it.*"

He didn't want to confuse the cat.

I'm in the twilight zone. That's the only explanation.

"Water," he says suddenly, heading for the kitchen. I giggle a little, watching Minnie bounce on his shoulder, tail in the air as he leaves, then finally turn my attention to Micah's apartment.

It is nothing like Kade's.

Where Kade's is modern and industrial, Micah's is warm and homey. Wood floors, warm walls. Soft colors and fabrics. It's like a...nest. Somewhere you'd want to hole up for weeks. The focal point in this room is floor to ceiling bookshelves. I'm green with envy, looking at his collection. There must be over a thousand books there, and I'm itching to explore them.

I slide myself to the edge of the couch, slowly pushing to my feet, keeping my weight off the air cast. I'm ok for a second, before a wave of dizziness hits me and I stagger backward, dropping heavily back to the cushions. I vaguely hear a shout, then feel Micah's arm around me, carefully rubbing my back. I swallow back the bile, trying to breathe through my nausea. That was a bad idea.

I hear a groan of frustration before his guttural "Bed." I reach out, tangling my fingers in Micah's shirt, trying to ground myself.

"Ok," I whisper. "Carefully."

Careful he is. He picks me up like I'm a priceless treasure, carrying me delicately. He sits down on a bed, settling me in his lap. I freeze at the new position, breathing through a spurt of panic. But he does nothing more than rub my back, breathing quietly.

Finally, I open my eyes. I'm in a huge bedroom. It's bigger than the whole main floor of my home with Brent. There's a mound of pillows against the wood headboard, and I want to wiggle into them until I feel like I'm in a fluffy cloud. I see an attached bath, and my heart stops.

"This is *your* room," I say, easing away from him. Of course it is. I don't know why I'm disappointed. It's exactly what I expected after all, but I guess I thought his promise that I would be safe with him would last a day at least.

Micah gently lowers me off his lap onto the bed before sliding to crouch beside me.

"It's the main bedroom, but I don't sleep here. My room's on the

other side of the apartment. Do you think you can be comfortable here?"

I'm stuck on the fact that he doesn't sleep here. "Why don't you sleep in here? Was someone else staying here?" And was it a woman? It's none of my business, but I still want to know.

His eyes fall to the ground, then he tips back until he's sitting on his bum, stretching his legs out in front of him. He looks sheepish. *"I stayed in here when I first moved in, I just… couldn't sleep."* He shrugs his shoulders, looking uncomfortable.

I shouldn't push. He doesn't look like he's eager to talk about it, and I know better than most people that pushing can backfire. But I'm so intensely curious about this man. Far more than is healthy. "Why couldn't you sleep?"

He studies me thoughtfully before finally replying. *"Actually, you might understand better than most people. I couldn't stay in here because it felt too open. Like there were too many places an attack could come from."*

I exhale, leaning back on my hand. How many times had I slept curled up in a corner, too afraid Brent would come at me from behind? And the shelter…well that was both better and worse. Better because I was away from Brent, but worse because there were so many other dangers to look out for. "Yeah. I guess I do understand." I tell him, then answer his earlier question. "This room is nicer than anywhere I've ever been, so yeah, I'll be comfortable."

His body relaxes. *"You're still dizzy, right?"* I nod carefully. *"Do you think you can sleep for a while longer? I stayed in bed for three days after my last concussion, so you're already a badass for being up and talking."* He winks at me, and heat travels up my neck. This version of Micah, the smiling, flirty one, is a lot to handle.

I have to snort, though, at his use of badass. "I'm so far from a badass, I'm not even on the same continent." Becca's a badass. Strong, kicks ass, never lets anyone hurt her. Me? I let my husband beat me for years. No, I know who I am, and it's a lot closer to coward.

"Holly...badass," he snaps, his familiar glare on his face. *"I see you. You are so strong. Can't you see it?"* Wincing, I shake my head.

"How?" he asks, eyes wide. *"You built a life for yourself, despite all the shit you've had to live through. By yourself,"* he emphasizes, his eyebrows raised, hands flying. *"You know how many women would just stay? And what about coming to work at the garage? You're there with all of us, keeping us in line. Fuck, you keep all of us in line, Holly. Can't you see how amazing you are?"*

I can't take the way he's looking at me. He doesn't truly see me. He can't. I let myself imagine for a minute that I am someone strong, a woman in control of her life, but it fades away. Because it's not true.

"I'm tired," I tell him, closing my eyes to block out his knowing look. "I'd like to sleep now." I can feel his eyes on me. Judging. But I can handle it. I've handled it my whole life. It's a safe, familiar feeling.

"Bathroom?" he asks quietly. I startle, opening my eyes to find him leaning over me. I shrink back instinctively.

"No," I shout. No way do I want him going in the bathroom with me. It's just too much. My eyes fill with tears. "Please. Just go."

He studies me, his face tightening before nodding and pulling away. "Sleep...Holly," he says and softly closes the door.

I carefully pull myself backwards on the bed until I can nestle into the pillows. Away from his piercing eyes, I finally feel like I can let go. I let the tears flow, carrying away my helplessness, my fear, my sadness. Until I feel like I'm empty, barren. Only then do I drift into sleep, wishing I could walk across the room and lock the door.

Just in case.

12

MICAH

Holly sleeps for the rest of the day. I check on her a lot, more than necessary I'm sure, but now that I have her here, under my roof, I'm having trouble staying away from her.

Every time I go in, I have to go right to the bed. She's so far into the pillows that I can barely spot her head. I moved a few so she wouldn't suffocate in her sleep. I know that can happen to babies, and clearly she's not a baby, but better safe than sorry.

I thought I would settle down once I had her here. Instead, I'm even more worried about her. Is she sleeping too much? Does she need anything? Did she fall out of bed? Does she need a cuddle? It's getting ridiculous.

I finally grab Minnie, pull the new Eve Dallas novel off my shelf, and settle down to read. I only look at the clock a million times before settling into the story. I jump up when I get notification that the nurse is on her way up. Holly's going to have to wake up now.

I let the nurse in, and we make quick introductions on the way to Holly's room. I knock this time, pretty loudly, but don't get a response. I creep open the door, and see she still hasn't moved. I crouch down next to the bed. "Holly…wake," I say as I rub her arm. She wakes with a gasp, pulling her arms in tight over her chest protectively.

Fuck.

"Sorry…Holly…Ok." I whisper, staying right where I am. It takes her a minute, but her breathing finally slows and her body uncurls. Her blue eyes meet mine, and I smile at her, despite my strong desire to put my fist through the wall.

That reaction wasn't a normal startle, that was a learned reaction. She just told me, without saying a word, that she's been woken up by a beating.

She pushes her tousled hair away from her face, slowly sitting up. "W…what time is it?" she mumbles.

"Nine," I tell her, as I motion the nurse closer. "Kathy," I say pointing to her. When I'm sure Holly's awake enough to see, I sign, *"The nurse I hired. Kathy will come in the morning and night to help you change and take care of anything else you need her to. I'll be here, but I thought you might be more comfortable with a woman helping?"*

"Oh…ok." She looks at the nurse. "I really would like a shower. My hair still smells like smoke."

"I'll carry you to the bathroom," I say, eagerly opening my arms for her. After the way she woke up, I can't bring myself to reach for her. Forcing any kind of touch on her right now feels wrong. So I wait, holding my breath, while she studies me. Finally, she scoots closer. I meet her in the middle, carefully picking her up. And I can breathe again. "Got…you."

"Oh Micah," she exclaims as we enter the bathroom "you shouldn't have."

Oh yes, I should. Anything she needs is mine to provide. Even if it's just handrails on the toilet and a shower chair. She doesn't need to know about the after hours emergency plumber who installed the handheld shower attachment. "You…needed." I tell her gruffly.

I'd explain to her that I'd do anything for her, but that

would mean putting her down and I'm not quite ready to do that. Instead, I carry her through to the walk-in closet, pulling out the top drawer, revealing brand new pyjamas of every variety. "Pick," I tell her, wanting her to feel clean and cozy. She leans forward, trusting me to hold her as she picks up a soft yellow set. Then I carry her straight into the huge shower stall, setting her carefully on the chair.

"Thank you," she says softly, watching me as I back slowly out of the room. I can't seem to go far, sliding down the wall next to the bathroom door. I want to be close in case she needs me. I close my eyes and relax, letting the women's muffled voices lull me into a doze.

Finally, the door opens.

"She's all set, Mr. James," the nurse says. "She did really well, but it took a lot out of her. She's going to need her pain meds pretty soon." I stand and thank her, heading straight for Holly. She's still on the shower chair, but now she's wearing the buttery yellow pyjamas, the fabric stretched around the air cast. Her hair is wet, combed back from her face.

I wince at the look on her face. "Hurt," I say in sympathy.

"Yes," she breathes, reaching up for me.

She actually reached for me.

I don't let the fact that she'd be stuck in the shower all night if she didn't want me to pick her up dim my pleasure at the simple sign of acceptance. I scoop her up again. "Come eat," I say, carrying her out to the living room. I deposit her on the couch and sit on the coffee table in front of her.

"You need food in your stomach for the pain meds. Is there anything you feel like eating? I ordered a few things, but I can get you anything you want."

"You ordered a few things? Like…" she prompts.

"Ah…" I rub the back of my neck. *"I ordered Chinese, and Thai. Then I got pizza. Some salads. And I have lots of sandwiches, too."* My face is hot.

Holly's smile grows as I list off item after item, then she

giggles. I swear time stops. Just fucking stops. It's the best thing I've ever heard. I'm smiling so big it's got to be touching my ears. I don't care that she's laughing at me. She's laughing! *"I know. I went a little overboard. I just wanted you to have something you'd like. Does any of it sound good?"*

"Can I sit at the island so you can show me?"

Um, yeah she can.

I settle her on the massive granite island, then carefully open the my commercial sized fridge. I have to catch a falling take-out container when I do. Peals of laughter ring out.

"You're unbelievable." She's giggling and snorting and it's fucking adorable. "Did you order everything on every menu?" She watches in awe as I pull out container after container of food, about ten sandwiches, then three pizza boxes, filling the entire island she's sitting on.

"Pretty much," I admit. *"I haven't had time to get to know you well. I'll learn, though. I promise. By the time you're better, I'll know exactly how you like your coffee, what your favorite food is,"* and where you like to be kissed. Of course I don't sign that last part, but it's going to happen. I was hooked before, but the woman smiled at me, so now I'm fucked.

Completely hers.

She reaches over and starts opening containers, humming or scrunching up her nose at what she finds inside. When we have all the lids open, I grab a plate and some spoons. I slowly work my way through them, adding items based on her yes's and no's until she tells me to stop. "More," I order, frowning at the too-empty plate.

"I don't need any more. Are you trying to fatten me up?" she teases.

I run my eyes slowly down her body, over the curve of her shoulders, the soft swell of her breasts, imagining them overflowing even my large hands. When I finally drag my eyes back to her, I say the only thing I can. "Perfect." She is absolute perfection. I put the plate down, wanting to make sure there's no confusion. *"You are absolutely perfect, every single bit of you. I want you to eat enough to help you heal."*

Her eyes are dazed, and she just stares at me as I pick up the plate. "More?" I ask again, pointing at the next dish.

"Ah..." she clears her throat, "just a little more. I'm still a little nauseous." I nod and add a little more to her plate, then pop it in the microwave to warm.

"Your turn," she says. I smile and get another plate out, piling it high. She watches, her mouth dropping open as I keep adding. "You didn't eat?"

I put my plate down near the microwave, stepping closer to her, my stomach almost brushing her knees. *"I wanted to eat with you."*

She smiles nervously, glancing away. "What are we going to do with all of this?" She asks, gesturing to the twenty plus containers on the counter.

I snort, putting the things she liked back in the fridge, then pulling my phone out of my back pocket. I snap a photo and send a quick text, then run and prop open the door. I pull down the plates and dump cutlery on the table.

"Watch," I say, reaching for her. She comes into my arms willingly, and I hop up to sit on the back counter with her in my lap, so she gets a good view.

The elevator dings.

Their voices are tumbling together as they push past each other to get out first. Colt and Declan are wrestling in my doorway. Pretty sure Declan has his finger up Colt's nose. Jonas drops to the floor and army crawls past them, popping up and running straight for the food. He grabs a plate and piles it high, glancing behind him quickly, grabbing another slice of pizza and getting out of the way. He's just in time too, as Colt and Declan crash into the island. Holly startles in my arms, but she's smiling, eyes wide. Jonas settles at the table, his arm wrapped around his plate to protect it as he takes big bites of the pizza in his hand.

Colt and Declan are busy filling their plates when we hear another ding. They speed up as Maverick and Nick come straight for the food, desperate to get their fill. They're both wearing suits, unlike the rest of the guys who look like they came up from the gym.

Holly tensed in my arms when the guys first came in, but I could feel her start to relax as they completely ignored her, zoned in on the food. Eventually, a little laugh escapes. "Do they not have food at home?" she asks, watching them with wide eyes.

"Always...hungry," I tell her with a laugh. Another ding from the elevator and out comes Kade and Becca. Becca drops her gym bags, running full tilt for Holly.

She stops just in front of us and bursts into tears. "I was so scared for you! I kept checking but he," she says, pointing at me accusingly "wouldn't let me in."

"Sleeping!" I growl at her. No way was I going to wake Holly up just so Becca could snot all over her. She has a concussion, for fuck's sake. "Asshole!" Becca growls back at me, making me smile despite my annoyance, then gingerly hugs Holly.

"I'm so glad you're ok," she says softly. "When I saw those pictures of your building...well it was horrible."

Holly leans into Becca, soaking in the affection in a way she won't with me. But she reached for me today, I remind myself. Baby steps.

"It was horrible," Holly whispers. "The smoke was so thick and everyone was screaming..."

My arms tighten around her, my heart pumping hard. Imagining her crawling through the smoke and fire has me on edge all over again. I wish again that I could have been there for her. I'm not a fucking fireman, but no way would I have ever left that building without her. She won't ever be afraid or in danger again.

I'll make sure of it.

After I get my heart rate under control, I take Holly over to the dining table, we all have the same twelve seater, and settle her next to Colt, knowing she'll feel safe with him. I hurry back to the microwave, pulling out her steaming food and popping mine in. The guys didn't bother to heat anything up.

They never do.

Maybe it's because most of us were so hungry for so long, or maybe because we're not patient enough to share one microwave. Either way, the guys are already plowing through their food.

I fill a glass with water, bring it and the plate to Holly, then grab my food and our forks. I settle next to her and start eating, keeping a careful eye on her and her plate. She said she was nauseous, but I hope she can eat it all. She needs to keep up her strength. I have this bizarre urge to get up and cook her something. Like a fucking steak or spaghetti. But since I can't fucking cook, I have to settle for takeout.

My brothers are their usual selves; loud, annoying, and rude. The fact that Becca and Holly are at the table doesn't seem to change anything.

Becca, I get. She's just one of the guys, but I'm surprised that their behavior isn't better with Holly around. I keep checking in, worried they're going to upset her, but she actually seems to be enjoying their nonsense. They're not ignoring her, sliding her small smiles and the occasional wink when they lock eyes, but for the most part, they're letting her be. Her eyes are jumping from one of my brothers to another, the corner of her mouth creased with a smile.

The elevator dings again, and I look up, nodding at Ransom as he walks in. He grabs a few slices of pizza, then sits across the table from Holly. He dressed in his full *Ransom Kyle - Billionaire* outfit, and I'm worried Holly's going to feel intimidated. Not because Ransom will try to make her feel that way, like he did with Becca, but because it's just who he is.

Holly's carefully avoiding looking at him, and my hackles rise. I shoot him a quick look. He nods, my unspoken order clear.

"I'm glad to see you looking better Holly," he says in a quiet rumble.

Her eyes widen. "Better?"

"I was with Micah at the hospital yesterday," he explains. "How are you feeling?"

Her face flushes, glancing between Ransom and I. "I...um I feel a bit better. Still sore."

I shove away from the table, heading to the prescription bottle on the counter. I shake out a pill and bring it back to her. She's eaten enough that it should be ok for her to take it now. I pass her the pill, pushing her water glass into her hand. She gives me a funny look, but swallows the pill quickly. I smile, then point across the table. "Ransom," I tell her.

Her wide eyes dart back to him before glancing away again. "Ah. Hello. Nice to meet you."

I hold in a laugh at her tone of voice, which doesn't match her words at all.

"Dude, seriously?" Becca interrupts, waving her fork around. "You growled at me and told me to watch my back when we met! And Holly gets 'how are you'. You're playing favorites, dude!"

Holly's eyes get even wider, and her hands drop to clench together in her lap. I reach over and rub my fingers over her knuckles. "Ok," I tell her when her eyes shoot to mine.

"I don't play favorites. I respond to the situation appropriately Becca. Holly's injured. You were not." His words are crisp, aloof, but we all see the wrinkles around his eyes. He's trying pretty damn hard not to smile. Becca has that effect on him.

"I'd been attacked by a knife wielding psycho! Sorry Holly." She says, slapping a hand to her chest dramatically. "Didn't I deserve a little bit of nice Ransom?" She asks, her voice rising.

The corners of his mouth are twitching. "You called me dude," he deadpans.

Becca gasps, fire in her eyes. Kade doesn't make any effort to stop her, instead sitting there laughing while she loads her fork up with noodles and launches them at Ran.

Everyone else at the table freezes, all of us holding our breath, poised for battle. Becca has no idea what she's started. Ransom looks down at his noodle spattered suit before raising his eyes to Becca. "This means war," he says coldly, a sinister smile erupting on his face.

From Holly's other side, Colt screams, "I'll save you Becca!" before launching a slice of pizza across the table at Ransom, who easily ducks.

Jonas sighs heavily. "Not another one."

"Another one what?" Holly asks. I realize she's tense, but the guys are long past caring there's an audience.

I'm about to explain when Colton yells, "Food Fight!"

The words are like an electric charge, striking everyone at the table. Holly gasps as I dive in front of her, wrapping myself around her as the food starts flying. I hear her suck in a breath. It explodes out when the first slap of curry hits the back of my head and slides down, plopping into her lap. My chuckles turn into full belly laughs as I feel more splatters. The guys are howling with laughter, and I hear Becca cackle, "I'm a ninja, motherfucker. You gotta try harder than that to get me!"

The chaos around me stills as Holly's small hands rise and grip my sides, slowly sliding them up under my arms. My entire body hardens as I focus in on that small, soft touch. I tilt my head until I can see her eyes. They're darting side to side, trying to look around me. I don't want to risk her getting hit accidentally, so I stay wrapped around her.

A pile of noodles rains down on me, some of them hooking over my ears, slapping wetly on my cheek. Holly reaches up and pulls at the noodles, watching as they stretch, then slide off my ear. Then she snorts, giggles, and sinks down in her chair in a puddle of laughter. The sound is free and joyous.

I'll start a million food fights if it means hearing her laugh like this.

When the food finally stops flying, Micah carries me to the island, coming back with a wet cloth. He carefully wipes food droplets off my cheek, my hair, and my shoulder. His touch is featherlight.

I stay still, not wanting his careful care of me to stop, but predictably, my anxiety rises and I pull away. He smiles, carrying me back to the bedroom where Becca helps me change my dirty pyjamas. Once he had me settled on the couch, he moved back to the dining room, helping the others clean up. The guys all know where the cleaning supplies are. They work like a well-oiled machine, gently shooing a snacking Minnie away, making it pretty clear that this is not their first food fight.

I laugh again, thinking about it. I never would have imagined that this group of grown-up men would play like that. The part of me used to living in poverty is dying inside watching them scoop so much food into the garbage can. I could have fed myself for a week on what they're garbaging.

I've eaten worse, and it wouldn't be the first time I've eaten food from the floor. Brent used to dump my dinner plate on the floor after a particularly frustrating day at work.

He'd sit there, boots crossed under the table, eating his meal while forcing me to scoop mine off the floor with my hands. My stomach would be in knots, knowing it's just a prelude to a beating, but I would force myself to eat slowly and deliberately, hoping that maybe he'd cool off and I could avoid the pain. It never worked, but I lived in hope that it might.

Hope.

That was the only thing keeping me moving most days.

The guys are still laughing as Micah hands out garbage bags. My breath stutters in my chest and I sink down into the couch until I'm peeking over the top. The men are all stripping out of their clothes, shoving them into the garbage bags. Becca strips off her shirt and leggings, leaving her in a tank top and boy shorts, the cut of the material emphasizing her strong body and heavy breasts, then runs towards me, diving over the back of the couch to flop at the other end. She crawls down the couch until she's snuggled up next to me. A bouquet of Chinese, Thai and pizza wafts towards me.

"Your hair is completely covered," I say with a laugh.

Her grin is manic. "It was worth it. That was so much fun. Do you…" She drifts off as her gaze snags on the men. Kade's joined the others, stripping off until the hard planes of his body are revealed.

The look on Becca's face makes me blush. She's looking at him like she wants to devour him. I let my eyes trace over him quickly, but don't linger. It seems wrong to look at my friend's boyfriend when he's naked. He's wearing his boxers, but still. I slide down a little lower, studying the long limbs and powerful muscles of all the guys. I didn't think men looked like that in real life, not unless they lived in a gym.

While all the men are big, the shortest still over six feet, it's easy to see the differences. Kade and Colton are clearly the most muscular, both of them looking like they could bench press a train. But Colton's muscles seem to have muscles. I wonder how he makes it through the door. The other men are slightly leaner, like, bench press a car instead of a train lean, and equally beautiful. My eyes are dancing over the array of tattoos covering their bodies when Micah walks past the others. Busy handing out the garbage bags, he's still wearing his dirty clothes. The front, where he was pressed up against me, is still mostly clean, but his entire back is covered in stains and food particles. I shift in my seat, remembering the way it felt, having his big, laughing body covering me. The way his body shook with his laughter. How good it felt.

I shift my eyes quickly to Becca, worried she'll call me out for staring, but she's completely focused on Kade, mumbling something about ties and climbing, so I go back to gawking. As I turn back, a laughing Micah reaches back and pulls his t-shirt over his head.

I was wrong. Micah's bigger, more muscular than Kade for sure, but not quite as big as Colton.

He shifts, peering at the seat of his sweats, shaking his head and dropping his pants, stepping out of them, kicking them up in the air and catching them. My greedy eyes sweep over his form, from the dusting of hair on his legs, skipping over what's hidden by his boxer briefs to the line of dark hair traveling out from his waistband. My fingers twitch, wondering what that hair might feel like under my fingertips, wanting to touch and stroke. I never felt like this with Brent, not even on our wedding night, before everything turned bad. This heat, this fascination, is new.

I thought I was being sneaky, but when I look a little higher, I meet Micah's laughing eyes. He winks, and with a cough I carefully slide all the way down until I'm lying on the couch. I slap my hands over my blazing cheeks, groaning in embarrassment.

A giggling Becca's weight drops beside me on the wide couch. I elbow her in the side, glaring at her to shut up, but of course it doesn't work.

"He caught you looking!" she teases, shoving me back.

"Micah and Holly, sitting in a tree, k— oomph." Her tongue comes out and licks the hand I slapped over her mouth.

"Ew," I squeal. "You're disgusting!"

Becca pokes her tongue out, then settles her head next to mine. We're pressed together tightly in a safe little bubble.

"How are you really?" she asks quietly. "Your body went through a lot in the last two days."

I nod, mentally cataloging my injuries. "I'm ok. I've been through worse." As soon as I say the words, I wish I could take them back. They're true, but bringing Brent up in this place that was so filled with laughter only seconds ago is like throwing water on a fire.

"I hate that for you," she says, covering my hand with hers. Her warmth sinks into me, but a stray thought, that it doesn't feel as comforting as Micah's, shocks me. "You've never really talked about him. About what you've lived through…"

I turn my head to study her. She's shared some of her pain, the death and grief she dealt with after her father's cancer battle. "No. I don't think it's something I'll ever share with you." I tell her honestly.

Her eyebrows arrow down. "You need to talk to someone, Holly. I'm a good listener, I swear."

She's so earnest, truly believing that she could handle the darkness that was my life. I slowly shake my head. "I love you. You're one of the best friends I've ever had. But I will never share that part of my life with you." I cover our clasped hands with my other. "Your life has been pretty blessed. You've mostly seen the good, and I'm so glad. But the things I've lived through…well I don't want those things to have to exist in you too. They're too big a burden for you to bear."

A tear rolls over the bridge of her nose and down her cheek. "You need to talk to someone," she says, her voice thick. "I'm pretty tough, Hol, I can handle it."

I smile, but don't respond. There's nothing she could say

to convince me to share. I don't want her thinking about how weak I was. How much I let him hurt me. How awful the things he did to me were. That would be the only thing she'd see when she looks at me, and I don't think I can take it.

She wiggles even closer, pressing her forehead to mine. "Promise me you'll talk to someone about all of it."

I exhale, suddenly exhausted. "I've talked to lots of people, Becca. Counselors, doctors, social workers." So many that their names and faces blur together.

"But so much has happened to you recently, with Brent and now the fire." Her eyes are pleading.

"Stop it," I say firmly, done with this conversation. I let a little of the anger simmering below the surface bubble up, pulling my hands away from hers. "I'm a fully functioning adult. I don't need or want you to be my keeper. Stop treating me like I can't take care of myself, because I can Becca. I've been doing it my whole life. I don't have to promise you anything."

My heart is racing, my palms damp. It's a familiar reaction. The same thing happened anytime I spoke up for myself in the past. But Becca's not going to beat me for speaking up. No, what she could do would be so much worse.

She could walk away.

Decide being my friend is not worth it. That I'm not worth the trouble. I close my eyes, blocking out the hurt in hers.

I should take it all back. Smooth it all over. Tell her I didn't mean it. It's what I've been trained to do. But I resist the urge.

I exhale heavily. "I can't have another person in my life treating me like I'm stupid. Like I'm helpless." I carefully pull myself to sitting, mindful of my ribs, and turn to look down at her. "I got myself out Becca. I built a new life. And yes, I've had a crappy couple of months, but I'm still breathing. I just need to rest for a little while, then I'll find my way. You have to let me. Please."

She's studying me, the hurt bleeding off her face. Finally

she nods, "I hear you. I'm really sorry. I know I can be a bit much. Just tell me to fuck off if I overstep. Ok?"

"Ok," I murmur, leaning into the corner of the couch. I let her apology settle over me like a warm weight. No one's apologized to me in years, and now I've had two in as many days.

I like it, not always being the one in the wrong.

"Are you doing ok here with Micah? You're welcome to come stay with us." She says hesitantly.

I smile, turning to watch the guys. Most of the food has been picked up, but the guys seem to have stopped cleaning to… "What are they doing?" I ask.

Becca sits up and looks at them, choking out a laugh. "Picking up noodles with their toes. It's gotta be another stupid bet."

They seem to have divided themselves into two teams. They're cheering on their teammate as he picks up a noodle with his toes, then hops it over to the garbage can, lifting his foot to drop it in.

"He looks so disgusted," I say, watching one guy who looks like he's about to vomit. I cover my mouth to hold back the giggles, not wanting to interrupt this bizarre competition.

Becca's laughing so hard tears are running down her face. "That's Jonas. Oh God, I can't believe he's playing. He hates being dirty. And the feeling of the noodles between his—" We both break into hysterical laughter as Jonas gags, dry heaving as he grabs a noodle and hops frantically to the garbage can. He collides with Colton.

"Jesus, Colt!" Becca yells suddenly. "You have the flexibility of a rock."

She's right. He can't seem to raise and twist his foot enough to drop the noodle, instead hopping back and trying to drop it in the can straight legged. He flips her the middle finger. Meanwhile, Jonas is still dry heaving, and some of the other guys have joined him, alternating between gagging and yelling at Jonas to stop gagging.

I honestly can't believe what I'm seeing. "If you'd told me this morning that I'd be watching a room full of half naked billionaires pick up food with their toes..." I trail off, not even sure how to finish that sentence. It sounds like some sort of fetish porn. Becca seems to get it though.

"I know," she says, still laughing. "They're nothing like you'd imagine. They're all so tough, so accomplished. And Ransom," the giggle snorts are starting watching him take his turn. "Ransom is hard as nails. He scares the piss out of the rest of the world, never letting them see what's underneath. The only people who get to see him like this are family."

Her smile is knowing as she looks between the guys and me. The implications of her simple words rattle me. "Family?" I ask. Wanting...no, needing to understand.

"Family," she confirms. "They would never act like this around outsiders. They're like the lost boys when they're together. Never wanting to grow up. Maybe it's because they didn't really have a childhood. They're making up for it now. I don't know, really. But the fact that they're all over there in their tighty-whities means that as far as they're concerned, you're family."

I let that sink in for a moment. "Because I work for them?"

She shakes her head, still smiling. "No Hol. Not because you work for them."

I scowl at her, fed up with her dancing around the subject. "Why do they consider me family?"

"Because Micah claimed you." She says simply, watching me carefully.

I sit back with a shudder, her words ringing through me, sparking panic. I force myself to breathe evenly, not wanting to show how terrifying those words are. She sees it anyway.

"It's not like that Holly," she says gently. "He doesn't want to own you, or control you. He just...wants you."

Wants me.

What does it mean to have a man like Micah want me? With Brent, want meant that he wanted someone to dominate. Someone to manipulate. Someone to bend to his will. Someone to use. And lucky girl that I am, he picked me.

Want is terrifying.

"I don't care what he wants." I gasp through the tightness in my throat.

"You don't have to. He hasn't put any pressure on you, has he? I'll kick his ass if he has."

"No," I admit, "he's been...kind." And considerate, and so gentle.

She nods, unsurprised. "You can come next door with us right now, Holly. We have a guest room, and we'll figure everything out. You don't have to stay here."

"You're running the garage, though, aren't you?"

She shrugs. "Yeah. But it's no big deal. Kade can take over at the office and that way I can be home with you during the day." She smiles, like she has it all worked out. What kind of person would that make me, though? Taking advantage of her friendship? Kade was making himself sick trying to run the garage day to day while managing all the others. Plus, they would never have a minute alone in the apartment.

I don't want to be a burden.

I am a burden, though. Micah dropped everything for me. Did everything he could to make me comfortable. He hired a nurse, for heaven's sake. And despite myself, I'm getting comfortable here. Would it be so bad to stay?

I'll admit to being a bit nervous still, but Micah really has proven that I can trust him. I can't say that I actually *do* trust him, but he hasn't done anything that makes me think he's lying.

"I really appreciate the offer, but I'm already settled in here. It's been ok so far. Besides," I say, shrugging, "it's only for a few days."

She nods, looking satisfied with my answer, for now at least. "OK. But please know if you change your mind, I'll have you moved over so fast your head will spin." I smile, knowing she would commandeer all the guys and have them move my things over in minutes if I asked her to.

I don't need her to though, I realize, as the guys' game breaks up and Kade wanders over to scoop up a giggling Becca, blowing raspberries in her neck. Because despite my temporary panic, I'm starting to see that not all men are like Brent, or my dad. Watching Kade and Becca love each other has been eye opening. She's not diminished by her relationship. Instead, she seems brighter when they're together.

Micah promised me he'd respect my boundaries, and so far he hasn't pushed me into doing anything I don't want to. I'm keenly aware that if he wanted to hurt me, he could, and there would be nothing I could do to stop him. But being that vulnerable isn't new to me. I live it every day. I'm sure most women my size feel the same way.

The guys all smile and wave as they trickle out carrying their garbage bags of clothes, still completely unconcerned that they're in their underwear. I can't make eye contact with them without blushing, so I focus on their eyebrows as I say goodnight, privately thrilled that I get my own smile and 'Night, Holly' from each of them.

Finally, it's just me and Micah. He's doing another pass over the floor with a mop, making practiced, smooth strokes. Seeing a man as physically and financially powerful as he is, mopping his own floor is...pretty amazing. In the seven years I spent with Brent, the only time he touched the mop was to give it to me, or more specifically, hit me with it, then drop it on top of me when I fell. According to him, I'd been lazy and did a crappy job cleaning the kitchen floor.

It was perfect. I made sure of it. But the truth didn't matter to Brent. He'd make up any excuse to take out his frustrations on me, and a dirty floor was as good a reason as any for him.

A wave of exhaustion washes over me, and I give in, sinking further into the couch. The pain pill's done its job, dulling the bone deep aches and the pain in my ankle. Without the sharp pain to deal with, my body can finally relax. My eyes drift shut, only to slide open when Minnie's warm, soft weight settles on my chest. Her little paws making biscuits on my breasts, her purr like a tiny outboard motor. I rest my hand on her back, and close my eyes again, letting her soft rumbles lull me to sleep.

A soft rubbing on my cheek wakes me up. I'm too relaxed to move, so I crack open my eyes to see Micah crouched down next to me. "I like the way you do that," I mumble, "Crouching down instead of looming over me."

He hums, still stroking my cheek. "Bed...Holly?" He asks. I nod my yes, sitting up and easing Minnie to the couch. She meows at me, but goes straight back to sleep. Micah keeps his eyes on me as he slides his arms carefully under me, then lifts me into his arms. I gasp as I'm tucked into his bare chest and he freezes. "Hurt?"

"Ah...no. I'm ok." Just a little warm. My slitted eyes travel over the sprinkling of hair on his chest. I'm tired, and curious, so I let my cheek rest on his skin, letting the hair tickle me. I can still smell his soap, but over that is the same Eau-de-Takeout the rest of them were wearing.

Wrapped up in the warmth of his skin, I don't realize we've stopped outside the bathroom. I raise my eyes to meet his. His cheeks have a flush to them, and his eyes are glittering as they lock on me.

"Bathroom?" he asks quietly. I let the wave of panic flow through me before nodding my yes. I'm feeling all kinds of awkward as he carefully stands me in front of the toilet, waiting until I've got a firm grip on the rails before letting go. *"I'll be right outside. I won't come back in until you call for me."*

"Promise," he says as he exits, pulling the door closed behind him.

I hurry to finish up my business, wishing I had asked him to turn the tap on or something. Anything to disguise the sound of peeing. Oh God, what happens when I have to poop while he's waiting for me? He's going to come back into a stinky bathroom.

That horrifying thought consumes me while Micah helps me to the sink to wash up, then tucks me into bed, making sure my air cast isn't snagging on the covers. I'm mesmerized by the way he smooths the blankets at the edge of my body. Both of us watch the motion of his hands.

Finally, he seems satisfied and backs away from the bed. I want him to stay, but I also really want him to go so I can escape the penetrating way he looks at me. I blame my confusion on exhaustion, letting my eyes slide closed. "Goodnight," I whisper.

I hear his, "Night...Holly," as I slip in to sleep.

14

MICAH

"Sleeping…too…much?" I ask Kathy when she arrives Friday morning. It was so fucking fantastic to have Holly laughing and engaged on Tuesday night. The contrast between that and the last two days has been especially jarring. I've had to wake her when Kathy arrives and to get some food in her, then she'd immediately drops back into sleep.

The deepest sleep I've ever seen. She barely moved, for fuck's sake. This morning when I checked on her, she was in exactly the same position as last night, straight as a pencil, head turned towards the always on light in the bathroom.

I've been Googling concussions for the last hour, and now I'm freaked the fuck out. What if she has a brain bleed? What if the smoke inhalation was worse than the doctors thought? I'm tempted to drag one of the doctors here to check on her, but I don't want to leave her alone long enough to track one down.

"Mr. James," Kathy says in her soothing voice. I liked it when I hired her. She seemed calm, and I thought Holly would like her. But I don't think she's taking this seriously enough. "She's had a rough week. Every concussion is a little bit different, but Miss Clarke clearly needs it. Her body is telling her what she needs."

I run a frustrated hand through my hair, then pull out my cell phone and open a blank note. *She's only awake while you're here. She's sleeping 22 hours a day. That can't be ok.*

"Is she hard to wake up?"

"No," I admit.

"That's good. What about her mood? She seems clear-headed when I'm here. Do you agree?"

I think about how sweetly she's been waking up. Smiling at me, eyes hooded, clearly tired but still responsive.

"Yes," I admit grudgingly. I'm a selfish prick. Wanting her awake more than two hours a day has more to do with me than her. I'm craving the sound of her voice and jonesing for her soft hands on me.

Anywhere. Any kind of touch.

"Ok then Mr. James. We'll check in this morning and see how she's doing. But we really do need to let her lead here."

I nod and jog to the bedroom door, knocking softly before pushing it open. I'm met by the best sight in days. Holly is awake, sitting up in bed, her hair mussed. Unlike the last few days, her eyes are clear and alert.

"Good morning," she says shyly, eyes darting between the two of us.

A wide grin stretches across my face. "Morning!" I basically yell at her. I have zero cool where she's concerned. A smile creeps across her face, and I'm struck dumb at how bright she shines. I stand there, staring until a finger pokes into my side. I shake out of my daze, turning to see Kathy smiling behind me. "Sorry," I mumble, moving out of the doorway so she can come in.

She and Holly have the morning routine down pat, so I stand around waiting to be called to assist. Within an hour she's dressed in a soft, light blue, wide legged lounge set. She looks so fucking delicious. So huggable, so kissable.

After escorting Kathy out, I settle Holly into the couch, then sit on the edge, studying her. "Tired?" I ask her. *"You've been sleeping so much...I was getting a little worried."*

She tilts her head, a small smile on her lips. "I feel much more awake today."

"That's good. You look good. I mean, you always look good, but you..." I drop my hands with a groan.

Her smile grows, and my face heats. *"I just mean that your concussion must have been pretty bad to make you sleep so much."* I'm worried about her headache. I hate the idea that she's still in pain, and I wish I could take this on for her. Take all the pain, all the scrapes, all the bruises. I'd rather be the one hurting.

She bites her lip, picking at the hem of her t-shirt. Her eyes sketch over my face. "I...I don't think it was just the concussion."

I shift my body towards her, so our legs are almost touching. She's usually so reserved. I'm desperate for any hint of what's going on in her head.

"I...I think I've been in survival mode for nearly a decade." She says in a whisper.

"Tell," I say hoarsely.

She frowns, tucking her hair behind her ear. "The last two years have been about survival. Trying to feed myself, find someplace safe to live, get out of the shelter. I could never fully relax knowing that he was looking for me. Then during my marriage...I couldn't rest. Not my brain, not my body. I was always analyzing, trying to figure out what might set him off. Is the house clean? Did I iron his shirts? Will he like the supper I made? Then when he was home..."

She trails off, and I reach out to stroke the top of her bare foot. "Tell," I urge her again. *"I can take your pain, Holly. I've lived through my own hell. I don't want to compare trauma, but you need to know nothing you can say will change the way I feel about you."*

"Tell...me," I beg again, dropping my hand back to her foot. I desperately want that little connection with her. You'd think I had a handful of breast, the way my dick is standing at attention.

Her eyes are on my fingers, a flush coloring her throat. A surge of satisfaction travels through me. I knew there was a possibility, fuck, a likelihood that she wouldn't ever respond to me, so to see her reaction now sends fresh energy into me. "Holly...tell."

"W...When" she stammers, still watching my hand, "he was home, I had to be on guard." She wets her lips, eyes darting to mine before falling away again. "I couldn't predict when things might go bad. Sometimes it was before supper and ran all night. Sometimes he was calm. And sometimes at night..." She trails off, either not able or not wanting to finish that sentence. Maybe it would be smart to drop the subject, let her retreat. But I can't. So I let that hideous, nauseating word come out of my mouth instead, wanting to spare her that pain.

"Rape."

Her breath stutters, and her eyes fly to mine.

"Sometimes at night he'd rape you." I sign. She swallows repeatedly, then, oh so slowly, nods her head. Even though I suspected, I work harder than I've ever worked in my life to school my features, not showing her the rage coursing through my body.

I know it in my gut. If she sees it, I'll lose her. She doesn't trust me enough yet to know I'm a different kind of beast from her husband, one that's hers to command. So I'll hide it. I'll wait.

"It never starts out bad, does it? My dad didn't start in on us until I was about six." I drop to the floor, sliding forward until I'm sitting right next to her, facing her. If I turn my head just a little, I can rest my chin on those cute thighs of hers. *"I think it was losing his job that finally set him off."*

"What do you mean? Why would that set him off?" Her breathing's evened out, now that we're not talking about her, so the words come out quiet, but clear.

"I don't know for sure, but I think that when he had money, he'd head out with his friends and spend his anger on the streets." I pause, thinking of those days. *"He'd come home with split lips, and bruised knuckles, and go straight to sleep. So when the money stopped, he was stuck at home, and all that anger got directed at us."*

"Did he hurt you a lot?" Her words are soft. "Or was it mainly your mom?"

"First...Mom." I can almost hear her screams, his shouts. *"Then he'd move on to me if he was still feeling energetic. He'd beat her until she stopped moving."* I remember lying against her chest, reassured by her breath brushing my cheek, telling me she was still alive.

Tears well in Holly's eyes, spilling over to drip down her cheek. I reach over to wipe at them gently. She leans into my touch and I want to shout at that small sign of trust.

"Brent would do that too," she says tightly. "I learned to stay down. If I stopped reacting. Stopped screaming, then he'd walk away."

"Smart...girl."

She laughs wetly, leaning out of my reach and rubbing her eyes with the palms of her hands. She looks like she'd like to get up and leave, so I change the subject quickly.

"Holly," I say, wanting her eyes back on me. *"How did you learn to sign? You said you knew someone who was deaf?"*

"Ah...there was a little girl in my second-grade class, Robyn. She was hearing impaired. She wore hearing aids and could read lips some, but...I didn't have very many friends, so I tried to learn as much as I could. She became my best friend."

"More," I ask her with a smile. I want more of her stories, more of everything.

Her eyes are hazy, unfocused as she travels to the past. "We muddled along in elementary school. Then in Junior High and High School I took ASL as an elective. Then there were classes in the community. I got pretty good. I loved it."

"Love...what...part?"

"I loved feeling like we had a secret language. Robyn and I could talk across a crowded cafeteria, or at a football game. Not that I went to many of those." She says with a rueful grin. "It just felt like something special. But maybe you don't feel that way about it."

ASL has mostly felt like a tool, a way to cope, but when I think about it, she's right. *"Actually, I do...sometimes anyway. All the guys learned when we were teenagers, mainly through books and videos from the library, so our gang could pass messages anywhere, as long as we were in sight of one another. It came in handy more than once. But sometimes it's frustrating to have to use it."*

"What's w...I mean, what happened?" She flushes at her slip.

Wrong.

I've been asked what's wrong with me too many times in my life, but from her, I wouldn't mind.

"You haven't heard this story?" I'm honestly surprised Becca hasn't shared everything.

"I want to hear it from you."

Wincing, I tell her. *"My dad beat me really badly when I was about eight. I ended up in the hospital. The doctors said I had permanent brain damage in the language center of my brain. It makes speaking hard for me. The words are clear in my mind, but they don't come out the way I want them to."*

Her eyes are sympathetic. She opens, then closes her mouth, looking like there's more she wants to know.

"Ask," I urge her. *"I don't have any secrets. Not from you, anyway. You can ask me anything. You won't offend me or upset me. I promise."*

Holly nods and clears her throat. "I've noticed that you tend to say only two or three words most of the time. Is that because it's all that comes out or...?"

"I don't know if I can fully explain what happens between my brain and mouth." I admit with a frown. *"When I was a kid, I would stutter and struggle to get any word out. The kids were brutal."*

My hands clench into fists as I picture the taunting faces, the bullies. *"Then, as I grew, the teachers started treating me like I was stupid. Putting me in remedial classes or ignoring me all together."* The frustration and embarrassment of those years comes flooding back. *"It made me so fucking angry. So for a while I tried really hard to get my words out clearly. But by the time I got to three words, one of two things would happen."*

"One," I say, holding up a finger. *"Whoever I was talking to would get bored and either walk away or start guessing what I was trying to say. Or."* Two fingers go up. *"I would work so hard to get the words out clearly that I was done. I couldn't do anymore. Like my brain turned off."*

Holly's leaning towards me, and I have to resist the urge to pull her in closer so I can breathe her air.

"And is it easier for you now to get the words out? Is it still exhausting?" She asks gently.

"Not...hard."

"But three is still the limit?"

"It depends on the situation, really. I'm more likely to talk more around people I'm really comfortable with. But it's still pretty stilted, and I stutter a lot more. It's easier to sign honestly."

"That makes sense." She's biting her lip again, and I'm staring. "Did you get help with your speech after you were hurt?"

I shake my head. *"No, I was from the projects. Maybe I was supposed to? I don't know. All I know is I never did, and after I was released from the hospital, no doctor ever talked to me about it."*.

"And you've never gone since? I know speech therapists can be a huge help in situations like yours."

"When we finally started making money, Ransom asked. A few times. But I didn't really see the point."

Plus, I really didn't want bad news. As far as I'm concerned, ignorance is a valid choice, in this situation at least. Shaking the tightness out of my shoulders, I change the subject. *"How do you know so much about speech therapy?"*

Her bright smile is back. "I used to volunteer at the hospital. Brent hated me doing most things outside of the house, but volunteering at the hospital was something he let me do. I think he figured it reflected well on him to have a wife who was so involved in the community. I loved going there so much. I made friends with a bunch of the nurses and doctors and I loved talking to the patients."

I smile back at her. "Candy...striper?" I ask with a wiggle of my eyebrows. She rewards me with a tinkling laugh, and I feel ten fucking feet tall.

"No!" she says with a grin. "I did all kinds of things. I was there a long time, so I got to work in a bunch of different departments. Sometimes I worked the front desk. That was more directing traffic, or escorting people to find their loved ones. The ER was a tough position. When people are coming up to me at the desk in the E.R., they're usually in a panic because something bad has happened." Her smile shifts, softening. "And sometimes I got to rock the babies in the nursery and NICU. That one was my favorite. They all smelled so good. They were so tiny and innocent. They would soak up the love."

She's so fucking kindhearted. I'm so glad that she had somewhere to escape him. How was she able to stay such a good, kind woman, despite it all? "Good...Girl," I say with a smile.

My heart fucking sinks as her face whitens, and she pulls back from me. "What?" I ask, signing frantically, *"What's wrong? Are you hurting? Did I say something stupid?"* I can't stop myself from scooting a little closer to her, putting my hand back on the top of her foot, needing a physical connection with her. "Please."

Please tell me what I did so I can fix it. Don't pull away, beautiful girl.

Her breathing is erratic, so I rub small circles on the top of her foot with my thumb. Hoping she'll focus on that. "Ok... Holly...Ok."

"B...Brent always called me that, when he was..." she says, breath shuddering in her chest, eyes filling with tears. She breathes deeply again, and her eyes stab at me. "Even before it was...rape...I didn't like being with him. But it got so much worse. 'Be a good girl and scream for me', ' be a good girl and stop fighting me', 'be a good girl and let me in'."

She sobs, wiping her eyes angrily. "Let me in," she snorts, "Like I could control that. Any time he came near me, my whole body tensed up. I...don't ever call me that."

I pull my hand back before I accidentally hurt her, clenching them both into fists until they turn white, trying to find the threads of my control. "So...Sorry," I stutter, *"Never again, I promise."* I consider leaving it there, but this woman has shared pieces of her soul with me. I have to do the same. *"I mean it Holly. Never again. You will never have to live in fear again. I will fucking make sure of it. Nothing touches you."*

Her face is shuttered, the warmth from minutes ago long gone. "You can't make that promise," she says flatly.

"Holly," I say quietly, waiting for her attention. *"I absolutely can. I am a big, scary motherfucker. I am rich as fuck. Everything I have, everything I am, it's yours."* Her big blue eyes widen. *"I'm yours. You need something from me, you take it. You don't even have to ask."*

"What?" she stops to clear her throat. "What do you mean, you're mine?"

"Exactly what I said." I lick my lips. *"I...am...yours."* I rub my hand over my heart. *"I have been since the day you showed up at the shop. I'm sorry I did a shitty job of showing you that. But it's true."*

Out of the corner of my eye, I catch Minnie carefully climbing down the cat tree. She hops up onto the back of the couch, walking softly to Holly. Her purring announcing her arrival.

I swear I'll feed Minnie tuna for the rest of her life in thanks for the smile that spreads on Holly's face. She reaches up and carefully pulls the cat into her arms and Minnie curls up on her chest like she belongs there. She's rubbing Minnie's cheeks and stroking down her back, and I can actually see the tension in Holly's body dissolving. I sit, content to watch her, until her eyes finally meet mine.

"What exactly do you want from me?" She asks, still guarded.

"Wrong...question." I tell her. Her forehead furrows in confusion.

"I told you I'm yours," I explain. *"So honestly, it doesn't fucking matter what I want. The real question is, what do you want? Because if it's in my power to get it for you Holly, I will."*

"So, what, I tell you I want a mansion and you'll just go out and get it for me?" She asks in disbelief.

I pull out my phone, and open the contact for the realtor we work with, a fucking shark of a woman, then hand it to Holly. Her eyes dart from me to the phone as she takes it.

"That's our realtor. Text her what you're looking for, and she'll get on it. She'll start sending you listings ASAP."

"You're certifiable," she says, shoving the phone against my chest. I don't take it. "You're not buying me a mansion."

"You...want...get." I nudge the phone closer to her chest. *"Go on, message her. I'll take you to look at a few as soon as you're feeling better."* I don't mention that I have every intention of going with her if she moves, even if I have to live in a shed in her backyard.

She's staring at me like I have two heads. She clicks the screen off and drops it in her lap. "You're serious."

"Yep."

She rolls her eyes. That little sign of sass makes me feel lighter. More hopeful. "I don't actually want to live in a mansion."

"Ok." I shrug. *"As far as I'm concerned, this place is your home. If you decide you don't want to be here anymore, we'll go somewhere else."*

"We?"

Whoops.

Fuck.

I rub the back of my head. How am I going to dig myself out of this hole? I can't take it back, so I might as well lay everything on the table. *"So what you want is number one. You've had too many years of not having your needs met. I won't allow that to continue."* Her eyebrows raise at the word allow.

I take a deep breath, exhaling heavily as I go all in on the most important gamble of my life. *"But you asked me what I want? The answer is simple. You. Any way I can have you. If that means I'm the best friend you've ever had, then so be it. But I hope, with time, you might come to love me like I love you."*

"Love...you." I tell her, needing to say the words, to let her see the truth of them on my face.

Her eyes are flipping between mine, searching. I don't hide from her, letting her look her fill.

"You don't even know me." Her voice is barely a whisper, though her disbelief is clear.

"I know you." I tell her, capturing her eyes with mine, letting her see the truth. *"I see you. You're the kindest, most beautiful woman in the world. You're an amazing friend. You have a laugh that could light up Times Square. And you have the softest skin I've ever touched. You're the perfect package."*

She shakes her head, leaning back on the couch. "Why are you saying all of this?"

"Because it's true. And I don't want to play any games with you. I want you to have all the power here, Holly. Every bit of it. You need to know exactly where I stand."

"So what, you want to…marry me?" She stutters over the word marry. I get it. Her experience of marriage was worse than shit.

"I'd give you my name in a heartbeat."

Her mouth drops open and her eyes dart over my face. She licks her lips, and tension settles into her shoulders. "I don't like sex. I don't think I want a relationship. It's…they…I don't want that."

I shrug again, not at all surprised at her vehemence. "Ok…friends." I say with a nod. *"Want to play a game? I stocked up on board games."*

She freezes, her face stunned at my easy agreement. I hop to my feet, taking a few steps away before turning back to her. "Holly," I say, infusing her name with all the heat, all the want, I feel. *"What you had with Brent was not a marriage. If I were your man, you would never touch a mop again. I would eat fried worms if you went to the effort of cooking them for me. And in bed, baby? I would make you feel so good, you'd order me to put my mouth on you every chance you got. I'd never make you beg. Because serving you? Giving you what you need? That's what I live for now."*

I take a minute to admire her flushed cheeks, wide eyes and the heaving chest bouncing Minnie up and down, before turning away to find the games. And if I'm walking a little funny, well, it's a price I'm fucking happy to pay.

15

HOLLY

How can he be this calm?

He dropped a huge bomb in between us, then just asked me to play games like it's no big deal. My mind is spinning and I can't seem to focus on anything. And the touches. My God, just when I got used to having him carry me, now he's constantly touching me. Little caresses on my foot, tucking pillows under my leg, brushing my hair back, all day long.

It's maddening. I should hate it. It should scare me. But heaven help me, it doesn't. I think I'm actually starting to... crave them, maybe? I've never craved before, but I imagine this is what it would feel like, the tugging in my belly, the restlessness.

"C4," Micah rumbles, snapping my attention back to our game. He's on the floor again, smiling up at me as he announces his move. He's got me and he knows it.

"Hit," I mutter, hiding my smile as I put a red peg in my aircraft carrier. I haven't sat and played like this in so long. "We didn't have games at home. I haven't played Battleship in twenty years."

"You didn't play games with your family?"

"No," I say "My parents are very…religious. They didn't approve of idleness."

Or joy. Or laughter. Or free will.

"Game…idle?" He says with a frown.

"That's what they said. My time was better spent in prayer or doing chores. We spent most days at the church. It was…strict."

"Where I grew up, we always had this TV show image of how regular families grew up. Sunday dinners, moms helping with homework, and kisses on the forehead at bedtime. No hitting, no going to bed hungry, no roaches." He pauses, studying me with a wry smile. *"I guess TV families are easier."*

"I used to watch those shows at friends houses sometimes and wish I had a family like that, too. My parents are…hard people. They're strict and cold and impossible to please."

"Do you speak to them much? Did they help you with Brent?"

My mouth tightens, an unconscious echo of the way they always looked at me. Like I was wrong. Not good enough. "I haven't spoken to them in years. By high school, I was avoiding being home as much as possible. I would go to the library at night to read or do schoolwork so I got pretty good grades. I got a partial scholarship to go to college, and took it. I thought it would be harder to leave, but I felt…free, finally."

"Free?" He asks. *"Because you were away from them?"*

I nod. "They controlled every aspect of my life. They approved my clothes, what classes I took, who I hung out with. I didn't get to make any decisions."

"They really fucking hated you leaving for school then, didn't they?"

"Oh yeah," I breathe with a sad laugh. "They were so angry with me when I told them I was going. They weren't going to support me in any way. When I told them I had a scholarship and would pay for everything myself, well, then they froze me out." I let the old sadness flow through me.

"They didn't speak to me the whole summer. Not one word. They wouldn't even make eye contact. My Mom wouldn't even set a place for me at supper." I felt like a ghost in my own home. It would have been better to be yelled at, or punished.

At least then I would have felt seen.

"Assholes," Micah mutters. His eyes are blazing again, but it's clear it's anger for me, not directed towards me. It feels... good. Like I might have someone on my side. *"How do you treat your own child like that? That's not family."*

"It was horrible. I felt like I was invisible. F8." I think I've got him now.

He shoots me a cocky smile. *"Miss. How did you cope that summer? With your parents being dicks?"*

I suck at this game.

"I escaped to Robyn's house. Her family actually was like a TV family. They laughed so much. And they always made me feel like I was welcome there. It was...wonderful."

"Do you still talk to Robyn?"

I shake my head. "We kept in touch through college. She went across the country, but that didn't matter. We still connected. But when I left school and married Brent...I couldn't." It's still one of the biggest regrets of my life, the way I just let her go, the way I gave up.

"Why?" He asks, sliding a little closer.

"When you're spending your day just trying to survive, it's hard to always put on a happy face, you know?" I pick up one of the little game pegs, rolling it between my fingers. "Robyn would be telling me about a party she'd gone to, or how awful her finals were. She was living this big life. And I...well, what could I say when she asked how I was?"

"You didn't want to tell her the truth?" He asks, frowning. *"Why?"*

How on earth do I explain my weakness to a man who can bench press four of me? "Because I felt stupid! I made a really stupid choice, and then I was stuck. I felt like I was living on a different planet than everyone else."

He's quiet, studying me with kind eyes. *"Did you tell anyone about Brent?"*

I shift uncomfortably. "I told my parents. It was a few years after we got married. I asked them to let me stay with them. They told me I made my bed, and that it was my job to submit to my husband. I didn't try again after that."

Micah's lips are curled in disgust, and I feel smaller. Less.

It's not my fault, I remind myself. But when someone looks at me like that, I can't help but internalize the disgust. Because it was me that stayed.

"Fuckers," he says fiercely, reaching up to rub my arm. It's hypnotic, watching those scarred, tanned fingers brush my pale skin. "How...get...away?" He's still stroking me, touching me. Distracting me from my story.

"Um...it was Evie." His fingers are creating little ripples of electricity, traveling up my arm, into my shoulder. Tingling into the back of my neck. All of it from a simple touch on my arm. In all the years of my marriage, I never once felt anything near this powerful.

"Evie," he prompts, eyebrows raised.

"Evie right...she was a nurse at the hospital I volunteered at. We were close, I mean as close as I let anybody get." My lips curl remembering her bright smile. "She had the best laugh. It was so big, it would draw you in. I loved being around her and her energy. She was everything I wished I could be."

"Holly," he says, drawing my eyes. I like how he does that, just says my name, and waits patiently. He would be well within his rights to get frustrated with me. Looking away from him takes away his option to communicate. It's a rude thing to do.

"She sounds great. I'm glad you had her. How did she help you get away?"

I drift in the memories of my old life. Of the woman who saved me. "She's so smart. She worked with the babies in the NICU, so we'd talk while I rocked them. Some of them were so fragile, but it helped, you know?"

He tilts his head. *"What helped?"*

"Some of the babies were born addicted. They would have to detox, and often the mothers either couldn't or wouldn't be there. I used to tuck them right against my chest." I cup my hands, pressing them just above my breasts, remembering the slight warm weight of the babies I held. "The nurses always said it helped them, that their scores got better."

Micah's eyes are locked on my hands. I slowly lower them to my lap. His eyes don't follow them like I expected. No, his eyes are glazed as he stares right at my breasts. He seems frozen. I carefully reach over, using my forefinger to tip his chin up. His sheepish gaze meets mine. *"You can't blame me for looking. I can't help it."*

"Brent used to stare, but…it never felt like this."

His eyes sharpen. "How….feels?"

"Ah…warm." I cover my red cheeks. Micah's gleeful chuckle makes me smile despite my embarrassment.

"Anyway," I say, clearing my throat. "Evie invited me to grab coffee in the cafeteria after a shift, and I said yes. Brent was working late that day, but if he found out I didn't go straight home, I had a cover story ready."

"What was the cover story?"

"Another volunteer was late for their shift, and I had to stay a bit longer." Best to keep things simple. I learned quickly that if the lie got too complicated, Brent would pick it apart in seconds. Apparently I have tells, since Brent could always spot when I was lying.

He nods approvingly. *"Simple. Clean. Smart."*

"That's what I thought. Anyway, when we sat down, she laid it all out…she had been recording every bruise she saw, every time I acted stiff or sore, and wrote it all down in a little notebook." I swallow thickly, the panic of that day still fresh in my memory. "I was terrified that she'd tell someone, that she would force me to make a report."

"But she didn't?"

"No. She laid it all out, then told me when I was ready she had cash and a phone number for someone who could help me get out. She told me about an underground network of people who help women in my position." I tear up, remembering her generosity. "She's a single mom, Micah. Every penny she had went towards supporting her baby. But she had saved every extra penny she could for me."

"She sounds like a pretty incredible friend."

"She was. She is."

"What happened after that talk?"

"Honestly, it took me a while to wrap my head around actually leaving. I was so used to all the decisions being made for me, you know? It sounds stupid now, but it felt like if I didn't have Brent's permission to leave, then I couldn't go."

"How long were you married?"

"Seven years. I married him a few months after we met. I was twenty-one."

"Still a kid," he says, wincing.

"I didn't think so at the time." I say, glancing away. "I was old enough to drink. I figured I was old enough to get married. I didn't really understand how bad it was going to be until our first anniversary. By then, I had no support system left. Nowhere to go."

He leans even closer. *"So, what was the tipping point? How did you decide to leave?"*

My eyes flood with tears, thinking of that night. The joy, the dread, the pain. And eventually, the loss.

"I got pregnant."

A hoarse sound comes from Micah, and he rocks forward onto his knees, carefully moving Battleship off my lap. "Wait," he says. *"I need to hold you for this, Holly. I don't think I can handle it without touching you.*" The V between his eyebrows is deep. "Please."

At the garage, I've seen this man laugh like a loon with another mechanic, curse like a sailor - in words and sign - after dropping a car part, and terrifying a customer who was giving me trouble. But seeing this big strong guy tearing up around me just breaks me. Knowing he feels that deeply, that he's letting me see it, somehow makes me feel stronger.

That little voice at the back of my mind telling me that it's an act, that he's going to change, is getting quieter.

I exhale and nod my head yes. He stands, lifting me like he does multiple times a day, then sits in the V of the couch, settling me so my head and back are still supported at the corner, and my legs are extended on the cushions. Then he pulls his arm from behind my back.

"Is this ok? I need to be near you, but I think I'm going to need to ask questions."

I didn't even consider how we'd talk if he were hugging me. The adjustments he has to make to ensure he can communicate is mind-boggling. Apps make most things easier now, but what happens when he has to call someone?

"Holly," he nudges. *"I lost you. Where did you go?"*

My face flushes. "Sorry…I just started wondering how your…speech might affect you every day. I never really thought about it when we were working together. But now?"

His shoulders relax. *"It used to be harder, but with texting, it's way easier. And if I get in a situation like with you? Having to get to you at the hospital? Well, one of my brothers come."*

"So you just ask them to come and they drop everything?" What would that be like? To know someone cares about you so much, they'd drop everything.

Wait.

Isn't that exactly what Micah's done for me? He put his whole life on hold to take care of me.

"Sort of. Ransom came, but I didn't have to ask him. We were all

trying to track you down, and as soon as I found out where you were, I was gone. Ransom met me there."

"He just came? Just like that?"

"They're my family." He says with a casual shrug of the shoulder. *"I know your family is different, but we've got you now. In our family, if one of us is in need, we're all there. No one has to go through hell alone."*

"Coming to the hospital was hell?"

"Yes." When I look at him doubtfully, his mouth firms. He cups the back of my head briefly before signing. *"All I knew was you were in a fire, and at the E.R. I spent the whole drive over losing my shit. I ran through all the worst-case scenarios in my head. I was terrified that you would be really fucking hurt, or worse. I tried not to think about the worse."*

I swallow tightly, thinking about the worse too. "I haven't said it...but thank you for coming. And for taking care of me. That first night I was in so much pain...anyway, thank you for being there."

I can't meet his eyes, but he's not going to let me get away with that. He nudges my chin until my eyes are tipped up to his. I hold my breath as he brings our faces together. Just when I think he might press his lips to mine, he turns, sliding his stubbled cheek over mine, stopping when his lips are pressed to my temple. And if his touch stole my breath, well, his words they fill me with life.

"Always...be...there..p-promise."

16

MICAH

I can feel my heart beating in my ears. I don't think that's normal, but right this minute, I don't give a fuck. Because Holly's in my arms and all's right with my world. We're about to get into some heavy shit, I know it. And it's going to fucking gut me, but I need her to know I can handle all her dark parts. All of her pain. I want to savor her closeness, the softness of her skin, the faint smell of strawberry on her skin, but it's time to pull off the band aid.

I let my mind muddle through the word for a minute, so I can get it out clearly, before finally asking, "Pregnant...tell." She stiffens, her breath rattling in her chest, so I wrap my arms around her again, careful to keep my arms loose. She's been giving me more and more of her trust, and I don't want to fuck it up by making her feel trapped.

"Tell," I beg her again.

She takes a deep breath, pressing her cheek against mine before sliding her head back to look at me. Her hands rise to play with the neck of my t-shirt. "I was...Brent controlled everything. He didn't want me on birth control. But the idea of bringing a baby into my marriage was...terrifying."

"Need...baby...safe."

Her eyes slide away. "Partly...but honestly, I knew if we had a baby, I'd die."

My throat closes up at the certainty in her voice. At the idea of her not being on this earth. At the possibility of never meeting her.

"Explain."

Her mouth twists. "Brent is very regimented. Dinner at 6:30. Pants ironed on a pleat. Bathrooms cleaned on Tuesdays. Babies don't respect schedules. Dinner might be late, or I won't get to the ironing because the baby's fussy. So messing with that schedule, well, I was pretty sure he'd end up beating me to death. Following his schedule, his rules, was the only way to keep myself safe. So for my sake, I never wanted a baby." She bites her lip, watching me nervously.

"Good...smart," I reassure her. Wanting her to stop hurting that soft lip. I reach up and gently pull her lip out of her teeth, smoothing my thumb over it until the marks are gone. Focusing on her enticing mouth, it takes me a minute to realize she's panting. Her cheeks flushed, her eyes cloudy. Need and invitation written all over her face.

A stupid man would respond to the invitation. But this stunning, sensual woman doesn't even realize what her body's asking for. She hasn't known need or pleasure. So yeah, a stupid man would push it.

I'm far from stupid.

Instead of giving into my instinct to plunder, I slide my thumb from her lip to her cheek, and give her a grin. "Talk...woman."

She returns my smile, the dazed look slowly fading from her face. I mourn it, but have every confidence that I'll see it again. I'll make sure of it. She's so fucking responsive it will be my absolute pleasure to make her look at me like that again. And again.

"Ah...where was..." she clears her throat "right. So I knew a baby would be bad. I got on the pill when we got married, but right after our first anniversary, Brent started to make a fuss about them. He took them away. So one day, while Brent was at work, I drove to the next town over and got an implant in my arm. Then I never refilled my prescription. Brent figured he'd won and would get what he wanted."

"He…wanted?" I prompt.

"Another way to control me, I think. He never seemed to have any interest in kids. But a baby would be another tie binding me to him."

I hum, knowing she's right.

"Then…how…preg…preg…preggo?" I take a few deep breaths to calm myself, my stuttering a clear sign I'm getting emotional.

Holly giggles at preggo, so I wink and playfully scowl at her. I'll sing her the fucking alphabet song, stuttering the whole way if it gets her to light up like that.

I used to hate people laughing at me. Shutting them up with my fists was really fucking effective. But Holly's laugh is different. It's not mocking or mean.

Her smile fades, eyes turning stormy. "Implants are only supposed to last for three years. I was able to get it replaced once, but by the time I got pregnant, I was overdue. I knew that wasn't smart, but getting away to get it replaced felt impossible. I got a couple of shots at the clinic in the hospital, but those are only for 3 months. And then every time I had an appointment for another Implant, I couldn't go. Because Brent beat me, or he forced me to cancel my volunteer shift and I couldn't get away. And then, my period didn't come." She blushes when she says period. I'm no expert on women, but I'm a grown fucking man. She doesn't need to be shy about her body with me. I have plans to learn everything about it, and what it needs.

"*So your…*" What the fuck is the sign for period? That's something we never learned as kids. Maybe we should have spent a little less time learning to swear in ASL. "*What's the* *sign for…*period?" She smiles and shows me. *"So your period was late. That must have been scary."*

"It was terrifying. I'd been afraid of it for months, and finally it happened. I didn't know for sure, but I grabbed a test and took it during one of my shifts at the hospital."

"I can't imagine. Seriously. I've had my brothers by my side for more than twenty years. Anything big happened, I had a support system. You had no one."

"No, I had no one. Except Evie. I told her a couple of weeks later. And I asked her if her offer was still good." A teary laugh escapes. "She pulled that envelope right out of her locker, Micah. She had it there waiting for me. She'd even added more to it. We made a plan together. I knew Brent had a double shift coming up. It coincided with one of my volunteer shifts. After he left for work, I packed a backpack and any jewelry I had, which wasn't much admittedly, and headed to the hospital. Evie was there. She had the money, of course, $650, and she also packed me a bag of food. She drove me to a pawn shop to pawn my jewelry, then she took me to the bus station where I made the first phone call."

"Say the word, Holly, and I'll get you in touch with her. Fuck, I'd like to thank her. More than thank her, kiss her feet. She helped save your life, love. It would take Declan minutes to learn everything about her and get you her phone number."

Her lip trembles. "I thought about calling her so many times over the last two years. And I am worried about her. I knew Brent wouldn't give up, and with the resources he had access to through the police station, well, I was afraid he'd be able to track me too easily."

"Call… Declan?"

She considers it, then slowly shakes her head. "Thank you, but maybe soon? I could ask him myself maybe, when I'm ready."

"Okay," I say, content to give her a bit of time on this. Now that she's here with me, she can take all the time she needs. But if I have anything to do with it, Evie's going to be set for life.

"What happened after you ran?"

"It was a blur honestly, moving from house to house, then motel room to motel room, and then finally I got to a shelter. Along the way, I managed to get my new ID. I got to pick my name," she says with a smile. "I've always loved the name Holly. It always seemed happy and reminded me of Christmas. I never want to go back to Hannah. I don't want to be Hannah anymore."

I don't like the way she says her old name. The hint of disdain in her voice. *"I'm positive Hannah was equally wonderful. You're you."*

She narrows her eyes at me. "Hannah was a doormat. She let people hurt her."

I narrow my eyes back. "Bullshit," I say with a growl. *"Hannah got away from her shitty parents. Hannah learned sign and made an incredible friendship. Hannah volunteered at the hospital, and Hannah escaped. She's a fucking badass. No way am I going to let you talk bad about her. You want to stay Holly, that's fine, but don't you dare put down Hannah. I think she's pretty incredible, and I'm a fucking great judge of character."*

Her wide eyes are searching mine for a hint of deception, maybe? She won't find it. I mean every fucking word. She swallows heavily. "Micah..." Chills run up my back at the grit in her voice. The rasp. I lock on her mouth as she licks her lips. "Micah," she says again, "what would happen if I... kissed you?"

I freeze, licking my suddenly parched lips. "Anything... you...want."

Her head tilts adorably as her eyes lose focus. "What if I don't want you to touch me?"

"Ok," I squeak, fucking squeak, and shove my arms behind me, locking my hands together. My eagerness makes her giggle adorably. With her still on my lap, our lips are almost lined up. She braces those tiny hands on my shoulders, and I have a moment of epic self doubt. She's so fucking small, so delicate.

And I'm just...not.

I'm big, I've solved most problems in my past with my fists, I'm scarred and damaged. I should let her walk away, find someone who can handle her gently. Because right now, I'm a man on the fucking verge.

"I..." she whispers as she hovers her lips above mine. "I just want to try."

I nod, but as she comes closer I pull back, suddenly flipping the fuck out. "Kiss...back...scare?"

She bites that lush lower lip again. "Can you...just stay still for now? I...I've never kissed anyone but Brent. I just want to...taste you."

I'm not even a little bit ashamed of the groan that escapes me. I fucking dare you to have a woman as hot as Holly tell you she wants to taste you, and keep your cool. No straight man with a pulse could.

"Ok," I choke out.

She leans in again, before pulling back. I almost whine. "Can you tell me if I do something wrong?" she asks anxiously.

I scowl and I have to draw my hands forward so we can get this perfectly clear. *"I'm going to spell this out, so you don't have any doubt where I stand. I told you I was yours, and I meant it. Anything you want to do to me is going to feel fucking fantastic. You couldn't do anything wrong."*

"That's not true. What if I used my teeth and hurt you or..."

I bark out a laugh. "Baby, *I'm about ready to come in my pants just from your hands on my shoulders. I mean it when I say anything you do will feel good to me. If you want to experiment, you tell me what to do, and I'll do it. I'll lay down and let you do whatever you want to me. I'll even have my fucking brothers come and tie me down for you, so you know you're in total control. What-ever it takes."*

She shifts restlessly, pressing her legs together and I have to slam my eyes shut, trying to pull the threads of my control back together.

They slit open when her delicate fingers trace over my face. I watch her as she explores me, floored by the want on her face. She's not hiding anything from me. She looks drunk off the simple touches, and I can't stop myself from imagining what she'll look like splayed out on my bed, letting me drive her higher and higher.

She slowly brings her lips back to mine, and I hold my breath, not wanting anything to distract from the moment her lips first touch mine.

It's better than anything I've ever felt in my life.

Better than beating up every bully in elementary school. Better than opening the garage. Better than finishing a custom job and seeing the owner tear up. Better than all the money in my bank accounts. Better than any sex, with any woman I've ever been with.

One simple, barely there kiss, and I'm wrecked for life.

She's making soft, breathy sounds as she explores my top lip, licking and sucking, before moving to the bottom. She gets braver and adds tiny bites that make every muscle in my body clench. I haven't come in my pants since I...fuck, I've never come in my pants. But this tiny, one-hundred-and-fifty pound woman has me on the fucking verge. The little black spots dancing in front of my eyes finally force me to suck in a deep breath. And it gets worse. Her scent is driving me mad. I swear she smells like fucking apple pie. I'm drowning in her, and I don't give a damn.

She pulls her lips away, pressing her forehead against mine. I memorize everything about her. The soft blonde brown of her eyebrows, the small freckle on the corner of her eye, the white lines of long healed hurts at her hairline.

The scars are a sobering reminder of the many invisible hurts still riddling this beautiful woman. It makes controlling my instinct to claim her easier.

I miss her before she even pulls away. Knowing that from this moment on, I'll always feel colder without her in my arms. Like a fucking piece of me is missing. To have her touching me, trusting me is everything. "You...ok?" I ask her through the tightness in my chest.

Her eyes are dazed as she slowly touches her lips, rubbing them wonderingly. "I didn't know," she mumbles, bringing her other hand to my lips. I can't resist giving her finger a tiny little nip. Her breath catches in her throat, her body jumping. I capture her eyes with mine, letting her see what she's done to me. Her dazed, "Woah," pulls a chuckle out of me.

I slowly bring my hands between us, briefly cupping her cheek, then moving to sign. *"Are you ok? Was that ok? Need to gather a bit more data?"* I smile, unable to resist teasing just a little. I love the way her cheeks pink up when I do.

"I'm ok...I didn't know."

"Know...what?"

"That I could...it could feel like that." Her voice is slow, wondering.

"You...feel...good?"

The tiniest of smiles graces her lips. "I feel really good."

I exhale heavily, the last little worry leaving my body. She liked it. And hopefully, if I keep making myself available, like really available, we'll do it a lot more.

"You can experiment with me anytime. I will dedicate my body to the cause."

Her snort makes me chuckle. She's coming out of her shell, feeling safer with me.

She's lost in thought for a while, and I'm content to sit, watching her. I slide my arm behind her back, giving her a bit of support, and she relaxes against me easily.

Win after fucking win today.

I still don't know what happened to her baby, but I don't want to break this peace we've found. It's a question for another day.

"Could you take me to get some crutches?" She asks suddenly.

"I'm here. I can help you get around. I'm happy to do it." I fucking love carrying her around, having her close to me.

She looks down, twisting her fingers together, then takes a deep breath and looks me straight in the eye. "I need to be able to get around on my own. I'd like some crutches."

"Ok…we…go." I scoop her up and stand. Her mouth drops open at my easy acceptance. She doesn't believe me yet, but I made her a fucking promise that I'd give her anything she wanted. No way I'm going to fail on the first fucking request.

17

HOLLY

How is this my life?

Somehow, my trip to get crutches got hijacked. Micah wanted to take Jonas's minivan. He kept muttering something about airbags and freckles. Declan and Colton were at Jonas's and wanted to come, too.

So suddenly I was in a van with four giants. It's the stuff of nightmares, for me at least. But I was surprisingly ok with it. Sure, a bit shy, but otherwise I wasn't worried about my safety. And it wasn't just Micah's presence. It was the guys. They look at me, talk to me, like we've been friends forever. I don't understand how they can be so kind, so quickly. Maybe it's pity? Though I've been looked at with pity, and it doesn't feel like this.

So here we all are, at six at night, in a massive medical supply store. How do they not have anything better to do on a Friday night?

My cheeks are blazing as the salesman and I watch the spectacle before us. I somehow feel like a parent explaining to the teacher why their child pulled their pants down in front of the whole class. "I'm so sorry. They...well they've been cooped up." The boys are in fine form tonight.

Silly me, I thought the First Annual Naked Noodle Challenge, as it's been dubbed, was an anomaly, but I'm starting to realize it was just the tip of the iceberg that is the Brash Brothers.

They scattered as soon as we got in here, Micah only staying with me until I was settled in a wheelchair. He ordered the salesman to get me anything I need. Then he saw something shiny and took off.

Oh, he's checking on me, always looking over to make sure I'm ok. Checking on me while he and Colt lay on the adjustable bed, traveling up, then down, over and over. Or during a wheelchair race with Declan. Or sitting in the safety bath while Jonas studied the sealing mechanism. Thank God there's no one else in here for them to run over. They're completely unfiltered and uncontrollable, goofing around like children.

I really want to play too.

Play's never really been a part of my life. Not when I was a child, and definitely not while I was at college. Between schoolwork and working at the cafe, I barely had time to sleep. It was exhausting.

That's probably why I fell for Brent's lies. I was so tired of being alone. I let the dream of having a TV perfect husband and marriage convince me Brent was exactly who he said he was. That he fell madly in love with me when he saw me. I ignored the red flags, and I just...let him take over. Take me over.

"Oh, there they are. That's exactly the knee scooter I was mentioning to you!" The salesman is pointing as Jonas scoots by, his knee resting on a padded spot on the odd-looking scooter, his leg sticking out behind him, using the other leg to push himself around the store. He stops in front of us.

"Holly," Jonas says, completely ignoring the salesman. "This is a much better option than crutches. I did some research, and crutches can be very dangerous. You could slip, or strain your shoulders, causing further injury. This would be a much safer choice for you. It's very easy to operate. Would you like to try it?"

He's so earnest. So serious. And he researched for me? I smile up at him, still a long way up even though he's one of the smaller brothers. These men are massive. "I'd love to try it."

Jonas slaps at the salesman's hands, moving to help me out of the wheelchair himself. He asks for permission before wrapping an arm firmly around my waist, letting me use his other arm to balance as we take a few steps to the scooter. As I'm trying it out, Declan, Colt and Micah go tearing by on knee scooters too. I laugh in disbelief, my wide eyes meeting Jonas's.

"We're children," he says calmly.

"It's a little unexpected."

He hums, nodding in agreement. "We weren't always like this...well this bad."

"What do you mean?"

"When your childhood gets cut short the way ours were, there's no time for play. We were too busy surviving. When we were all together, we'd goof around some, but mainly, we were focused on building something that couldn't be taken away from us. Something that was just ours. We've done that."

"And then some," I say with feeling.

"And then some," he echoes with a small smile. "Now, we play. A lot. None of us have to work, but we do because we enjoy it. But now, we play too."

"Most guys as rich as you all are would be racing cars and flying around the world, not racing around on knee scooters."

"We've done some of that," he says, distaste coloring his voice. "It got boring fast. Having fun together, playing the way we would have if we'd all lived different lives...well I'm sure psychologists could write a large book about our dysfunction, but..." He shrugs his shoulders, unconcerned with what anyone thinks.

I watch the guys zooming around the store as I sift through flashbacks of my life. All the times I wasn't allowed to be a child either. "I get it." I say softly. "My life has felt like an exercise in survival. When I got away from Brent, I finally had a chance to do some of the things I'd always wanted to."

"Like what?" he asks. He doesn't meet my eyes, but his focus is now completely on me, seemingly tuning out the yells and laughter behind him.

"Little things really." I say, embarrassed. "I started crocheting again. I'm not very good, but I always enjoyed it. Brent hated it. Thought I was being lazy. I made a blanket." I smile up at him, remembering how proud I was to lay it on my cheap couch. My smile fades. "It's gone now."

"I am very sorry that you lost your home, Holly." His words are so formal, but I can feel their sincerity.

I blink back tears. "Thank you, Jonas."

Colt, Declan and Micah pull up in front of us. Micah dismounts, crouching in front of me and my knee scooter. *"How's this working for you? Want to take it for a spin?"*

I laugh, nodding. "Why not?"

Jonas disappears, reappearing with another scooter, and the guys escort me around the store, or 'the track' as they call it, weaving around displays of compressions socks and toilet risers.

And I laugh.

More than I think I've ever laughed in my life.

We come to a stop in front of the salesman, all grinning like loons.

"Sold!" Colt bellows to the poor guy.

"Ah, yes, sir. Of course." He smooths down his fluffy white hair and extends an arm to the front of the store. "Ma'am, if you'll come with me, we'll get you rung up."

I follow him through the store, dissolving into giggles

when I realize I look like a mother duck leading a train of big, highly muscled, scooter riding ducklings. The salesman's eyes are wide as we all pull up to the counter.

"Crutches...too." Micah orders the poor guy. I glare at him, and he adds, "please," with a cheeky smile.

The man hurries off, coming back quickly with a pair of small purple crutches. When he sees my raised eyebrows, his cheeks redden. "It's the only pair we have in stock for someone your uh...height."

There's a snort behind me. "Cause you're itty bitty," Declan sings.

I turn to glare at Declan. "We can't all be gargantuan apes now can we?" I ask sweetly.

He winks and the rest of the guys snicker as I turn back to the salesman. His head is bobbing between us like he's watching a tennis match. "Ah. Ok, with the scooter and the crutches, the total will be-"

"Scooters," Colt interrupts, waiting for the salesman to look at him. "We're taking all of them, man." He waves to the ones he and the guys are still occupying, rocking them back and forth like they're toy cars.

"Ok. Right. Of course, sir. Would you like me to arrange delivery?"

AND JUST LIKE THAT, WE'RE BACK IN JONAS'S MINIVAN WITH MY crutches and knee scooter, four more on their way to the condo. I just about swallowed my tongue when I saw the total Micah put on his credit card, but I didn't argue. I need to be mobile. What if there's another fire, or something else happens? I don't want to be helpless again.

And maybe I'm testing him just a little bit. The $250 he just spent on me is a drop in the bucket for him, I know, but I still wonder what it's going to cost me. Brent always collected. Always.

"Where…going…Jonas?" Micah asks suddenly. The men insisted I sit in the front, even though I can fit in any of the seats easily. They're piled in the back, looking quite comfortable, clearly not their first ride in this van. I didn't even notice we were going the wrong way.

"Craft store," Jonas says, both hands on the wheel, "Holly needs yarn."

My eyes widen. "Oh Jonas, no it's ok. I don't need anything more tonight."

His eyes shift to mine briefly before staring back out the window. "Yes. You do," he says firmly.

"I've never been to a craft store before." Declan says. "What, they have like, paint and shit there?"

I turn back, surprised to see all three of them looking intrigued. "Ah, yes. Paint, canvases, yarn. Things for baking and making jewelry. Lots of yarn."

"Fuck Yeah! Let's go." Colt says, pumping his arm and wiggling his eyebrows. I face forward, giggling the whole way to the parking lot of the big box craft store. As I look up at the massive store, I thank God we couldn't fit their scooters in the van.

When we get in the doors, it's a repeat of the health care store. The guys scatter, only this time Declan takes Micah aside for a moment, speaking quietly. Micah nods and slaps him on the back before coming back to me. *"Is it ok if Declan hangs with you for a bit? We'll meet you guys in the yarn section."*

Puzzled, I nod yes, then let Declan escort me as I beeline on my scooter for the yarns. I've actually been to this store before. It has the right combination of price and selection for someone with a budget as tiny as mine is. Declan stays by my side, shooting glances at me until I'm completely unnerved. Unable to take it anymore, I stop at the end of an aisle. "What?"

He turns to me, pushing the hood of his sweater back. His hair is in a mohawk. It's mostly bright red, but his dark roots are growing out. His eyes are devastated. "It's my fault." He blurts, locking his hands behind his neck.

"What's your fault?" I ask, already lost.

"I'm the reason Brent found you."

lack spots dance before my eyes. I sway, and Declan's hands are there, keeping me from falling. He helps me shift until I'm sitting on the scooter.

"Explain," I order him, my panting breaths making the words come out in a whisper, rather than the assertive order I intended them to be.

He kneels in front of me, devastation written on his face. "I ran a background check. It's standard for all new employees, but yours came back with some...anomalies. Enough that I had to dig deeper."

"They told me my new identity was solid." The only thing that let me sleep the last two years is believing that. Finding out it's a lie is rocking my entire foundation.

"It is," Declan assures me. "It would get past almost any background check. But I'm really fucking good at digging... so I did." He gently touches my hand, eyes tight. "As soon as I found the first file, I should have stopped. But I kept digging. I fucked up. I should have stopped sooner, or gone all the way and learned everything there was to know about Brent. Stopping where I did gave him the information he needed to find you. I didn't know he had access to those systems. I swear I didn't know. I would never have left you vulnerable like that."

I lick my dry lips. "He...he worked for the police. He was a civilian contractor, but he worked on their computers, and had a lot of friends who were cops."

"I know that now." He hangs his head, apology in every line of his body. "I am so fucking sorry. I will do anything to make it up to you, no matter how long it takes. Just tell me what you need, and I'll do it."

He means it, the apology, the sorrow in his voice unmistakable. I understand that feeling. Of making a mistake and wishing you could take it back, make it better. But I don't want this man bearing the weight of this guilt. There's no reason for it. I'm alive, and Brent is behind bars.

"You don't need to do anything, Declan. I accept your apology. Brent's in prison, and I'm ok. The rest of it is in the past."

He eyes me in disbelief. "The man came for you with a knife, Holly. How can you be ok with that?"

I smile. "Because the day he showed up at the garage? That's the first time anyone ever stood between Brent and me. I lived seven years under his boot, no one willing to help me. To protect me. Until that day. That day, there were four people I knew Brent would have to get through to hurt me. It was the safest I'd felt in nine years. I hated that they were in danger, *hated it*, but I was so thankful it happened the way it did."

"But it could have been so much worse! What if you'd been alone? What if he'd followed you home?"

"There's no point in playing the what if game. I'll admit I had some sleepless nights, those same thoughts keeping me awake." Lots of nights actually, but he doesn't need to carry that. "But there's no point. I have to believe it all happened the way God intended it to."

His lips curl briefly before he hides it. I've seen that cynicism before. He tries to hold it in, but finally asks. "Do you honestly believe that it was God's plan to have your husband beat you for years?"

I smile gently. I've asked myself the same question, so I can't fault him for it. "I think that I must have a purpose on this earth, because despite all the times I could have died, I didn't. I always believed there was a bigger plan for me." I shrug. "I can't say that I believe most of what my parents forced down my throat as gospel, but I can't help feeling a connection to something...more."

Thankfully, he lets it drop. I don't want to defend my faith to him, especially since I'm not sure what exactly I believe anymore.

He sighs heavily, standing. "Are you sure there's nothing I can do?"

I feel sorry for him. He's stewing in regret and I wish there was something..."Oh!" His eyes sharpen on mine. "Actually, there is something you could do for me, though...maybe not yet."

"Anything." He says simply.

What is it with these guys, making indiscriminate promises?

"I had two...friends that I've lost touch with. I tried making a fake Facebook profile to find them but I didn't have any luck. The phone numbers I had for them are out of service."

"Give me whatever you have. I'll find them." He says with absolute confidence.

"But, just find them, right? I...there's so much I have to make up to them for. I just need a little time."

"Just find them, I swear. I'll give you everything I find on them and let you make the first move."

I believe him, so I give him everything I know, all the details I remember. He doesn't say a word, taking notes on his phone and nodding. My stomach swirls with nausea now that I've made the first move. A spiral of self doubt is starting.

What if they don't want to talk to me? What if they can't forgive me?

Just as those inner voices are ramping up into a scream, Micah appears in front of me. His smile fades as he takes in the tension in my body. "Move," he tells Declan as he shoves past him, coming to squat down in front of me. "*What is it, love? What do you need?*"

What do I need? So many things. But right now, in this moment. I can only think of one thing. And only one person I want it from. Asking for it feels like an epic act of faith. "I could really use a hug," I whisper.

Micah groans softly, pushing forward as he gently spreads my thighs, careful not to knock my ankle. Then he wraps one of those big arms around me. I gasp and throw my arms around his neck as he pulls me off the seat and stands, settling an arm under my butt. He's cradling me to him like a parent would a child, but nothing about it feels parental.

It feels...like my spot.

The solid weight of his arm pulling me into that wide chest. The way he hikes me up until he has our faces level. His eyes are so serious, so warm. The promises in them flowing through my limbs, chasing away those painful doubts, quieting the voices.

I tighten my arms around him until I'm pressed as close as I can be, brushing my cheek against his as I fold forward, collapsing into his arms. Trusting him to bear my weight.

For the first time I can remember, I accept the comfort of a man. Without worrying about how he might hurt me next. Or worrying about what it might cost me. I just...fall in and let myself breathe in the moment. It won't last forever. It can't. So I memorize the feel of him, the simplicity of this moment, so I can pull them out and relive them when I'm alone.

It could have been minutes or hours when he breaks the silence. "Home?" he asks.

I pull back. "No way." I say, shaking my head and pointing to the back of the store. "Take me to the yarn."

I don't let go, content to stay in his arms while he carts me around. My self consciousness from earlier in the week is gone. Any worries about my weight, or Micah's ability to carry me faded away. I smile over Micah's shoulder, seeing Declan hunched over the short, perfect for me scooter, crab walking as he follows us.

Micah stops suddenly in the aisle, "The...fuck?"

I drop my cheek against Micah's forehead, laughing, watching Colt and Jonas sword fight with giant crochet hooks. They're not quiet about it, nearly knocking into a small elderly lady, who turns and beans Colt with her cane. "You ruffians. This is a place for civilized people. Smarten up! Put those away right now. Now," she orders them. Wide eyed, they do as they're told, then stand, awaiting judgment. "Well," she sniffs, pointing at the top shelf with her cane, "make yourselves useful and get me three skeins of the cream wool."

"Skeins?" Colt asks me, looking cowed.

"Three balls of the beige wool." I clarify for him. He nods, pulling them down and carefully putting them in her cart.

"Good. Now I need some baby yarn. Come along, boys." She toddles off, tapping the cart with her cane and eyeing Jonas, who just stands there.

Colt whisper yells, "Grab the cart Jonas," as he meekly follows the crusty old woman.

"Do...should we...rescue them?" I ask, tears of laughter streaming down my face.

Declan snorts. "No fucking way. She's scary as hell."

And there it is.

As I relax in Micah's arms, directing Declan to the yarns and hooks I need, the differences between these men, and all the men I've known in the past are glaring. No way would

Brent, or my father, or any of the men from our church let a woman treat them like this. Or like that old woman did.

They seem almost...doting. Happy to help me, happy to be together. "You guys really don't care what anyone thinks of you, do you?" I ask.

Micah chuckles. "Nope...except."

"Except?" I ask, tilting my head. He smiles at me, then turns to Declan, raising a brow.

Declan explains. "We don't care what anyone thinks about us, never really have, unless it serves us."

"Serves you? How do you mean?"

"Well, sometimes it's easier to let people think we're dumb" he says nodding at Micah, "or snobs, or anything else we want them to think. We've gotten a lot of great intel over the years using that strategy. So we care what they think of us, because we want to make sure they're getting the impression of us that we choose. Make sense?"

"I think we all do that to some extent." I say, thinking of the masks I've worn over my life.

"Like?" Micah asks.

"Like playing the perfect wife, agreeing with everything Brent said, even when I thought he was wrong. It was safer for me to be what he wanted. It served me."

"Exactly," Declan says softly. "The only opinions that actually matter to us? Well, it's the nine of us, and you and Becca. That's it. Everyone else can go fuck themselves."

I feel like I just grew an inch, at least. "Becca, I understand. She's one of you. But me?"

"Holly," Declan says with a wry smile, "we've all known Micah wanted you from the day he met you. You matter to him, so you matter to us."

I'm going to tuck away the tornado of feelings that sends up at me, for now anyway.

I carefully avoid Micah's eyes. "But, we're not together. Until this week, we barely spoke."

Declan slides his hands into the pocket of his black hoodie. "Doesn't matter."

"I don't understand you guys. At all." Shouldn't they protect themselves more? Be more jaded or cynical? How can they just…draw me right into their fold?

Micah growls, moving towards Declan, swinging my legs up and placing me into Declan's arms. I'm staring, wide eyed, up at Declan's smiling face when Micah says my name, "Holly." When he has my attention, he starts signs, "*I told you I loved you. I meant it. This*" he says, pointing between us "*is not new for me. I didn't think I was good enough for you, but I always wanted you. I didn't try to hide it from my brothers. I made sure they knew, so they'd look after you.*"

"Look after me?" I squeak.

"*If anything ever happened and I couldn't be there for you, I wanted to make sure you'd have someone.*"

Something about the way he said it made my heart sink. "You knew about Brent?"

"Yes." He says calmly. "*Declan and Kade shared everything with me. I always knew.*"

I can't speak, too horrified by the idea that they all knew about my past this whole time, even before Brent showed up.

"W…What did you see?" I turn to Declan. "What did you show him?" Most of the scars of my marriage are internal. Brent was usually pretty careful not to damage me anywhere that clothes couldn't hide. But when I tried to get help, at the beginning, there were pictures. Reports. Nothing ever came of them, but they exist.

"Nothing." Declan's words are emphatic, his eyes begging me to believe him. "I would never violate your privacy like that. I only shared enough so that everyone would be on guard. We didn't know about Brent specifically, but we knew you were hurt. I should have dug everything up. We could have ended it sooner."

I nod, shifting to study the row of yarns behind us. I guess

I'm not surprised they know everything, but I wish my mistakes, my shame weren't the first things they learned about me.

"Hey...what....thinking?"

"I...I tried to leave. And I did fight him. I didn't always just...give in."

Micah stares at me, wide eyed. "Fuck!" He yells, shoving his hands into his hair. He paces away, breathing heavily. I watch his shoulders heave, as mine round in.

"Can you put me down please" I whisper to Declan. He's so incredibly kind, but I don't want to be this close to him. It feels wrong. He carefully lowers me until I'm settled with my knee on the scooter. My ribs are throbbing, and I'm feeling a little dizzy. Maybe going from sleeping for two days solid to a shopping spree wasn't the best idea.

Micah storms back, dropping to his knees in front of me. *"You don't ever, EVER, have to justify yourself to me. To anyone. You are fucking alive. Whatever you needed to do to get yourself out, is RIGHT."* "Hear...me...Holly...no....s..sh..shame." His muscles are bunched, eyes fierce, nostrils flaring.

The conviction in his voice brings tears to my eyes, but I shake my head. "There were so many things —."

"No," he says firmly. *"I didn't protect my mom. When my dad would beat her, I didn't always try to protect her. Sometimes, I just hid. Do you blame me?"*

It's not the same. Not at all. "Never, Micah...but you were just a child—."

He stands suddenly, looming over me, bringing his body inches from mine. His size suddenly overwhelming. My head only reaching his chest, his forearms thicker than my biceps. I swallow thickly, feeling panicky.

"Holly," he pleads. I force my chin up and meet his gaze. He keeps us pressed together, glancing at Declan with pleading eyes. Declan nods.

"Brent was smaller than Micah, but still a big guy." He

says, "You had no training. No way to defend yourself." He exhales heavily. "There is no way you could have stopped him. No way. Just like there is no way you could stop any of us if we wanted to hurt you."

He comes forward, crouching in front of me. Micah drops back to his knees too. Over their heads, I see Colton and Jonas, eyes dark, brows drawn at the end of the aisle, blocking us from prying eyes.

"Holly," Micah says, *"You are absolutely safe with us, because we would never choose to hurt you. I would protect you with my life."*

"Placing one's body in a submissive position when interacting with victims of abuse is shown to reduce cortisol," Jonas says "helping the victims feel less threatened."

My eyes bounce from Jonas, to the men in front of me, back to Jonas. A hysterical giggle escapes me.

"It works." Jonas assures me, nodding earnestly.

"That's why you guys are always crouching down in front of me?" I ask, looking at Declan and Micah, shoulder to shoulder in front of me.

Everyone but Colton nods. He strides forward until he's right in front of me, then lowers his chin so he's staring right at me. "See," he says, pinching the skin under his jaw, startling a laugh out of me, "double chin. Crouching gives you a better angle to admire my awesomeness."

These men are unbelievable. I've been on an emotional rollercoaster tonight and I'm on the verge of a meltdown. My body is so primed for conflict it sees a threat in everything they do. It's got to be tiring for all of them.

I never meant to be so much work.

"Could we go home now?" I ask, tired to my bones. And so sick of myself. Micah's been bending over backwards, dealing with broken me. I don't know how he can do it. How does he stay so level?

The guys hustle to grab the yarn and supplies I point out,

then we head to the checkouts, Colton and Jonas pushing carts full of...well I don't know. I refuse Micah's offer to carry me, trying and failing to ignore the hurt in his eyes. He deserves so much better than me. He deserves someone strong and whole.

Someone more like Becca.

19

MICAH

She's pulling away from me, and I don't know what to do. I watch the back of her head as we travel through the dark city, hoping she'll look at me, but she won't. There's an ocean between us and I don't know how to bridge it.

I should never have let the guys come. Her request for crutches interrupted a really fucking serious conversation, so I thought she'd appreciate the distraction that is my brothers. Plus, I want them to get to know her, to love her. But it feels like we've gone backwards, and all I want now is to get her back to my condo and rebuild the bubble we created today.

This wanting someone who doesn't want you back shit is hell.

She lets me carry her into the condo. "Hold...tight," I tell her as I use the hand supporting her back on the scanner to let us in. The guys follow, carrying bags of yarn and supplies. Declan wheels her scooter in. They say soft goodnights and leave quickly, Holly giving them small smiles as they go.

Then it's just the two of us, her small frame still in my arms. She feels so right there, I wish she wouldn't get better. But that's fucked up, and I don't really want that for her. I want her healed, but still happy to be carried around, like a fucking Queen. That would be perfect.

Shifting uncomfortably, I eyeball the door to her bedroom, then suck it up and take her in, settling her on her bed. *"We were out late and Kathy couldn't come later. You're stuck with me tonight. What can I help you with?"*

Her hands grip the mattress beside her hips. Her gaze sliding from me to the bathroom, and back again. "Ah... you've helped me to the bathroom before. Maybe just bring me some pyjamas and I can get changed myself."

SHE'S BEEN IN THERE FOR TWENTY MINUTES, AND I'M READY TO break the door down when she calls for me. I burst through in a Kramer worthy entrance, mentally kicking my own ass for my lack of cool, and find her still sitting on the toilet, tears in her eyes.

"Oh...Holly," I crouch next to her. Her lounge pants are still on. She's managed to pull the nightgown over her head, but it's pooled at her waist. I put my hand on her knee, waiting for her to tell me what she needs.

She rubs her eyes angrily, "I'm so sick of being weak."

I growl at her, "Not...weak."

Her laugh is sarcastic. "I know who I am, Micah. You don't know me. My whole life I've been quiet, meek, going along with what everyone else told me to do. It's pathetic."

I slide down the wall facing the toilet until I'm sitting. "Not...weak." I say firmly. I'll say it as many times as I need to until it sinks in. *"We talked about this Holly. You are not weak. You've got a fucking backbone of steel woman. How can you not see that?"*

"Right, so because you said it, it must be true? Because you're a man and that means you know better?"

Oh fuck.

"That's not what I meant." Christ, she's stewing for a fight.

"You've known me for two months. You know some parts of me. You know some of the crap I've been through. That doesn't mean you know me."

I draw my knees up, resting my arms on top of them. We study each other, her jaw locked and eyes tight.

"You're right," I admit. *"I don't know your whole life. But I've watched you at the garage. I couldn't take my fucking eyes off you. And I see who you are out from under Brent's thumb. Can you allow for the possibility that you might be stronger than you think?"*

"I can't even stand up, Micah. My legs are shaking." She says, biting off the words, launching them at me like little daggers.

"Over...did...it." I mutter. *"I should have told the guys no extra stops. I'm sorry. Your body's been battered, you're getting over a fucking concussion. I should know better."* Her mouth firms, another argument on the tip of her tongue.

"I...help?" I ask gently, heading her off. *"Please. I need you to be comfortable."*

She finally nods, and I move the two feet separating us to kneel at her feet. She puts her hands on the grab bars around the toilet and lifts herself up. "Shoulders," I tell her, waiting until she's got a firm grip on me to move. I lock my eyes with hers, watching for any hint of panic as I pull the hem of her blue T-shirt nightgown down to her thighs. Once she's covered, I run my palms up the side of her thighs until I reach the waistband of her pants. "Panties?" I choke out.

She tightens her hands on me. "I want them on." Her voice is tense, the words wobbly.

I nod, then move my fingers into the waistband, running them back and forth until they're between her panties and the pants. My knuckles are against the skin of her stomach and I swear I've never felt anything softer. Being this close to her, on my knees in front of her, I swear I can smell the sweet scent of her sex. I am so gone over this woman, I'm seconds from coming in my fucking pants. Again.

I have no self-control.

Watching her, I slowly pull her pants down, letting them pool to the floor on one leg, working the fabric carefully off the air cast on the other. "Step," I mutter. She steps out of the fabric and I toss it into the shower stall next to us. "What…next?"

Her cheeks flush, her eyes focusing on my forehead. "I…I have to use the…"

I smile, "Boss…me…around."

Her eyes flare at my teasing, but some of the red recedes. "My legs are shaking pretty badly."

"Know." I can feel the trembling in her whole body. I want to take over, strip her, help her pee, then tuck her into bed. I know she's embarrassed, but I want to care for her in every way. I want that right, and that privilege. But I'm not going to scare her again.

"Pull my panties down…don't look please," she begs. The hands on my shoulders are gripping so tight I might actually bruise. I want her marks on me, just not like this. Because she's afraid and weak. No, I want her nail marks in my shoulders as she shoves me down to pleasure her.

I slam my eyes closed but the image plays on the back of my eyelids like a move. I threaten my cock with bodily harm, then slide my hands back up until I've hooked the panties, drawing them down past her knees. I feel her body shift as she sits. "Give me a minute, please."

"Ok," I say with a smile, exiting the bathroom. As soon as I close the bathroom door behind me, I fold over, bracing my hands on my knees, gasping for breath, trying to regain control of myself.

I've got my dick somewhat handled by the time she calls me back in. We follow the same routine in reverse; me pulling her panties up with my eyes closed. I give in to my need to hold her by wrapping my arm around her waist at the sink, taking all of her weight as she washes her hands and brushes her teeth. When she's done, I scoop her up and take her to the bed, leaning down so she can pull the bedding back, helping me slide her in. The soft glow of the bedside lamp creates dancing shadows along her face. I slowly move to sit on the bed, facing her.

Her glassy eyes are ancient, weary.

"Today was heavy." I say, exhaling. *"And I don't know how to make it better for you. I'm sorry I pushed or tried to mansplain your own life to you. You're right, I guess. What I think of you doesn't really matter. I just…"*

"You just what?"

I almost can't bring myself to say it. *"I used to get so angry with my mom when she would fight him. The beatings were always so much worse, so I didn't understand why she'd do it."*

"She fought back so she could live with herself." She says flatly.

Wincing, I replay the beatings my mom took, looping the past like an old strip of film.

"I'm starting to see that. She used to fight all the time. Then some of the time. Then not at all. Then she was just…gone. She left us."

Her hand fists on blanket. "She left you behind? With him?"

"Yeah." I say quietly. *"It's good she left. He would have killed her."*

"Why didn't she take you with her?"

I shrug. *"You might be able to tell me."*

Her mouth tightens. "Trying to run with a child would be…agonizing." She says apologetically.

"Explain," I beg her, desperate for some insight into my mom. I want to understand why she chose to leave me behind. I need it.

"I had a network of people helping me, and it was still

terrifying. Most days I felt like a robot, going through the motions. In the back of my head was this...certainty...that he would find me. That I would die. I was in my most basic lizard brain."

She shifts, reaching down to trace a crease on the sheet. "I saw some mothers in the shelter. They looked so...worn. They never ate a full meal, always giving extra to their kids. Their focus was on the children as they themselves were wasting away."

"Were you afraid that was going to happen to you?"

Her eyes flash, and she nods slowly. "I was terrified of it."

"Of raising a baby?"

"I didn't do a very good job keeping myself safe. The idea of being responsible for a baby was overwhelming. And the idea that I would be connected to Brent for the rest of my life...I hated it. Maybe that's why I miscarried. Maybe God knew I wouldn't be a good mom."

There's so much wrong with that statement. I clench my jaw so I don't explain to her how wrong she is. How amazing she is. *"How did you feel about losing the baby?"*

Her fingers are picking at the sheet now, and I can't stop myself from reaching out to cover her hands. She looks at me, searching for any sign of judgment. She won't find any with me, ever.

One tear spills from her eye. "Sad, but also relieved. I would have taken care of the baby, but it was a scary time. Having a baby on the run...was not how I would want to do it."

"Course...not." I want to hold her. She's experienced so much loss, I don't know how she stands it. *"Babies are miracles. You should be coddled, and loved, and not have to worry about anything when you're pregnant."* I want to be the one to take care of her, especially then, when she's round with my child.

She smiles sadly, eyes falling to the bedding between us. A big yawn cracks her jaw.

"You...sleep." I say as I ease off the bed. "Night." I back away. I don't want to take my eyes off her until I have to.

"Micah...wait." I freeze, waiting for her to continue. "Can...will you sleep in here tonight?"

My eyes widen, darting from her to the empty side of the California King bed. I swallow twice before asking, "How?" Hoping she understands my question. But I don't want there to be any confusion. I would sign, but suddenly I can't feel my body. I need her to spell out exactly what she wants from me.

"Maybe you can wear your pyjamas and sleep on top of the covers?"

I nod, my head bobbing repeatedly. It's so hot in here, sleeping on top of the covers will be fine. "Ok...back...soon," I tell her, then make my escape.

I run across the apartment, Minnie lifting her head from the back of the couch to watch me, then bang into my room. What the fuck do I wear for pyjamas? I don't own fucking pyjamas. I spin in a circle, unable to remember what clothing I own. Or where I keep it. Or who the fuck I am.

I sink down on the edge of my bed, trying to get my head on straight. I can't go to her with this manic energy. Maybe I should take a shower, rub one out to calm down.

I've tried that though.

It only buys me a few minutes of relief. The second I see her again, my cock will be fucking saluting her. No, I don't want to leave her waiting too long. I can't risk her changing her mind.

I throw on a tank and athletic shorts, brush my teeth, then grab a throw on my way back through the living room. I knock softly, waiting for her invitation to enter. I leave the door propped open. "Minnie," I explain at her questioning look. Holly hasn't moved, still sitting up. She watches me circle the bed, a tired smile slipping over her full lips as I hover, staring at her.

"Lay down Micah," she orders softly. It's like my body was waiting for her to release it. I collapse into the mattress, trying to settle before popping back up to pull eighty pillows off the bed. Fucking interior designer. Then I lay back down with my one pillow, sighing in satisfaction. Her soft giggle makes me smile.

"Sleep...Holly." I whisper, turning on my side to face her. She turns the bedside light off and rolls on her side to face me, carefully adjusting her foot. The light from the bathroom shines behind her, hiding her face from me. Her breathing is rapid, and I pray it's not from fear. I wish I could snap my fingers and she'd believe in me. In the way I feel for her. That she'd know, keep in her gut, that when she's with me she's safer than she's ever been in her life.

Minnie's weight lands on the end of the bed with a small meow. She pads up the bed, stopping to let Holly give her a rub under the chin before padding over to me. With years of practice, she settles herself on the pillow, right in front of my head, and begins to groom herself, stopping once in a while to lick my forehead. I don't bother to wipe it off, knowing she'll just lick me again.

Over Minnie's purr, Holly's soft laughter rings out. I smile at her, and slowly reach my left arm towards her, letting my hand settle on the bed between us.

An invitation.

Holly stares at it before slowly reaching out, wiggling her fingers until they're tucked inside mine. She closes her eyes, a small smile on her lips, and drifts to sleep. I keep my eyes on her, the soft movement of her chest, the tiny squeak of her breath, not quite a snore, but nearly.

And for the first time in my whole life, I fall asleep with a smile on my face.

20

HOLLY

He has a cat on his head.

Sometime between last night and this morning, Minnie draped herself over his head, spread eagle. One of her little paws is resting on his nose, her chin on his forehead, her back legs stretching down the back of his head. He hasn't moved at all, even when she stretches and flexes those sharp little nails. She couldn't be closer. Looks like Minnie and I both have a little crush.

Micah didn't move all night. But I did. When I woke up on his side of the bed, my nose was plastered to his chest, my right leg thrown over his. My nightgown bunched around my waist.

Thank God I kept my underwear on. Micah's arm is wrapped around my back, holding me snugly to him. The other hand is holding mine to his chest. I've never slept with a man like this, wrapped up. In bed with Brent, I clung to the edge, unable to bear touching him. Even in my sleep, I was repelled by him. Apparently, my body has very different feelings for Micah.

It's not a surprise, really. It's been giving me hints of how I feel, how much I want, all week. It's my brain that's getting in the way. I've been fighting it. Fighting him all week. Unable to believe that he might truly want me. But more, unable to believe that I might want him. That he really is different from Brent. But somehow it's this little cat that's convinced me who he truly is.

It seems like a simple thing. I mean, she's just an animal. What effect could she possibly have on the way I feel about Micah? But I can't help but remember every time Brent came across someone with a pet, in our neighborhood, or out for a walk. He loved to 'promenade', he called it, wanting to look the part of the dapper gentleman and his biddable wife. So we walked, and I pretended that everything was ok. That I hadn't just been pushed down some steps and cracked a rib.

I loved visiting with the pets, though. I got to snuggle and love on all the dogs, and the occasional cat rolling in the front yard. But not once, in the seven years of our marriage, did an animal approach Brent. More than that, when Brent would attempt to play nice with a dog, it would snarl or back away. Animals did not trust him.

Micah, and all the guys really, seem to be wrapped around Minnie's little paw. It's so easy for an angry person to target an animal. But she doesn't show an ounce of fear around them. That has to mean something.

It has to.

Maybe I'm reaching, but I feel safe here too. My gut is telling me that Micah would never raise a hand to me. And if I'm really honest with myself, my gut told me Brent was not the man he presented himself to be. But I ignored it. I put myself in harm's way.

Micah's arm tightens around my back before relaxing. He's awake. I can feel the warmth of his gaze on the top of my head. Gathering my courage, I raise my head.

"This...ok?" he asks carefully.

A giggle takes over my body. "I should be asking you that. Looks like the females have invaded your space."

He smiles, crossing his eyes to look at Minnie's paw on his nose, but doesn't move her.

"Like...you...space."

My cheeks heat, but I don't look away, my gaze moving from his warm eyes to the cat, and back again. "You're not ever going to hit me, are you?" I ask, a thread of certainty in my voice.

"Never." His voice is strong, sure. His glittering eyes locked on mine.

"You're never going to rape me, are you?"

He flinches, a rumbled, "Never,"coming from deep in his chest.

I move to sit up, getting tangled in the blankets. Micah lifts up to help me, Minnie sliding off his head onto his pillow. She rolls over and goes right back to sleep.

Micah helps me adjust the stupid cast until I'm sitting comfortably facing him. I take a minute to admire the acres of golden skin, the flattened spots on his dark hair. I swear I can see a Minnie shaped outline. But his eyes, those warm brown eyes, are locked on me, like I'm the only thing he can see.

"When Brent asked me to marry him, I thought it was too fast. He seemed so mature and smooth that I sometimes felt like an immature child around him. And I was flattered that he wanted me. I was...shy. Quiet. Stuck in my books. But he came into the coffee shop at the university when I was on shift, and stayed for hours, flirting with me." I meet Micah's eyes briefly before looking back at the hollow of his throat. "I...liked the attention. I hadn't had any boyfriends in high school. My parents were...very strict. So when I got to college, I felt left behind, I guess? I didn't know how to interact with most of the guys. So I focused on school, and I worked to make ends meet."

"Scholar...ship?" he asks.

"It covered my tuition and books, and my dorm room. I

had to handle food and everything else. I made it work." He nods, encouraging me to continue.

"Brent took the lead in our relationship, completely. He did most of the talking, and then he kept showing up when I was on shift. He'd asked my manager, and she told him my schedule." He scowls at that. I feel the same way...now. I don't understand why she thought it was ok to share that information. Aren't women supposed to look out for each other?

"At the time, I was flattered by the attention. He was handsome, put together, and he seemed to want me. So when he pushed me to marry him, I said yes, even though in my gut I knew it wasn't the right choice. But I ignored it, Micah, and I paid for that mistake with everything that I was."

He exhales heavily, pushing his hand through his hair. "Right," he says heavily. Those eyes are shuttered now, hiding what he feels from me.

"My gut," I say, watching him carefully, "tells me I'm safer than I've ever been in my life when I'm with you."

His eyes flare with surprise. He swallows thickly. *"I thought you were going to say something different."*

"I know." I say sadly. "I've been pretty all over the place this week. Battling my head and my body. And then you told me..." The words he gave me feel so massive, I don't think I can say them.

"Love...you." He says with a quirk of his lips.

"Yeah. That. I...It was a lot." I say, an apology in my tone.

"I never meant to overwhelm you, or push you into a corner." He signs urgently. *"My feelings for you are mine to handle. If you don't feel the same, or—."*

"It's not that. I feel lots of things. Most of them are completely new to me. But I also feel...vulnerable," I explain, scowling. "I'm dependent on you for everything right now. I'm living in your house, eating your food, wearing clothes you bought me. I needed your help to get changed last night, for heaven's sake."

He looks down, gently petting the tip of Minnie's paw with his pinkie. "Need...time." He says gruffly.

"Yeah, I do. Just when I think I have some control over things, the rug gets yanked out from under me. I need a chance to figure out how to be me again. How to not be so scared all the time. How to trust myself."

I take a deep breath, feeling my whole face flush in preparation for this next part. But if I want even a hope of things working between us, he has to know where I'm coming from.

"I've never had an orgasm, Micah. I have never had sex without pain. Not once have I done something in the bedroom because I wanted it. I don't know what I like. What feels good. And I'm terrified that if you and I ever got to that point, all I would be able to think about is the way Brent hurt me. I'm afraid he'll poison everything that could be between us. I'm afraid we'll be ruined."

Micah's eyes are glassy, his hands fisted in his lap. His deep chest moves rhythmically. *"I hoped that he was kind to you at the beginning, at least. That he would take care of you on your wedding night."*

"He told me it always hurts the first time. He was abrupt, and I wasn't ready, but I thought it would get better. It didn't. And when I learned that he would force me, even when I didn't want to...I had to get resourceful."

"Re...re...sourceful?" His face is pained, tight.

I hate this conversation. I don't want to share all these intimate details, but I also don't want him to have any illusions about me.

"It hurt so much," I whisper. "I would bleed...I wanted to avoid the pain. I couldn't stop him, but I could stop some of the damage, so I went to a sex shop. The lady there was so nice. I didn't tell her what was going on, just that sometimes things were...dry. She suggested some lube."

Micah groans, shifting in bed, shoving his palms into his eyes, pressing his elbows into his knees. I hesitate, not sure he wants to hear the rest. "Finish," he says harshly.

"I would...apply...it without him knowing. He would use the fact that I was wet against me, telling me how much I wanted it." I lick my dry lips. "I didn't want it. I never wanted it. But at least I didn't...tear anymore."

Micah makes a choked sound, then launches off the bed. I hear him retching in the bathroom, then finally the toilet flushing. He stays hunched over the sink as he rinses his mouth.

I watch the lines of his back, enjoying the flex of his muscles, letting my brain drift away from those horrible memories, wondering how he maintains all that muscle. Maybe all the heavy lifting he does at the garage is enough. I don't think I'll ever get tired of looking at him.

He comes back into the room, moving to sit back on the bed. His face and hair are wet, drops of water traveling down his cheek.

"I'm sorry," I say softly.

He snarls. *"Don't you ever apologize to me for telling me the truth. I'm the one who should be fucking apologizing. I've been pushing you, Holly. I had the best intentions, but I still pushed you. I knew that you'd been through a lot, but hearing the specifics... I promise I'll do better. If you want to talk, then I want to hear it, I promise. I just might have to go down to the gym and hit something later."*

"Ok," I say over the lump in my throat.

Micah's cell pings on the nightstand. "Kathy...coming," he says. *"Also, Declan and Colton would like to come talk to you. Declan says he found your friends."*

My heart jumps in my chest, excitement and dread mingling until it's a messy swirl.

21

HOLLY

My stomach is still swirling as I watch Colt and Declan walk in. I rolled myself to the head of the table this morning, the couch somehow not formal enough for this conversation. Not terribly logical, considering the last time we sat at this table, there was a massive food fight.

These are not formal people.

Declan's eyes are serious this morning, his trademark black hoodie over a white tank and black track pants. Colton's wearing a plain black t-shirt and sweats, both stretched tight, pulling over his massive frame. I wonder if he just outgrew his clothes or does he like them tight? He's massive, but I know he can afford clothing that fits.

Declan settles on my left, Colt next to him. Micah brings over coffees, then sits on my right. "Morning," I finally manage through the frog in my throat. It's not good news. I can see it on Declan's face.

"Mornin' Holly," he says. Colton smiles and waves happily, making me grin despite the heaviness in the air.

"That was really fast. I didn't think you'd have anything for me this quickly."

Declan smiles softly. "Computers are kind of my thing. Finding people who aren't hiding is easy. Took me less than an hour last night to pull everything together."

He did in an hour what I couldn't do in a year. The scope of their resources, their abilities is a bit overwhelming sometimes. If I had run from Micah, if he were my husband, he would have been able to find me so easily.

Thank God they're good guys.

"Tell me." I say, locking eyes with Declan. "It's not good, is it?"

His mouth twists, and he opens the file folder in front of him. "Let's start with the good stuff. I tracked Robyn down to California. She's teaching at a school for the deaf out there. She's married and has a three-year-old son."

I cover my mouth, the reality of how much I've missed of her life hitting hard. When we last spoke, she tried to talk me out of marrying Brent. She was frustrated with me, convinced I was making a mistake. She's lived an entire life without me. But a good life. She has a son! But if she's doing ok then...

"And Evie?" I ask, bracing myself.

Declan blows out a heavy breath. "This is where things get tougher. You said Evie worked in the NICU when you left?"

"Yeah, she'd been there a few years. She had just adopted a little girl. A baby she'd been taking care of in the NICU for nearly a year. She was one of the best nurses there. Completely dedicated to the babies." I want him to know how amazing she is.

He nods, shoulders tight. "There's no easy way to say this." Declan's eyes are dark. "About a month after you left, she was fired from the hospital. Rumors were circulating that she stole opiates. The hospital didn't press charges, on the condition that she not work as a nurse anywhere in the state of Ohio."

I slap my hands on the table, anger pouring through me. "No chance! No way in hell would she ever do that."

"After I pulled her history, it seemed pretty unlikely." He agrees calmly. "But she took the deal and left." He hesitates. "Looks like CPS took her daughter."

I moan, slamming my eyes shut, knowing the destruction of her life is because of me. Because she helped me. "Tell me she got her back, please."

Declan nods carefully. "It took her about six months, but she did get her back."

Thank God.

"It was Brent." I say harshly.

"Yeah, it was. We know Brent spread a story about you when you left. That you'd stolen his 401K, emptied the bank accounts, and split. He had some friends on the force that helped him. The same guys that buried your police and medical reports." His tone is low and deadly. "I don't know exactly how he did it, but he and those cops planted evidence. From what I can tell, the hospital bought it hook, line and sinker. They still don't have a clue that she was framed. Neither does CPS."

"She saved my life," I say, voice cracking, "and they destroyed hers." Micah's warm hand covers mine, and I grab onto the lifeline he's offering.

"What happened to the cops? Can you prove they did these things?" I ask, eyes filled with tears.

"That's why I wanted Colt to hear this." Declan says, tilting his head towards him.

When I look over at Colt, the joking happy guy, the one who waved hello this morning isn't there. In his place is a hard man with a steel cold gaze.

"Colt is head of security for The Brash Group. He handles everything from logistics to counter espionage to surveillance and personal security. And I think he's going to want to help with this."

Colt's smile is feral. "Damn right I want to help. This woman sounds like a saint, and they blew up her fucking life." I've never seen this side of Colton. As safe as I know I am with him, a little shiver still runs down my back.

"Where is she now?" I ask, looking back at Declan.

He pulls more paperwork out of the folder, along with a couple of photos. He places one on the table in front of me. Colton moves to stand between us so he can see, too. Looking up from the photo is my smiling friend. Her rich auburn hair pulled into a ponytail, her round face wreathed in a smile. "This is the photo from her badge at the hospital." I tell them. "She has the best smile. She lights up the room when she walks in. Everyone loves her, and she always has a kind word." I say, touching it softly.

Declan nods, then lays another picture in front of me. It's still Evie, but the smile is gone. Her cheeks have lost their roundness, and her eyes are hard. A sob breaks free. "They stole her smile." What have I done? "This is all my fault. I never should have let her get involved."

"Holly," Micah snaps. "*None of this is your fucking fault. This is on Brent, and those fucking cops. Lay the blame where it belongs, baby. Be mad at them.*"

"He's right," Declan says. "This isn't on you. Don't make what she did for you, the sacrifices she made, count for nothing."

"She had a new baby, Declan, and she still scraped together money to help me run. That's how good she is." Breathing deeply, I wipe my tears. "Where is she now?" I ask, touching the second photo.

"She got a job as a custodian in a care home. She's making less than a third of what she used to. She picks up extra shifts whenever she can, but she's barely making ends meet."

"You pulled her financials?" Colton asks gruffly. Declan nods. "How much in her checking account?"

Declan hisses through his teeth. "Thirty-six dollars. She's been overdrawn twice already this month."

Colton's expression is grim. "Those motherfuckers are

going to pay. I guarantee it." He pulls the photos off the table, taking them both back to his chair. He traces his fingers over Evie's smiling face, looking lost in thought.

"I have to talk to her. I have to thank her. I have to do something for her." My mind is swirling, but one thought rises above all of them. I have to make this right. I owe her everything, and I can't allow the rest of her life to be destroyed for me. When I look at Micah, his eyes are calm, locked on me.

Waiting.

"Anything," he says clearly. I know he means it. He's already offered me everything he has. Accepting it for myself is hard. I'm still mentally calculating the cost of every egg I eat, every pair of pyjamas. He'd hate it, so I won't tell him, but I haven't been able to stop. But when it comes to Evie, I'm going to ask.

"I need Evie to be made whole. I need to talk to her and then I need her to have a better job, a safe place to live, a car. Whatever she's lost, I want her to have it back."

"And if she doesn't want it?" Declan asks.

"What do you mean?" I ask sharply, frowning at him.

"She's had lies spread about her, her reputation ruined, her child taken away from her. Going back to her old life may not be possible."

"Then we bring her here." Colton says, still tracing the lines of Evie's photo. "She wants to be a nurse again? We can get her a job with one phone call. She wants to take a break and just look after her little girl? We got her. We set her up in one of the apartments downstairs, and help her build a new life. She'd be way better off with us." He looks up, his eyes burning. "We'll take care of her."

"You will?" The generosity of these men still amazes me. But I don't understand it. "Why? Why would you do that?"

Micah's answer is simple. *"She's yours. You're ours. That makes her ours, too. And we take care of our own."*

My heart is pounding a strong, steady rhythm. With these guardian angels on her side, Evie's going to be ok.

"I want to talk to her."

Colton reaches into his pocket, pulling out a brand new phone. "I got you set up with a plan. I've got all our contacts in there already. I've put Evie and Robyn in too."

I take it slowly. "You got me a phone?"

"You needed it. Micah wanted to make sure you could always reach someone." He says, shrugging. "I'll show you how to use it."

He got me a phone. Not a basic flip phone like Brent allowed me to have, but a brand new iPhone. This feels monumental. A connection to the world I didn't have before.

Micah brushes a gentle finger over my cheek, then takes his coffee over the couch, settling into a patch of sun facing me. Minnie's up on his chest in a matter of seconds.

There's something about him giving me space to figure this all out that makes me feel stronger. He's letting me decide how to approach Evie. How to help her. He's not pushing any ideas on me, but I know he's listening and will help with anything I need. This level of support is almost dizzying.

After a quick iPhone crash course from Declan, I open up Evie's contact, and send her a message. I can't hesitate, if I do, I'll over think everything and never get it sent.

Me: Evie, this is Hannah. Can we talk?

I don't know her work schedule. It might take her hours to reply. Or maybe she doesn't want to hear from me, and never replies. I have to prepare myself for that possibility. That she hates me and blames me for all the horrible things that happened to her. So even while I acknowledge the very real possibility she won't reply, I still hold the phone close, hoping she will.

I jump when a ping comes from the phone. My heart skitters around in my chest as I read her message.

> **Evie:** Hannah. Are you ok? Are you safe? I'm at work but I'm on a break in ten. Can we Facetime then?

"Can this phone Facetime?"
Declan nods. A giggle sob escapes as I type my reply.

> **Me:** I'm safe. Brent's in jail. I'll be waiting for your call. I go by Holly now.
> **Evie:** Holly's a beautiful name. I can't wait to talk to you.

When her call comes in, I slap the phone in a panic, trying to accept. I've been on the verge of a meltdown for the last ten minutes, and when I see her face, I lose it.

"You're too skinny," I sob, looking at the sharp lines of her face. She must have lost fifty pounds. She looks worn and weak. Not that I would ever say that last part.

She's laughing and sobbing too. "I know," she says, not expanding. But I know it's because she's stressed, and probably skipping meals to take care of her daughter.

That sets off a new round of tears. "I'm so sorry Brent framed you. You saved me Evie. No way would I be alive if it weren't for you." I'm vaguely aware of Colton standing behind my shoulder, far enough that he's out of frame, but close enough that he can see the screen.

"That's all I wanted. For you to be safe. Brent is a piece of shit. Don't apologize for him. What he did was in the news. He's going to pay for what he did. Maybe he'll be someone's bitch in there." She smiles through her tears. "See! That idea makes me so happy."

She's trying to make me feel better. Still, after everything that's happened to her. "They took Mia from you."

Her smile fades. "I got her back. She's so beautiful, Hanna...Holly. She's three now, and she's so smart. She's counting and reading. She has a horrible singing voice." Evie's chuckle is warm and full of love. "And she's so sassy. She's perfect." She glances off screen, whispering to someone before coming back. "I'm sorry. I only have a few more minutes. I'm so glad you're ok. You are ok aren't you? All things considered, I mean."

"I'm ok," I say. "I have a lot to work through. But I'm safe. You don't have to worry about me." Her eyes drift to the side again, like she's checking a clock. I'm running out of time. "Evie...if you could go back to your old job, old life. Would you want to?"

Her lips firm. "I used to think I wouldn't. I was feeling very wronged. But I'm a mom. And I'm barely making ends meet. So yes, I would take any job that paid what I used to earn, even if I have to work with people who think I'm a thief at best, or an addict at worst."

Her answer makes things so much clearer. "What if I told you there's a job waiting for you here in Chicago? One that pays better than the NICU. And an apartment. Would you consider it?"

Her eyes widen, but the hope fades quickly. "I can't work in nursing. They made me sign something. I wouldn't be hired."

I catch Micah's serene eyes. "I know you have to go, but I want you to consider coming out here. You tell me when you have time off and we'll get you and Mia out here. Stay for a few days, explore your options, then make a decision. I've made some really amazing friends out here Evie, and they'll make that contract, and the whole incident, disappear."

Her eyes fill with hope, tempered by suspicion. "W... How? Why would they do that?"

"They looked into your life because I asked them to. They'd help you fix it, because they're good men. Promise me you'll consider coming out. It won't cost you a penny. We'll cover everything."

She brings a hand up to cover her face. "I'll think about it. I promise." She drops her hand. "I'm sorry, I have to go. I'm so glad that you're ok. I've thought about you every day."

"I've thought about you too," I whisper. "Goodbye." She smiles, hints of her old warmth still there, then disconnects the call.

I sit, staring at the phone in my hand, wishing that she'd said yes. Wishing that she could be on a plane out here tomorrow.

Something they said earlier clicks. "You guys have extra apartments in this building?" I ask, looking between the three men.

They all nod. "We have the floor below our gym floor. There's four two-bedroom units there."

What would it be like to have so much money you can have a few million dollars in real estate sitting empty? "Has anybody lived there? Why didn't you sell them?"

A smile finally cracks the granite of Colton's face. "We did sell them. Fuckers that bought them complained about the noise from the gym. The floor is a fucking foot of concrete. Made no sense. Anyway, we bought them back and we've kept them. We use them sometimes for guests or business associates. But no one full time for the last few years." Colton runs his palm roughly down his face. "We could have one ready for Evie in a day. We could fix up a bedroom for her little girl, paint it. Maybe buy a princess bed or something. You think she'd like that?"

I swear I never used to cry. Now, I just can't seem to stop. These men are too good. "I think she'd probably love a princess bed Colt." He grunts, deep in thought, then pins me with a firm look. "You have my number. You let me know when she gets back in touch with you, yeah?" He seems satisfied with my nod, turning back to Declan. "You have access to

Evie's accounts? Can you drop a hundred grand in there for me?"

I choke on my sip of coffee, spluttering and gasping. All three of them hover around me, yelling and patting my back. "Stop. I'm ok. Stop. Just went down the wrong way." I pin my stare on Colt. "You can't send her that much money."

He crosses his arms, glaring at me. "Why not? It's my money. I can do whatever the fuck I want with it."

"Yes, you can. But...I'd really like her to make the decision that's right for her. Selfishly, I want her here. I'm never going back to Ohio. And I don't think she has a very nice family, so there's really nothing keeping her there either."

"I'm not hearing the problem here." He says, scowling.

"She's proud. She's paid her own way her whole life. She started a family on her own. Dropping a hundred thousand dollars into her bank account is going to bother her Colt. She's going to end up pushing back."

He drops his arms. "She deserves some fucking help."

"I agree—."

"How...much," Micah interrupts, sitting down at the table again. *"How much did she give you? Maybe you can pay her back with interest. It should be enough to tide her over for a month. Give her a bit of breathing room while she thinks about things?"*

What a brilliant man. I give him a huge smile. "She gave me $650. I don't think she would ever turn that away, or deny me the chance to thank her by paying her back."

Colt grumbles, but gives in. Declan makes short work of transferring $800, and I send her a text.

> **Me:** I sent you some money. Your money helped me escape. Now that I can, I need to pay you back, with interest. Please don't say no.

22

MICAH

She's smiling as she texts on her new phone. I only mentioned it to Colt last night, so I'm glad he was able to get it for her so quickly. I hated the idea of her not being able to call one of us if she needs us. I'm still with her all the time, but I know that won't always be the case.

Evie's texted back a bit, thanking Holly for the money, and she's been back and forth with Robyn a lot today. She's done a lot of crying and it's worn me the fuck out. I hate seeing her cry, even if they are happy tears. But maybe she'll let me hold her again tonight, help her feel better. Because after falling asleep next to her last night, I don't think I'll ever be able to sleep any other way again.

"Micah," she says softly. The phone's face down on the coffee table and she's settled back into the corner of my sectional. I picked it because it was huge, and comfortable, but I hate it now. I have no valid excuse to sit close to her because there's so much room, so there's way too much space between us. I know I should have sat down closer, but things have felt...off...today. She's felt far away, lost in her thoughts, or her past. I'm not even sure she was aware of me most of the day.

"Come sit," she asks, patting the cushion next to her. I leave my end, moving to sit closer, turning my body so I can look at her over her extended legs. I'm nervous, but I can't pinpoint why exactly. It just feels like something monumental is about to happen. I put my hand on her foot, needing some small connection, and wait.

"Today has been…a lot." She licks her lips and I bite back a groan. "And we never finished our conversation this morning."

"I…know." I say, swallowing. *"Talk to me. Tell me what you need."*

"I need everything to slow down, just for a little while. I need to let my body heal and get back to work." She holds her hand up, stopping the words about to come from my mouth. "I know I don't have to rush it. But Becca is taking so much on right now. As soon as the doctor says it's ok, I'm going back. I like working, Micah. I like being in the garage. I feel…needed there."

"Ok," I give in, knowing it doesn't matter if she's here or at the garage. I'll be right there next to her, making sure she doesn't overdo it. *"When the doctor says it's ok. We'll go back."*

She smiles. It's wobbly, but there. "You know, Becca's always telling us in our self-defense classes to find our balance, our center."

"So you're prepared to defend against an attack."

"Yeah. And I'm realizing that I've never felt like I had balance. I was always being pushed around. By my parents, my church, then by Brent. And then when I got away? I was still at the mercy of the shelters, the landlords, and my bosses. Did you know the outlets at my apartment sparked?" She scowls, throwing her hands up. "I reported it to the super and the rental company so many times. They did nothing. And my building burned down! Do you know what it's like to not have any control over your life, Micah?" Her eyes are full of fire, but I know that fire is directed at the world, not just at me.

"Been...long...time." I say. *"My whole childhood was one of chaos. I was at the mercy of my father's temper. Then at the mercy of the social workers. It wasn't until Ransom brought us all together that I started to feel like I had my place. Even then I still felt...chaotic."*

"Chaotic how?"

"We'd made a name for ourselves, but I still felt like I was... defective." Her soft sound of denial is a balm, soothing the hurt caused by decades of feeling less than.

"I couldn't speak. I couldn't order food at a fucking drive thru. The only thing I had to contribute was this." I lift my balled up fist, turning it so she can see the white webbing of scars that crisscross it. *"I was so angry, I was nearly unstoppable when push came to shove. Between Colt and I, anyone who fucked with us ended up in the hospital. It was the only thing I had to offer. I can't talk my way out of situations like Maverick and Nick. So I fought. And I intimidated everyone."* Holly leans forward, reaching for my hand. I let her take it and give me a squeeze before pulling away with a grunt of frustration. *"I can't even have a fucking conversation while holding your hand."*

"Put your foot up here." She says, slapping the couch.

I cock an eyebrow, but when she pats the cushion next to her hip again, I lift my leg up, so it's running down the outside of her body. She wiggles to resettle herself, then rests her hand on the top of my bare foot, mirroring the way I'm touching her. She looks down and starts to giggle. "Your feet are so big," she says between snorts. "Look." She spreads her fingers wide, still only managing to cover a third.

I let myself soak in her touch. Her laughter. When I was sitting next to her hospital bed, this is everything I wished for. Her smile is fucking everything.

"Tell me when things changed," she prompts, shaking my foot.

"*When we got the garage. Suddenly, we had to figure out how to fix cars. Ransom knew a bunch, but the rest of us just had to figure shit out. Jonas brought us all these books from the library, and videos on automotive repair. I loved reading, and I picked up a lot of it pretty quickly. Ransom got his hands on some junkers, and we fixed them up then sold them. Then we bought more junkers. By then, word was getting out that we actually might know what we're doing, so people around the neighborhood started coming to us for repairs.*" I shrug. "Words...not...needed."

"So, how did you start doing the custom stuff? I've seen the invoices for some of those cars you fix up." She says, eyes wide. "They're more than the rest of the garage makes in a month."

"Ransom...won...bet." Laughing, I explain. "*He was always hustling. Coming home with random shit. He won this old, beat up GTO and he brought it to me. Asked me to see if I could figure out how to restore it. He figured if we could get it to a car show, we might be able to make a name for ourselves.*"

"It worked," she says with a smile.

"Nope." I say, chuckling at her crestfallen expression. "*That would have been a good story, though. We did everything wrong on that first car. We paid too much for parts, did a weird mix of restoration and customization, and it flopped. We barely got our money out of it. But I did a fuck of a lot better on the next car, then the next. Took me a full year to win one.*"

She wrinkles her adorable little nose. "You're wrong, you know."

"Me?... Never."

She laughs, nudging me with her foot. "It's a better story the way it really happened. You worked hard for it. If it had come too easy, who knows where you'd be now?"

"Maybe." She's probably right. Nobody handed us a damn thing. We scraped and fought our way out of the gutter. We became unstoppable because we had to be. No ivy league pissant who's been handed everything by Mommy and Daddy would have been able to build this.

"You...need...time." I say, steering her back on topic. I want her to finish.

"Yes, I do." She wets her lips again, eyes darting around my face. "I've been thinking about the empty apartments all day."

Pain shoots through my chest, like I just took a fucking punch to the solar plexus. The last thing I want is her gone. Christ, I'd rather move out and leave her here, in my space. Having her here has made it feel more like home than any place I've lived before.

I can't sit anymore, rising to pace the space between the coffee table and bookshelves. I run my fingers through my hair, trying to think of the right argument, the right words to make her stay. But that's the fucking problem, isn't it? Men overriding what she wants. It's what her husband did to her, over and over. No way will I ever let myself be like him.

I stop and face her. *"Do you want to move out?"* I sign, then hold my breath while I wait for her answer.

"It might be the smart thing to do. We went from hating each other to living together. It's fast."

"Never...hate...you. Never." If she believes nothing else, please let her believe that. "Never."

"I never hated you either," she whispers. "Do...do you want me to move out? Get your space back?"

"No." I tell her firmly. *"I want you here for the rest of my fucking days. The last week has only convinced me of that."*

Her lips quirk up. "Then if it's ok with you, I'd like to stay."

And just like that, I can breathe again.

"This is your home, Holly."

Her beautiful smile lights me up. I bask in its warmth until it falls quietly off her face.

She pushes herself straighter on the couch, squaring her shoulders. "There are some other things I need."

"Anything."

"I apparently have a really good benefits plan at Brash. It includes counseling."

We treat our employees like fucking gold, so that doesn't surprise me at all. And we waived Holly's probationary period after the first week. We know a good thing when we see it, and we, okay I, didn't want to risk losing her.

"I want...I need to start counseling. When I went before, it was different." She says slowly, her brow furrowed.

Dropping back to the couch, I wrap my fingers around her foot again. "How...different?"

"I was just learning how to live again, without Brent's boot on my neck. This time, I need to work through how to... move into a relationship. How to do us, in a way that won't scar us both."

"Scar?"

"Sex," she says, her face beet red. "I don't want to be intimate with you and have a horrible flashback or freeze."

I shudder. *That idea is fucking terrifying. I don't want that either. When we're together, I don't want you to even remember his name.*

Her shoulders relax, "I want that too. I know I asked you to stay last night. I..."

"Holly." I say, shoving down my disappointment. *That's my room,* I say, pointing at my room, then pointing to hers. *"That's yours. I'm only there if you invite me. I'm not going to assume a damn thing."*

"So, roommates then?" she asks, her eyes shining.

I grumble, scowling at her again. "No. My... love...Always."

23

MICAH

I haven't felt this pumping need in years. The need to hurt, to maim. But being forced to listen to Holly's pain over the last couple of days, hearing the way Brent destroyed Evie's life, and not react, has made my blood boil. Prison is too good for her ex. He deserves to suffer for every bruise, every sprain, every broken bone he's ever inflicted on Holly. I want him to bleed and beg, and I want to be the one to inflict the damage. To punish. To get justice for her.

Prison is too good for him.

The rage is rising, swirling in my gut, suffocating me. It's an old friend. One that I thought had left me forever. But it hadn't left, instead just hiding, biding its time.

I relish it, welcome it. Because I know what that rage can do. The havoc we can wreck together. We want to make bleed, to terrify, to pummel, but the focus of that rage, Brent, is out of reach. Locked up tight behind prison walls. And I can't fucking stand it.

I head to the door, saying a quick goodnight to Kathy, thankful she agreed to stay until I get back. It doesn't matter how hard the rage is riding me, my need to keep Holly safe is stronger. No way in hell would I leave her here alone.

Colton's leaning against the bank of elevators, gray sweat-suit already sweaty, eyes hooded. "You sure you want to do this? We can just go downstairs and spar instead, man."

I scowl at him. "Not...good...enough." The beast is riding me. *"I don't want gloves tonight. I don't want to hold back. I need it, man."*

He looks down, rubbing the back of his neck. "I don't think it's a good idea, brother. Go back, be with your lady."

"Go back inside? And what'll you do, man? Go upstairs and read a book? Make a cup of tea?"

His lips firm. He knows as well as I do that his demons are riding him tonight. I saw them crawl over his face as he learned the damage inflicted on Holly's friend Evie. He's burning with rage.

"You need it. You know you do. I'll admit I didn't understand before, but I get it now. Why you need the fight. Why you like to make people bleed."

He doesn't agree or deny it, instead turning to call the elevator. In the garage, we climb into my car and head towards the warehouse district.

Colt's quiet voice breaks into the silence. "It's not about making people bleed." I glance over at him, catching his serious eyes. I cock my eyebrow in disbelief.

"It's not. It's...simple there. It's just man against man. Both of us letting the aggression out. Strongest guy wins." He leans back in his seat with a sigh. "Our lives aren't really simple anymore. Before, we had to fight for our place every day. It's not like that now. We don't worry about blades and bullets anymore. Instead, it's corporate espionage and shady lawyers and fucktards who think they're bad. Fuck brother, sometimes I just want to use my fucking fists."

I get what he means. Most of our lives were a battle. When you're always primed for a fight, it's hard to stop. But I'm not like Colt. I like the lives we've built. I like not having to fight for everything.

"I'm...angry," I tell him, glancing over at a red light.

"I can imagine, man. Holly's been opening up?"

"Yeah," I mutter, hearing the gravity of all she's shared in my voice.

"We shoulda just arranged for that bastard to have an accident in prison. It would be easy. You know Johnny would do it for us in a heartbeat."

"Still...thinking...'bout." He would do it for us, even if it would extend his sentence. But I don't want to do that to him. He's sacrificed enough for us. And it's a little fucked up that Colt's even suggesting it. But then their relationship is a little fucked up.

"Good." He says, before asking carefully "Have you thought about what happens when you go home tonight with bleeding knuckles and a battered face?"

"Wait," I grunt, driving the last few miles in silence. When we pull up to the abandoned warehouse, I second guess this whole fucking plan. It looks exactly like a vampire hideout in every video game I've ever played, windows busted, doors hanging crooked. I see flickering lights inside, and a stream of shady and even shadier people heading inside. I rub my hands over my face, exhaling.

"I've thought about it, man. I'm afraid of what she might think. But I don't have another option here. The darkness is riding me hard. I can't spend another day being who she needs without releasing some of it."

"I get it. I swear I do. But wouldn't sparring with me help some?"

"No." I say, rubbing my tight neck. *"I need to let loose. I'm never gonna hurt you like that. Never. Same for any of you. We may fight, but we don't hurt each other. That's not who we are."*

"You're right," he says heavily. "I just wish you didn't have to do this brother."

"You're here a lot. What's the difference?"

"The difference is, I don't have anyone sweet and soft

waiting at home for me. It's just me and my fucking hobbies. If I had a good woman in my life, I don't think I'd be coming here."

"You...find...someone."

"Yeah, I'm not gonna hold my breath." He scrubs a hand over his beard. "You fuckers got lucky."

I don't like the sadness on his face, but he only lets it linger for a second before he shakes it off and turns to me. "Ok. If we're going in here, here's what you need to know. First, you can wear a mouthguard, but no gloves. Second, there aren't any rounds, it's fight until tap out or TKO. Third," he stops, frowning. "Never mind, there isn't a third."

What the fuck have I gotten myself into?

So maybe Colt has the right idea. My knuckles are split. So is my lip. My ribs are fucking killing me. And it's the calmest I've felt in days. The rage is gone, getting smaller with each punch, each kick, until it dissolved. Colt's energy has completely changed, too. The demons riding him seem to have released their grip on him. I haven't seen him that worked up in a long time, and I wonder what's been riding him.

"You think she'll come?" He asks in the dark of the car. I glance over, the passing streetlights lighting up his face briefly.

"Who?"

"Evie. You think she'll come?" There's something in his voice I haven't heard before.

"Hope...so." For Holly's sake, I hope she does. I don't want her feeling guilty for what Brent did to Evie. It's not her fucking fault, but that won't matter. As long as Evie's still struggling, Holly won't be able to settle into her life here. Her life with me.

"She shouldn't have to struggle, man. Why don't we just

go get her? I can take the Jet and have them here by supper tomorrow."

I frown at him. "Steam…roll."

He shrugs, unconcerned. "So maybe it's a little pushy, but that's not always a bad thing, is it?" I look at him, eyebrows raised, snickering when I see that not even he believes the shit coming out of his mouth.

"Wait…just…wait."

He drops his elbow on the door, resting his head on his fist. "You're right. I know. It just…fuck! Did you see how much she changed? In her hospital photo, she was…stunning." He swallows thickly. "She's so worn now. She looks like she's aged ten years."

I glance at him carefully. For a woman he's never met, he seems pretty fucking upset. He's dealt with some shady shit over the years, but I've never seen him like this. He's always level, cool, two steps ahead. Even the fucking fighting is calculated and serves a particular purpose.

"We'll…help" I murmur. I would do it for Holly anyway, but now, I know Colt needs it too. We won't let her fade away.

I OPEN THEN CLOSE MY FRONT DOOR QUIETLY, NOT WANTING TO wake Holly. But when I turn, my soul leaves my body and I about piss my pants when I see her sitting at the head of the table, eyes wide.

Kathy gasps from the couch. "Mr. James!"

I close my eyes, dropping my head to my chest.

"Micah," Holly says softly. "What happened?"

Kathy pushes off the couch, heading into the kitchen. "Let me get the first aid kit. We'll have you cleaned up in a moment."

She hustles back carrying the large bag. I raise my hand. "No…I…fix" I say, taking it from her. I open the door for her.

"Night...thanks". Her eyes dart from me to Holly, before nodding and heading out.

I stand, holding the kit, facing the door, scared to turn around. Afraid of what I'll see on Holly's face.

"Micah," she calls.

I take a deep breath, then join her at the table, busying myself with opening the kit and pulling out alcohol swabs and butterfly bandages. We all have these massive kits because, let's face it, we do a lot of stupid shit. They're well used and restocked often.

"Micah," Holly says again. The softness is gone from her voice, anger taking its place. "What happened?"

I raise my head, taking in her features. Her eyes are wide, darting across my face, then to my bleeding knuckles and back to my face. I wonder if I can come up with some story that will satisfy her. But the idea of lying to her turns my stomach. "Fight," I mutter, briefly meeting her eyes.

She crosses her arms over her chest. "With who? Why?".

"Underground fights. I went with Colt."

"Why?" she gasps. "Why would you do that?" She asks, eyes wide.

"I had to. I needed a...release." I admit.

"I...I don't understand."

I hate the turmoil in her eyes. I hate the wariness even more.

"I don't want you to look at me like that. I would never hurt you."

"But you'll hurt other people?" she challenges, frowning.

"I've hurt lots of people in my past. I never hid that from you. But tonight wasn't that. It was...an underground fight. Fights." I amend. Why? Fuck if I know. It would be easier if she thought it was one simple fight.

"How many people did you fight?" She asks quietly.

"Three."

"You fought three people tonight?"

I nod.

"You're just like him." She whispers, looking away from me.

She could stab me in the eye with a knife, and it would hurt less. This is exactly what Colt was warning me about. But what the fuck was I supposed to do? Let the rage eat me from the inside? Risk losing my shit in front of her? No chance.

"No," I say firmly. When she looks at me again, I sign. "*I am nothing like your piece-of-shit ex. Nothing. I would never lay a hand on you in anger, but if he were standing in front of me? I'd probably beat him to death. I'm not afraid to admit that to you. I've been listening to you tell me all the horrific things he did to you, and I had to fucking release it somehow. Release the anger. So I did what I had to do.*"

She clears her throat, still frowning. "And you feel better now?"

"*Mostly. I'm still angry that he hurt you. I probably always will be. But pounding on another big guy in a ring, just because? Well, it helps.*"

Her eyes widen comically. "You fought with someone your size?"

"*Wouldn't be fair otherwise. There's no challenge in fighting someone smaller, unless they have major skills like Becca. Colton spars with her all the time, and even though she's smaller, she still makes him cry.*"

"I've seen it." She says with a hint of a grin. She reaches out, pulling an alcohol wipe to her. Opening the package slowly, she looks lost in thought.

"What does it feel like, hurting someone?"

I shift uncomfortably in my seat. "*Hitting someone who's trying to hit you back is...satisfying. When I would scrap as a kid, I was so angry. This is different. It's not about hurting someone, it's about being completely in the moment, all your senses firing. Going into a fight knowing you're fighting just to challenge yourself...*"

fuck. That's not right. Most of those guys there tonight were there for money and to prove they're the best."

"But it doesn't matter to you?"

I shake my head no. *"I don't need money, obviously. I don't give a fuck what any of them think of me. I was there to release pressure. I did that. Now I'm done."*

She nods distractedly, reaching out for my hand. I watch, mesmerized, as she gently wipes the dried blood on my knuckles.

"I wish I'd been able to hurt him." She whispers.

"Know," I say. When you've been hurt over and over again by someone, you can't help but dream of all the ways you want to hurt them back.

"That's why I'm taking Becca's self-defense class. I don't want to ever feel that weak again."

"Good." I say firmly. *"You can always do more training. Becca and Colt would love to train with you. Or I could go with you,"* I offer.

Her shoulders lift slightly, and she gives me a small smile. Curling my fingers around the swab, she carefully gets to her feet. "Night," she whispers.

I watch her wheel herself away, praying my choices tonight don't set us back.

24

HOLLY

The last three weeks have been some of the hardest of my life. And I'm including the years I spent with Brent.

After cleaning up Micah's knuckles that night, my mind was whirling. Was I actually afraid of him again? Or was I angry that he had an outlet? Or maybe it was the easy power he commands. He's so strong, so capable.

And I'm so…not.

We danced around each other for the next couple of days, both extra polite. Both careful with our words. I'm sure he was following my lead, but thankfully, things seemed to settle down between us.

Going to see the physiotherapist a week after the fire was a relief. She agreed to let me go back to work part time, letting me switch to a smaller ankle brace since I was healing well. The next morning, I woke up excited to go back, nearly bouncing the entire elevator ride down. Micah kept side-eyeing me, but I didn't care. As I rolled my scooter towards Micah's car, I realized he wasn't behind me. Instead, he'd moved towards a dark blue luxury SUV parked right near the elevator.

"What is this?" I asked in confusion. "Does this belong to one of your brothers?"

"No...safer...you," he mumbled, opening the passenger door for me. I let him help me in, settling into the luxurious seat with a sigh. Everything about it was expensive, from the wood inlay to the buttery leather interior.

"So, this is your car? How did you find time to buy a car? We've been together pretty much nonstop for the last week?"

He snorted, flashing an arched eyebrow at me. "Billionaire," he said, tapping his chest, eyes twinkling.

I laughed, buckled in, and enjoyed the smooth ride. Eyeing this wonderful, beautiful man who bought a new car because it was safer for me.

Things at the office were different, too. Micah made a point of checking on me. Smiling every time he saw me. It was really distracting, but I didn't want to shoo him away. I loved that he was so open with his affection. I never had to wonder where I stood with him. It was freeing. So I shocked the heck out of myself by flirting with him.

It started small, an accidental brush of the hand when I passed him an invoice. Then I got a little more obvious, brushing my hand down his arm, touching him anytime I got the chance. I honestly didn't know I had it in me. I don't remember flirting with Brent, but I must have picked this up somewhere.

I kept waiting for Micah to break, or to pull away, but every single time I touched him, his eyes would heat and he'd smile so slowly that once I actually choked on my own spit.

That was embarrassing.

I didn't realize how much I needed us to dance around each other. Touching, glancing, smiling. It was like a long, slow seduction. At work anyway.

At home, things cooled off. I don't know how the man knows what I need before I do, but he does. It's like a switch flips when we walk in the door of the condo. Sexy, smoldering Micah gets tucked away, and my friend Micah takes his place. I stop the flirting, and just...be. We cook...well I cook and try to teach Micah. We get a lot of takeout, and I finally kick his butt at Battleship. It's so easy between us I have to pinch myself sometimes.

The only dark spot, really, has been the counseling. I found a great counselor, a survivor of domestic violence herself, and at my insistence we've been meeting three times a week either virtually or in-person.

It's intensive, and exhausting, and some days I wish I wasn't doing it. It's easy to convince yourself you're doing ok, until someone cracks your head open and forces you to spill all your deepest, darkest secrets. Being forced to examine your choices and reactions is hard. Trying to identify and undo all your programming is harder.

And then, there's the homework. By week three, I'd been tasked with bringing myself to orgasm. I argued with her for fifteen minutes before grudgingly agreeing, not seeing the point. I want Micah to give me orgasms. I'm not interested in flying solo. But she said there's no way I can be with a partner without understanding my own body's wants and needs. I guess I kind of understood. I still didn't like it though.

I ended up having to task Becca with getting me supplies, since I'm still hobbling around and Micah is my self-appointed chauffeur. But I should have known better. She ran amok in the adult store, bringing me a very heavy plastic bag. "I asked you to get me one vibrator," I hiss at her, moving to push my bedroom door shut. Kade and Micah were in the kitchen unpacking the Chinese, while I had a nervous break-down in my bedroom.

"I did get you a vibrator," Becca hissed back. "But then I saw the butterfly thingy, then a couple of natural skin dildos...feel this. Come on, feel it."

She grabs my hand, forcing it to the beige skinned

monstrosity. "I don't want to...oh, that's weird. And kinda real? But for sure, weird."

"Right!" she exclaims, happily tearing through the bag, tossing dildos and vibrators all over my bed.

I couldn't look anyone in the eye that night. Thoughts of all the...equipment I'd shoved under my bed filled my brain. More than once Micah asked me if I was ok, my squeaked "yes" not at all reassuring him.

But what was I supposed to say? 'No, I'm not alright. I have to go diddle myself tonight, and all the nights to follow, until I figure out what makes me orgasm. So that hopefully, one day really soon, I'll be able to do all the things with you that I've dreamed of doing.'

Luckily, I'm a great student. So I read articles and books, even watched a video or two. And every night I experimented, eventually opening all the toys Becca bought me. And I learned what kind of touch I like, and what kind I don't. I learned what fantasies turned me on, and which ones turned my stomach.

And I did it.

I had an orgasm.

It wasn't really what I was expecting. The way the books and movies go on about it, I thought it would be...bigger I guess. But it felt nice. And I cried when it was over. Not fully understanding until then why I had to do this stupid assignment.

Because, maybe for the first time in my life, I felt like my body was mine.

Mine.

Not for God, or for my husband. It was mine, and everything it felt was mine too, good or bad. And I learned I can choose what to feel. If I don't like something, I don't do it again. And if I do? Well, I have every right to do more of it. I was feeling pretty darn proud of myself.

Until she gave me my next assignment, that is.

25

HOLLY

I'm in my favorite corner of the couch, idly flexing my ankles as I study Micah, slouched beside me. My ankle feels strong. All of me feels strong, actually. And I don't have any excuses left.

"My counselor gave me homework. New homework," I blurt.

Micah pauses the movie, not lifting his head from the back of the couch, but turning it to look at me. I love when he does this. It doesn't matter what we're watching, or how into it he is. If I speak, he always pauses and gives me his attention. Well, I usually love it. Except when I'm so freaking nervous.

"New?...What...old?" he asks with an arched brow.

My face reddens, and I open my mouth to brush off his question, spilling my guts instead. "I had to learn how to have an orgasm. And Becca bought me a bunch of toys and I tried most of them, except some of them freaked me out. And I finally did it. But I had to practice. A lot."

Micah's frozen, except for his chest, heaving with his rapid breaths. His eyes are peeled open in surprise, locked on my face.

I stutter out the next part. "My new homework is to... touch you. I was hoping we could do that tonight."

I didn't think his eyes could get any bigger, but they do. I watch him swallow, then swallow again. He starts and stops a few sentences, then slowly raises his hands. *What exactly do you want us to do? I need you to lay it out, so I don't do anything wrong.*

This. This is exactly why I know he's the right man. His thoughts are always on me, and my comfort. But tonight, I want to take us both out of this friend zone we've built together.

"I want you..." I study the condo, finally settling on the plush rug in front of the fireplace. "On the rug, there. And... um...take off your shirt, please. I'd like to touch you."

He stands so quickly I pull backwards in surprise. He's moving to the rug and reaching back to pull his shirt over his head in the same motion. Chucking his shirt across the room, not caring where it lands, he stands, panting, waiting for my next move.

I swallow thickly, taking a minute to get myself under control. My nerves are off the charts right now, but they're mixing with a rising heat. Because Micah is...God, he's stunning. I've seen him shirtless, and always admired the view, but this is really different.

The glimpses of him I've had the last three weeks have been casual, pulling off a sweaty shirt on the way to his bedroom. Or my favorite, lifting the hem of his shirt to wipe his face. But this? The inferno in his eyes when he looks at me? The way he's holding himself back, waiting breathlessly for my next order? It's heady being the one in control. I could get addicted.

I circle the coffee table carefully, moving to stand in front of him. His body is frozen, waiting for my command, but his eyes are tracking every move I make.

I wonder if I should blindfold him. I don't think I'm into

that kind of thing, but I'm feeling really self-conscious and wish he wasn't looking at me. But I also love the clear heat and affection on his face. It makes me feel taller somehow.

So maybe, no blindfold.

Dropping to my knees, I look up his long legs, past the bulge at his groin to his face, as a low groan comes from deep in his chest. "Sit. Please," I say, patting the rug next to me. I keep my eyes averted from the tent in his sweats, not quite ready to go there. But it's not a *never* anymore, more of a *not right now.* I think that's pretty good progress.

He drops to his knees, sitting back on his heels, making no move to lie back. "Do…do you not want to do this?"

"No," he shouts. *"I'm just freaking the fuck out. Just give me a second."*

Tears welling, I tuck my hands between my knees. Of course he's freaking out. This was a stupid idea. Why did I think I should put him through this?

"Hey…no," he murmurs, leaning towards me. *"What's happening?*

"This is not fair to you, Micah." I say, swallowing back my tears. "You deserve to be with someone normal. Someone without all my baggage. This was a mistake. I'm so sorry." I move to stand, but Micah grabs my hands, holding me in place.

"Don't…go." He tightens his hands on mine, the crease between his eyes deep. "Please."

I want to get up and go, but doing that to Micah would be like putting headphones on in the middle of an argument with any other person. It's not fair. He's been so wonderful, I owe it to him to stay and listen. Then, I'll crawl into bed and fall apart. I let myself settle back, focusing on the middle of his chest.

"What the fuck is normal, Holly? Who exactly do you think I should be with?"

"I told you, someone without any baggage. Someone

who's been in a normal relationship. A woman who won't freeze up at the idea of having sex with you."

"That's the stupidest thing I've ever heard."

My eyes snap to his face. "Stupid? That is the-"

"Stop," he says forcefully, slapping his chest. "My...turn." Scowling, he signs *"Do you really not see it?"*

"See what?" I ask, crossing my arms over my chest.

"You believe in God, Holly. How can you not believe that we're meant to be?" I drop my arms, drawn in by the intensity of his gaze.

"Do you know how many women I've been in a relationship with? None. I had plenty of fun. I was never without sex if I wanted it. But not one of those women ever made me want more. Then you walked into my garage and I felt like I'd been hit by a fucking thunderbolt. I felt fucking alive. Something about you just drew me right in." He runs his hands through his short hair, taking a few long breaths.

"I never believed in God. I've seen too much shit in my life. But that day Holly, I believed. Ask me why." His eyes are fiery, trapping me with their intensity.

Clearing my throat, I ask quietly, "Why?"

"Because this woman that took my fucking breath away, this beautiful, perfect woman? She understood me. She knew ASL. She could have a fucking conversation with me. Do you know how long it's been since I could actually talk to a woman?"

I let the tears spill over, not wiping them away. "How long?" I ask, my throat tight.

"Never...only...you." He slaps his hands on his thighs, head bowed as he breathes. Finally, his head rises. *"You want to call your horrible marriage 'baggage' then fine. But even with all the baggage in the world, shit, even if we could never have sex, I still thank God every day that you're in my life. That's not going to end. Because if it felt like a thunderbolt when we met, my feelings for you now are a fucking comet. So you walk away, Holly? There's no other woman waiting in the wings. You're it for me."* He's glaring, pinning me with his gaze. Finally, seemingly satisfied with what he finds on my face, he grunts, "Touch...me... woman," and flops onto his back on the carpet, arms spread wide.

Giggling through my surprised laughter, I shift until our hips are pressed together and I'm looking up his body to that striking face of his. "So you're telling me that God gave me you?"

"Yep. And...you...me." He says, running a relaxed hand up and down his stomach. It's such an unconscious, manly thing to do. Brent did the same thing. But he never drew my attention the way Micah does. Because with Micah, I want.

So maybe he is right. Maybe God did have a hand in it.

When I was little, people always told me that God had a plan. And maybe it's true. I'm not sure I'll ever understand why Brent had to be part of it, but I do know that escaping him is what brought me to Chicago. Wanting to learn to protect myself is what brought me to Becca's self defense class. If Brent had been an average husband, or if I had never married him to begin with, would I have ever met Micah?

Would I change any of it? Knowing I'd have to give up Micah?

"Touch...me," Micah demands playfully, but I see a hint of the shadows I put in his eyes. I want them gone, so I smile at him and do exactly what I've wanted to do for weeks. Putting my fingers at the waistband of his black sweats, I thread my fingers through the trail of dark hair, traveling up as it turns lighter, until my palm is resting over his heart. My other hand joins it, then I run my palms over his sculpted pecs, stopping because I've run out of arm span.

I pull my hands back, studying the problem. I could just touch one side of his body. But that idea doesn't appeal. I want access to all of him. That means getting a lot closer.

I sneak a peek at him, then away as I explain. "My assignment is to touch you, respecting your limits, any way I would like. While still avoiding the um…sexual organs, I mean. You're not supposed to touch me. I'm in charge of all the sensation this time. She also told me to follow my instincts and enjoy touching with no expectations. Is that ok? Is there anything I shouldn't do?"

I peek back at him, and see Micah's eyes are shut tight. Lines of strain on his face. "*I'm yours,*" He signs, locking those brown eyes on me. "*So anything you want. Touch me however you want…but you should know I'm already on the verge. I'll warn you if I'm about to come.*"

I swear my cheeks feel as hot as they did in that burning apartment building. But I'm not going to question him. I'll trust him to tell me…that.

As I study the acres of golden skin and warm muscle laid out in front of me, I come to a decision. Thankful I'd already changed into my pyjama pants, I scoot forward, then carefully put my leg over his stomach, moving to sit on his lower abdomen. If I pressed back the tiniest bit, his dick would push against the seam of my bum. I let my weight settle on his stomach, watching as his eyes slam shut, a little worried about how quickly he's breathing. Sitting on him like this, my knees aren't touching the ground so I'm forced to rest all my weight on him. "Is this ok?" I ask, throat tight.

His eyes fly open. "Yes," he mutters through gritted teeth. Reaching out with both arms, his hands grip the plush carpet. He's strung tight, eyes somehow darker, making more of my shyness fall away. The sensation of having him under me is… indescribable. I can feel his heat through my pants. I can't decide if it was lucky to have skipped the panties, or if I've just made this harder for myself.

Unable to resist, I rock forward, enjoying the way his stomach muscles press against my clit. I like it so much; I do it again, revelling in his frantic mumbling. Returning my hands to his chest, I run them back over his pecs, leaning forward to reach his shoulders. I let my fingers trace the tendons and muscles of his shoulders and biceps. Laid out like this, arms stretched out and hands clenching the carpet, I can't reach all of him.

I don't like it.

I lean forward more, letting my heavy breasts rest on this chest as I tuck my mouth next to his cheek. "Let go of the rug."

"Can't," he gasps, wild eyes jumping around my face.

"You promised you'd never make me beg."

He chokes, letting go of the rug like it's a live wire. I sit up, moving to take one hand, then the other in mine. My counselor said he wasn't supposed to touch me, but I'm tired of letting everyone else tell what to do. I move his hands to just above my knees. "Hold here. Don't move"

He nods frantically, tightening his fingers until he has a firm grip. I can feel each individual finger pressing into me, but not hard enough to bruise. It's nothing like the grip he had on the carpet. Even as affected as he is by me, as big as his feelings are, he's still so careful not to hurt me. Emboldened by this knowledge, I run my fingers from the backs of his hands, up his arms achingly slowly. Stopping to tickle with my nails, or rub at any spots that make him twitch or groan.

There's a lot of groaning.

As still as he's trying to stay for me, his body is in constant motion. Muscles tightening and flexing. The ones in his stomach are rubbing against me in a way that's completely distracting, shooting heat through my center.

I rock my hips again.

26

MICAH

I'm dying.

My heart is about to fucking explode. That saying, 'he died a happy man', is total bullshit. If I die right now, while Holly is riding my stomach, I will gut a mother-fucker. I don't want to miss a second of this.

She's so beautiful, her blonde hair a wavy halo around her face, her cheeks flushed, gleaming with a sheen of sweat. She's so fucking turned on, and the surprise and shock in her face, the way she can't help but rock her hips, nearly pushes me over the edge. I'm going to come in my pants, guaran-damn-teed.

She hasn't even put her mouth on me, and I'm higher than a fucking kite.

She rocks on me again, pushing that hot pussy into my stomach, seeking friction. She's stunning. She's come so far in the last few weeks, but I had no idea she'd come this far. I had no idea she was doing orgasm homework.

I'm thankful I didn't know.

Pretty sure I would have rubbed my cock raw knowing she was in her room playing with toys, chasing that O. Maybe one day, if I'm very, very good, she'll let me watch.

Her weight drops forward onto my chest, and I just about shoot my load when her tongue laps at my nipple. I shout and buck, letting go of her legs to grab fists full of rug next to her knees instead. I'm losing control. No way will I let this end with her bruised.

She makes a happy little hum as she licks. Her fingers are playing with my other nipple while the long blonde strands of her hair tickle along my skin. Her soft, rounded stomach is pressing into my abs. And the rocking, the small uncontrolled rubbing of her pussy against me, continues. I've officially hit sensory overload.

"Sss...stop," I stutter, freezing her in her tracks. "Too...much...gonna...come." I pant, proud of myself for stringing together actual words and not just mindless gibberish. Her head rises slowly, those glittering eyes meeting mine. Our breathing is labored, and we suck in each other's air for a minute before her knees tighten around me. Planting her hands on my chest, pushing herself backwards, she lifts up, hovering over the cock trapped in my sweats, then lowers down until her pussy lips, trapped by her thin pants, are wrapped around the length of it.

I'm fucking drowning. "Gonna....come." I tell her more urgently, between gasps. I want to push up, grab her hips, and make her ride me. But my promise holds me back. This is her show, completely.

Shuddering, she licks her lips. I'm lost in her glittering eyes. We're burning up together. "I...I want to make you come." She gasps. "I want to ride you. Like this. Can I?"

I tighten my grip on the rug, feeling it rip under my fingers. "Yes." The answer will always be yes.

Forever.

She smiles, wiggling her weight deeper onto me, then starts rocking. Her movements are slow, but pick up speed, getting jerkier. Her mouth drops open, her eyes closing, small gasps and moans coming one after the other. Her breasts are bouncing in her top, and I'm desperate to get my mouth on them. Suddenly her moans rise in pitch. She's going to fucking come. That knowledge gives me the strength to hold out just a little longer, determined to let her get herself there.

Use me, baby, any way you want.

Her body is shuddering and jerking, and it's better than anything I've ever seen. I'm so wrapped up in her that my orgasm surprises the hell out of me, hitting me like a freight train. I do buck, unable to keep still as I empty my load.

In my shorts.

Called it.

She's still rocking over me, drawing shudders out of both of us, eventually falling forward, resting on my chest. My hands come up, hovering over her back. Am I allowed to touch her?

She sniffles, and my body goes rock hard.

She didn't like it. I mean, I fucking know her body liked it, but we're not just battling her body's reactions here. We're battling her mind and her nightmares. I carefully wrap my hands around her shoulders, pushing her up so I can see her face. She sobs, then jumps up, rushing for her room. "Holly... ok?" I yell after her, trying to stand. My legs are fucking jello.

By the time I make it to her door, she's closed herself off from me. I rest my head against it, feeling like I'm in purgatory. My body feels better than it's ever felt. I came harder than I ever have, and I wasn't even inside her.

But she's crying and I'm gutted.

"Holly...talk," I beg.

Her voice is raspy through the door. "I'm ok Micah. I just need a few minutes. Please, just a few."

"Ok," I say, rapping my fingers on her door, fighting my need to shove it open and take care of her. Awareness of the massive wet spot in my pants has me heading straight to my closet. As I strip, I smell her on me. No way am I showering that off. I'm keeping her with me tonight. I don't bother with a shirt, just throw on a gray pair of sweats, then head back to Holly's door.

I tap quietly, "Here…when…ready." Then slide down the wall to sit beside her door, resting my elbows on my knees, propping my head on my fist.

I don't know what happened, but I'm freaked that she's in there in the middle of some shame spiral. Based on everything she's said, that's got to be the first time she had an O with anyone else in the room. Maybe she got caught up and took things further than she actually wanted to. She could be regretting everything.

I don't know how long I've been sitting here, but with a soft click her door opens. She startles when she sees me so close to the door, but opens it wider to join me on the floor. She's wearing the same pants, and she smells intoxicating. Her eyes are red, but dry.

"I'm sorry I ran away…I got overwhelmed."

"I…do…something?" I ask hoarsely. *"I was trying to be careful, but I lost a bit of control at the end there. If I scared you, I'm so sorry."*

"You didn't scare me. I wasn't afraid, really." Her eyebrows arrow down. "I was…angry."

"Angry?" I don't understand her at all. I feel like she's living on another planet half the time. It's fucking frustrating.

"He stole so much from me, Micah." She explains. "My body became this vessel for pain. I didn't know I could feel good. I didn't know I could feel pleasure, or get so turned on just having you laid out for me. I hate that he took away my chance to explore that part of me." Her chest is heaving, hands fisted. She looks like she's ready to lay into someone.

Not someone, Brent. I wish I could hold him for her and let her wail away at him.

I reach out, slowly wrapping my hand around her ankle, carefully pulling her into me until her legs are spread over my hips. I force myself to keep my gaze on her face instead of dropping it down to the wet patch on her pants. But I really fucking want to look. To run my fingers over it. Run my tongue over it.

"You can explore as much as you want to now. There's nothing standing in your way, and you have a very willing volunteer in me. Anything, remember?"

She smiles shyly. "I remember...you're sure you're ok helping me with my homework? Is it ok for you?"

My eyes widen, shocked as shit she even has to ask. *"I came in my fucking pants like a kid. It was absolute torture, and I loved every second of it."*

She grins and ducks her head, peeking up at me through her lashes. "I thought you liked it, but I wanted to be sure." She bites her lip. "I just worry that this relationship is very one sided. It seems to be all about you giving me what I need." She takes a deep breath. "Is there anything you need from me?"

I'm almost afraid to ask for what I want. But she's opened the door, and I owe it to her to be honest.

"There is something I would like. Doesn't mean you have to do it, though."

"I know," she says softly. "Tell me."

"We've been...flirting at work. And I love it. Then we come home and it's like we're back to just being friends. I love being your friend." I rush to add, not wanting her to think I've hated anything about the last few weeks. *"But you kissed me a few weeks ago, and your mouth...it felt like coming home."*

I stop, checking in on her reaction. I will end it here if she looks uncomfortable. But her neck is flushed, and she's leaning towards me with wide eyes. It gives me the courage to continue. *"I respect that things need to go at your pace, but maybe, if you're ok with it, you could let me hold you sometimes. And maybe we could kiss sometimes."*

I feel like I'm trying to ask her to the eighth grade dance. I feel completely ridiculous, and I'm sure I sound it. But there's no one here but us, and I don't mind looking like a fucking idiot in front of her.

Her lips pursed in thought, she absentmindedly reaches out to hold my hand. She's done this a couple of times, unconsciously reaching for me, and it kills me every time. No way she ever reached out to hold Brent's fucking hand.

I soak in her innocent touch, mentally threatening my cock with an ice bath if he gets out of line, while she thinks.

"I was a little in my head the last few weeks." She clears her throat. "My homework was...a lot. And I guess it helped me relax to keep things between us...calm at home." I nod my understanding, waiting for her to continue.

"I think I got in a bit of a habit. But we've sort of let the gremlins out now, haven't we?" she says with a grin.

I smirk at her, quirking my eyebrow. "Little...bit." Sobering, I add, *"It doesn't have to mean anything though. We can go back to not touching at home if you need it."*

She's already shaking her head. "No. I don't want to go backwards." She leans closer, her voice a whisper. "I need you to help me not go back. I spent so much time avoiding touch that I'm good at it. It's hard for me to think of reaching out. Then when I do, I start doubting myself."

"Help...you...how?" I ask, leaning in too.

"By touching me. Just little casual touches, the way a couple would. You're doing it at work already, but maybe...more?"

Reaching out, I tuck her hair behind her ear, then cup her cheek. "Like...this?"

Her "yes" is breathy.

I bring the back of her hand to my mouth, giving it a little nip before rubbing it along my stubbled cheek. Her eyes are wide again, and my grin escapes. "Kissing?" I ask her.

Her eyes are hazy, unfocused. Gradually they sharpen as she registers my question.

"Kisses are good too."

No way I'm waiting for an engraved invitation. Wrapping an arm around her back, I pull her all the way into my lap, checking in for any hints of fear on her face. Her eyes are wide and I swear I see the pulse in her neck flutter. There's no hint of fear in her face or body. Cupping the back of her head, I bring us closer together, hesitating for a second before slowly capturing her lips. She opens so sweetly for me, so welcoming, but shy. The shyness fades as I sip and taste and tease.

She pulls her mouth away and frowns at me. "Stop teasing me!" Then takes my mouth with the same passion and intensity she showed when she was exploring me on the carpet. We sit there, making out like teenagers, laughing and teasing, until her cheeks are red from my whiskers and I'm about to lose control.

Riding that edge, I push it as far as I can before pulling back regretfully. Cheeks pressed together, I soak up the trembling of her body and her panting breaths at my ears. When our breathing has evened out, I press a gentle kiss to her neck, then loosen my arms, helping her crawl off me.

She stands, hands covering her cheeks as she runs her eyes over me. The appreciation and ownership I see there makes me puff out my chest like a fucking peacock. "Goodnight." She finally whispers, shooting me a playful smile. I smile back, then collapse back onto the floor, trying to catch my breath all over again.

This woman is going to kill me.

27

HOLLY

Becca hands me a beer from Micah's fridge, dropping heavily onto the cushion next to me. I watch, wishing I had had popcorn, as Micah and Kade try to pry a tape measure out of Colton's hand. He's been walking around, measuring everything, including me, and generally annoying everyone. It wasn't until he started teasing Becca and I about having us measure his dick that Kade and Micah lost their patience.

"Fuckers! It was a joke. Let go!" Colt drops to the floor, tucking the tape measure under his chest, squealing. It's hilarious, because I know how deadly he can be. I've watched him spar with Becca and others at the Dojo, and he's incredibly powerful. But he's not using any of that power here. Instead, the pitch of his yell changes as Micah and Kade, seemingly of the same brain, lick their index fingers, then stick them in Colt's ears.

"Eww," Becca and I groan, giggling at their stupidity.

"Kade better wash his hands before he comes anywhere near me." Becca says with a shudder. I snort, but agree. No way do I want Colt's earwax anywhere near me.

The guys finally pick themselves up. Micah and Kade both

jog over, planting goodbye kisses, hands behind their backs after some scolding, on us that leave us flushed, then head back to Colton, who's watching with a tight expression. We wave as the door shuts behind them.

"What are they doing again?" I ask. Micah and I have been together nearly 24/7 for weeks, so it's strange to see him go somewhere without me.

"Colt's got something he needs help with," she says with a shrug. "Maybe measuring something? I really have no idea." Throwing her feet up on Micah's wood coffee table, she takes a big swig of her beer, completely comfortable with herself. It's something I still envy. Her absolute confidence in her body and in her place in the world.

"So what are we going to do, Chickie? Movies? Gossip? Hit up the sex shop?"

The last suggestion leaves me sputtering, choking on my beer, and her cackling like a loon.

"Becca!" I scold, flushed.

"How can you still get so red? Haven't you been playing with the toys I brought you?"

I cover my face with a groan. "I can't believe you asked me that," I mutter.

"Holly, look at me."

I drop my hands at her serious tone.

"Your sexuality is nothing to be ashamed of. Not with me, not with anyone. You're not doing anything wrong, touching yourself."

"I get that here," I say, tapping my head. "But that's not how I was raised. It was a sin. My body was for God, and then my husband. Girls who touched themselves were… sluts." My tongue stutters over the word I heard my dad use more than once when talking about girls in our community that had sex. The vitriol, the disgust in his tone, stuck with me, making me certain that I never wanted to be a slut, even before I understood what that meant.

Becca's lip curls. "I can't believe people are still teaching their girls that shit."

"What did your dad teach you about your body?" How did she get to be so strong? So sure of herself? Is it really just a matter of how she was raised? If I'd been raised by her dad, would I have turned out as confident and capable as she is?

She laughs, snuggling into the cushions. The furniture in her and Kade's apartment is a lot more modern, not soft and welcoming like Micah's, and she seems to be loving his couch. "My dad wasn't that comfortable with puberty shit, but he still talked to me about it. Then when I turned sixteen, he explained that my body was the only one I was ever going to get, so I better be careful what I do with it, and who I share it with. Then he took me to the doctor and got me a prescription for the pill."

I can't even imagine my father being so matter of fact about sex. "I learned about puberty in a book." I admit.

Becca's eyes widen. "Your parents gave you a book?"

"No." I say with a snort. "I would have been locked in my room for a year if they ever saw something like that in my possession. I read it at the public library. They never said one word to me about puberty or sex. When I asked for pads, my mom just added a bit of money to my allowance to cover it."

"That's fucked up Hol." She says, lip curled in disgust.

"Yeah, I guess it is. I can't ever imagine not talking with my kids about anything important."

"Do you want kids?" She asks softly.

"I think I might." I say, speaking the dream I've held tight in the very core of me. "I always dreamed of being a mom. Of sticky kisses and giggles. The idea that I could have that with Brent was...enticing."

"And then everything went to shit, and you realized you'd married a violent, narcissistic asshole." She says through gritted teeth.

"Essentially."

"You can still have that Hol. Micah will give you anything you want, even babies." She's not laughing, her voice a whisper.

"Don't you think that's rushing things a bit?" I mean, we've been kissing...a lot. And I've been touching him. But we're not really a normal couple...yet.

"Nope." She smirks. "Micah's been in love with you as long as he's known you. You own him."

I shift uncomfortably. "I can't own another person. That's what Brent tried to do with me. It's not ok."

"It's completely different and you know it," she challenges. "You own Micah's heart, Holly. That means he lives to make you happy. Anything you need from him, he'll give it. But he's not giving that trust to some monster." Her gaze is pointed. "He's giving it to you. He's choosing you. Brent took you. That wasn't about devotion or love. It was about control. Can't you see the difference?"

I curl my feet under me. "I...yes, I suppose. But I'm not even divorced! How am I supposed to let him pleasure me if I'm still married?"

Becca sits up straight, turning to face me with wide eyes. "Wait a minute...pleasure you? Is this the homework thing? I thought you were touching him. There's more now?"

I scowl at her eagerness. "Yes, there's more," I mutter, "I'm supposed to let him touch me."

"Touch you or pleasure you?"

I blow out a frustrated breath. "He's been touching me. My counselor encouraged me to let him touch me casually throughout the day. Desensitization. So I stop jumping and I get used to him. We...ah actually started that before she suggested it."

She laughs. "Keener! And...it's working?"

My cheeks redden and I can't meet her eyes.

"Ah!" she screams, "It is working! He's turning you on!"

"He's just touching my shoulder, or my arm...and well,

there have been kisses. A lot of them. But nothing overtly sexual."

Becca's smile is warm. "It can all be sexual. Kade has this certain smile...well I'm like a fucking river every time he sends it my way." A river, what does she...oh. Heavens, can my face get any redder? "Oh Hol," she says through her giggles, "you're going to have so much fun."

"Sex and fun have never gone together before."

"They can. In good relationships, they do."

"But what if I can't...have sex with him?"

"What makes you think you couldn't? You're turned on by him, right?"

"Yes," I admit, digging my fingers into the leather underneath me. "But what if I freeze up? Or panic?"

"You take steps to put yourself in control first, but then if you panic? Well, you'll deal with it and try again when you're ready. Micah's not going anywhere."

"Steps to put myself in control?" My mind flashes to our first night on the rug. I felt in control that night. More than in control, I felt powerful.

"Well yeah. You can be on top, or you can just pick a position that makes you two equal. Am I right in thinking Brent was all about missionary?"

My thoughts are swirling, imagining Micah in a variety of positions, so I'm distracted when I answer, "Yes."

"So maybe you avoid that position, but there's a whole other world out there, my friend. And you know Micah would be on board."

"Um...like what positions would you suggest?"

Now she's the one flushing red, but not in embarrassment. "Oooh, there's so many good ones. For your first time, maybe face to face on your sides. No weight on you that way. Or go ahead and ride him. Or maybe on your sides with him behind you. Or you could sit in his lap, or you—".

"Okay!" I say with a strangled breath. "There's lots to choose from. I got the idea. I'm just not quite there yet."

"Well, what exactly is your next homework?"

"Ah…to let Micah pleasure me."

"Ohh…" She drifts off, a little smile on her face. "How do you feel about it?"

"Scared," I say flatly. "She says I don't have to do anything, but I think I want to. I'm just…Brent never touched me for my pleasure. It's new."

"You've never had a guy give you oral sex?"

"No." Somehow, I hadn't connected pleasure and oral until this second.

"Oh my God, are you in for a treat!"

A treat? I find that really hard to believe.

"I'm serious. It's so good if the guy is patient, and into it. You won't have any trouble with Micah."

"What, I'm just supposed to get naked, spread my legs, and order him to work?"

Becca bursts into hysterical laughter, tipping over on the cushion, clutching her sides tightly. "Jesus. I would pay to see the look on his face if you did that."

Giggling too, I admit, "The first night I asked to touch him, I thought his eyes were going to pop out of his face."

And there it is. We're locked in the giggle snort loop. Hanging onto each other, tears streaming down our faces. As she wipes her eyes, then her nose with her sleeve, a wave of gratitude crashes over me. "Thank you for being my friend," I whisper.

Her eyes well with fresh tears as she pulls me into a hug. It's deep, and wide, and cleansing. The kind of hug I used to share with Robyn. The kind only a true friend can give you.

"Thank you for being mine," she says thickly.

"How are you and Kade doing?" I ask her, sick of my own drama for a minute.

She groans, dropping her head to the cushion. "He's a

little squirrelly, actually. Keeps dropping hints about marriage. He thinks he's being so sneaky, but I'm onto him."

My eyes widen. "You're getting married? That seems fast."

"No, we're not getting married! It's way too soon. Kade's just…working through some stuff."

"I don't understand."

She sighs, looking up at the ceiling. "I think he's worried about me walking away."

"Why would he worry about that?"

"Because I told him I would." She says with a snort. My eyebrows raise in surprise and she laughs again. "He can get caught up in his own head sometimes, and go to some pretty dark places. I warned him when we got together that I wouldn't let him treat me like crap. That I'll walk if it happens again. So I think he's worried about fucking up and me leaving."

I'm not sure why I thought things between Becca and Kade are perfect, but in a weird sort of way, it's comforting that they're not. That they're still working on their issues.

We lay there, snuggled, relaxing. In the warm space between us, I admit a truth I've been hiding from. "Marriage is hard to walk away from," I say quietly. "I'm afraid I'll never be free of Brent. The things he did to me have changed me forever. And if he won't give me a divorce…there's no escaping him."

She growls out a breath and tightens her arms around me. "What does Micah say about that?"

"I haven't talked about it with him. I don't want to."

"Why? You know he'll be on your side."

"I know," I say quietly. "But I just can't. I have depended on him for everything the last month. Everything I'm wearing, he paid for. I'm sleeping in his bed, driving to work in a car he paid for. It's enough. I won't put anything more on him."

"Holly, please, know I say this with love...you're an idiot."

I scowl at her, but she's not finished.

"Everybody needs help at one point or another. Everyone. Right now, it's your turn. That's not a bad thing. I was sleeping in my car when I met Kade, remember?"

"I remember. But still...no." I say firmly.

"Can I make a suggestion?" She finally asks, after studying my mutinous expression.

"Can I stop you?"

"Nope," she says calmly. "Talk to Ransom. He's a problem solver. He might have some ideas."

"Not a chance." I say, laughing in disbelief. "The man is running a multi-billion-dollar corporation. He does not have time to talk to me."

"Let's see," she says, hopping off the couch and grabbing her cell phone off the counter.

"Becca! Don't you dare." I yell, chasing after her, hopping around her in an attempt to grab her phone. She quickly taps out a message, easily dodging me, then hits send. Holding the phone high over her head, she shoves her butt into my stomach, laughing at my feeble attempts to grab it out of her Amazonian sized hand.

I hate being short.

I freeze as her phone pings.

She tilts the screen and smiles. "Be at his office tomorrow, 10 am."

I stare, dumfounded. "Just like that?"

"Yep. Just like that."

"Why would he agree so easily?"

Becca's smile is gentle. "I think you should ask him that yourself."

MICAH

I haven't seen Colton like this before.

 He's the laid back joker of the group until he's not. Nothing seems to bother him. He's fucking Teflon. He's the voice of reason, the one with the psychology degree. He's calm, cool and collected until it's time to crack some heads.

 Calm, cool, collected, Colt is in the middle of an argument with a Santa Claus looking clerk in the paint department about how much glitter he can add to the cans of pink paint on the counter.

 Seriously, who the fuck is he?

 "It's not gonna be sparkly enough, man. You can barely see it. It needs more! Just dump another fucking scoop in there and swish it around." People in the aisles have stopped to watch. I don't blame them. A tattooed, tank sized man who could make a biker tuck tail and run, arguing about sparkles is not something you see every day.

 Santa Claus crosses his arms over his chest. "You'll see it when it's dry. You put any more glitter in there, you're going to affect the paint and end up with a shitty finish."

 Colt looks crushed. "But…she's three, man. She needs lots of sparkles."

Santa softens. "Look, you can give your girl the sparkles another way. Why don't you grab a can of glitter spray paint and use it to finish a mirror or a toy chest or something? I'm sure she'd love that. My granddaughter spray painted her entire bedframe. Fucking glitter was everywhere for the next two years." He scowls at Colt. "That shit will get in your hair, man." He leans in closer. "I swear I found it in my crack more than once. How the fuck does that happen?"

Colt looks worried, the crease in his brow deepening. "Your crack man? Fuck." Rubbing his hands over his head, his eyes bounce from Santa to the glitter and back again. "Ok, fine." He says, pointing a threatening finger at him. "I'm trusting you, but if it's not sparkly, you and I are gonna have words."

Santa scowls at Colt. "Yeah, yeah, I'm terrified. Now I got other customers to help."

Kade and I grab the paint cans and stack them in the already full cart and beeline for the checkouts, hoping Colt's done arguing.

"Why the fuck are we here, man?" Kade whispers.

"No...clue." I whisper back. *"He's fixating. I haven't seen him like this. He keeps asking if Evie's coming. He won't let up."*

"What is it about this woman that's got him obsessed? I mean, she's had a lot of shit piled on her, but we've seen people in rougher shape. We didn't fucking redecorate an entire apartment for them...I can't believe I fucking used the word redecorate."

I chuckle at the disgust in his voice. *"I don't know what caught him, though you know he's got a sweet spot for women in general, though this is on a whole other level. But I'm not going to argue with him. Holly wants Evie to come, so we might as well prepare."*

"Fuckers," Colt yells. "This way. I saw these unicorn curtains online. We gotta go find them."

"Fuck me," Kade says, his expression void of hope. He knows we're going to die in here.

TWO HOURS LATER, WE'RE ATTEMPTING TO ROLL GLITTERY PINK paint on the wall in the nicest apartment on this floor. It has a great view of the lake, and Colt insisted this was the perfect one for the girls. Sometime in the last few weeks he's gotten his hands on a princess bed, complete with canopy. It's propped up in the living room, waiting to be assembled. Kade and I are going to get stuck with that job, guaranteed, considering Colt is useless with tools. We own fucking garages, and he still doesn't know the difference between a Phillips and a Robertson.

"Fuck," Colt yells again, glaring at the ceiling. There's another blob of pink paint marring the expanse of white.

"Why the fuck didn't we hire somebody to do this? For fuck's sake Colt, last time we painted a wall was...never. We've never fucking painted." Kade's waving his roller around in frustration. He's somehow managed to get more paint on him than the actual roller. His eyebrow is pink.

"It can't be that fucking hard," Colt says, rubbing a frazzled hand over his beard, leaving a trail of pink glittery paint in its wake. "I mean, you just roll it in the paint, then slap it on the wall." We all eyeball the gobs of paint dripping down the wall.

"We...suck," I mutter. Colt's staring at the wall like he wants to light it on fire.

I slap him on the shoulder. *"It's ok. We'll call someone on one of the crews to come paint."*

Kade pulls out his cell to contact someone from our maintenance crew as I guide Colt out of the room.

"Ok?" I ask. I hate to see him looking so dejected.

He grumbles, pulling himself up to sit on the granite kitchen counter. These units are finished as nicely as ours are, but on a smaller scale. It really would be perfect for Evie and her daughter.

"Why do you think she hasn't agreed to come?" he asks, staring down at the light wood floors.

"Why...care?" I wait for his fiery eyes to shoot up to mine. *"Why do you care so much? I don't have a problem with it. I just wonder what's going on with you?"*

"I honestly have no idea. There's just something about her that I can't stop thinking about. I mean, she did the right thing, she fucking saved Holly, and what did it get her? Her fucking life was torn apart. It makes me so...angry."

"You want to fix it for her?"

"Yeah, I guess."

"Then that'll be it? You'll get her settled, then let her live her life?"

"Yes," he says, making it sound an awful lot like a question. I hide my smile, moving to look out the floor to ceiling windows.

"You...are...hooked."

He opens his mouth to deny, but stops. "I don't know. I just can't stop thinking about her." He slides off the counter, moving to stand next to me, bumping his shoulder against mine. "Declan had more photos in the file. Of her before, and of her little girl, Mia. She was hooked up to so many tubes and wires in some of them...she was so tiny and so sick. She should have a princess bed, you know? And Evie, well, she was so thick and strong...lush and healthy, you know? Now she's wasted away. I don't like it."

I study his face, seeing a hint of something that worries me. "Colt." I say in warning. *"I recognize that look on your face. Don't. Don't interfere in her life. Let her make the choice, man."*

He scowls at me. "Why shouldn't I interfere? She would be better off here, where I...we can help her."

"He's right," Kade says, walking into the room. "She would be better off here. There's no doubt about it. Sounds like she's in a shitty spot. Jim will be here in twenty minutes to finish the painting, by the way."

Wanting to ease some of the tension in Colt's shoulders, I throw Kade under the bus. *"Kade wants to propose to Becca."*

"You dumbfuck," Colt breathes, looking like he's been punched in the head.

Kade scowls and throws an actual punch at Colt's head, which Colt parries easily, of course. "Why the fuck are you saying it like that? What the fuck is wrong with wanting to marry the woman I fucking love?"

Colt exhales heavily. "Brother, take a minute and really think about your answer...why do you want to marry Becca?"

"Because I love her and I want to be with her."

"Ok...but she's in your bed every night. You're already with her. Why do you need the ring?"

"It's a commitment. A promise."

"What's the promise?"

Kade exhales, seeming to deflate. "That she'll stay with me always. That she'll never leave."

"Give the man a prize." Colt says, slapping Kade on the shoulder.

"It's desperate, right? I'm trying to make sure she never leaves me. So when the fuck do I propose? Or do we just... never get married?"

"You propose when you're no longer afraid she'll walk out on you. Not until then."

"What he said," Colt agrees.

"Well, fuck."

"What about you, man? How's playing house with Holly?" Kade asks with a smirk.

Fucker's deflecting, but I'll give him a pass. *"We're good. Great, I guess."*

"You guess?" Colt asks.

I exhale heavily, turning to lean my shoulder on the floor

to ceiling window. *"I took five cold showers yesterday. I feel like I'm going to crack from the second I wake up to the moment I go to sleep."*

They both laugh, but Colt's eyes are knowing. "Her demons riding her hard right now?"

"Yes. I'm walking on eggshells around her, always making sure I haven't said or done the wrong thing. She would be fucking gutted if she knew that, though. So I pretend."

"But things are progressing, right? She's getting counseling and making positive strides?"

Colt's so in your face most of the time, it's easy to forget he's nearly got his Masters in Psychology. Fucker didn't tell us until a couple of months ago. Well, he told Kade, but no way would Kade keep that shit to himself. So now everyone knows.

I shoot him a side eye, but nod. *"Yea, she's progressing. We're having a lot of fucking fun. I'm just worried about the day she's going to tell me she's ready for sex. I'm dreading it. In her head, it's like the last big hurdle before she can truly be mine. And I don't want to fuck it up."*

Colt rubs his beard, his mouth turned down. "That's pretty normal, brother. Watching you with her, it's clear she trusts you. You'll handle her right when the time comes."

Somehow, his confidence makes me feel better. Maybe I can handle things. *"So, I just keep doing what I'm doing? Follow her lead?"*

"Yeah, man, that's the only way. Also…um she's tiny. So maybe don't be on top. At least for the first few times." He scowls, neck red. "You don't want to make her feel trapped."

"Right." I mutter. I'd thought about that too. The idea of making her feel overpowered makes me feel sick to my stomach. *"I just wish…I was better for her."*

"There's no one better than you. No one." Kade says seriously.

I scowl at him, appreciating the sentiment, but not in the

mood. *"I wish I could talk to her. Just say what I'm thinking. I hate having to take my hands off her to communicate with her."*

"I thought you were at peace with your aphasia." Colt says.

"Was," I mutter, *"until I met her. Now everything feels different."*

Colt studies me with knowing eyes. "What do you need, brother?"

I study the boats out on the lake, and the little people in them that look like little ants. "Help," I admit quietly.

Colt's heavy hand lands on my shoulder. "There's a Speech Pathology program at the U. I can ask around, get you the name of someone good."

"Thanks," I say with a small smile. He nods, then shifts his gaze to the princess bed boxes. He rubs his hands together, cackling evilly.

"Now I'm going to set that bad boy up!"

Kade and I trade glances as Colt walks away. "Ah, Colt, maybe we should hold off until the room's painted. You know, assemble it in there."

Colt scoffs, "Nah, man. It's a single. We can carry it in there in a couple of big pieces. I've got my tool set here." He moves a huge purple toolbox into the center of the room, unsnaps it, then flips it over, dumping everything onto the floor. Tools, hot pink duck tape, candy wrappers and a fuckton of bouncy balls tumble out.

"Fuck," Kade and I mutter in unison.

Guess we're putting together a princess bed.

29

HOLLY

I think I'm having a panic attack. I was ok when I kissed Micah goodbye at the shop. I was ok driving here. But driving up to the front doors of this massive building is intimidating. It's not just a building, it's a compound.

I guess I was expecting a shiny high rise downtown, but this is more intimidating somehow. There's a security gate, with a serious-looking security guard, who seems to know exactly who I am. He directs me to the surface parking right in front of the building. The gleaming glass building must be at least twelve stories. As I drive up to it, I see large warehouses at the back of the property. Semi-trucks with the Brash Auto logo on them are backed up to open bays. There's a flurry of activity back there.

Turning off the SUV, I sit for a moment, gathering my composure. I double check my reflection in the mirror, smoothing wisps of hair back into my ponytail. I wore my happiest dress, with the bright flowers and long swaying skirt. Still feeling intimidated, I remind myself, again, that I've seen Ransom in his underwear, covered in food. He can't be that scary.

I enter through the glass front doors, approaching a desk. A smiling woman greets me.

"Hello! What a beautiful dress. I love all the colors," she gushes.

The kindness on her face and the enthusiasm in her voice make me smile back. I glance at her name tag. "Thank you Janey. I love it too. I'm here to see Ransom...um, Mr. Kyle." I flush at my mistake.

Just because I've tagged along to the last few family dinners doesn't mean that I'm family. It's obvious that he asked me here to keep some distance between us. He lives a few floors above us. It would have been easy to call me upstairs, or for him to come down. But no, we have to meet at the office.

"Of course, Miss Clarke," she says, handing me a badge. "Wear this please, and take the far elevator to the eleventh floor."

I'm surprised again that she knows my name, just like the guy at the gate, but I take the badge with thanks, and spend the ride upstairs deep breathing. When the doors open, my smile blooms. Colton's there, grinning, wearing a tailored black suit.

"Hi little Holly," he croons, extending his arm.

I snort, stepping out to thread my arm through his, finally relaxing.

"You look very nice," I tell him, brushing my hand along the sleeve of his jacket. "I've never seen you dressed like this."

He preens, reaching up to straighten his tie. "I know. I clean up good."

I laugh at his mock arrogance, and we fall into a natural banter. I barely notice the offices we pass, but I do smile and wave at Jonas and Declan when I spot them across the room. I consider myself privileged to know these quirky men. And quirky they are, beneath the thin veneer money has put on them. They're also kind and so incredibly generous.

"Have you heard anything from Evie?" Colt asks. He's trying to drop the question casually, but I can feel the tension in his body.

"We've been texting nearly every day. She's ok."

"Is she coming?" He presses.

I turn to look at him, spotting a splotch of pink paint in the hair at the nape of his neck. It's the same color Micah had on him last night. I desperately want to know what they were doing yesterday. "I really hope she does. I want the chance to be a better friend to her. I think she could use a good group of friends. She's been on her own a long time."

He meets my eyes, nodding, then pasting on the carefree smile again. "Here you go. The boss man himself." He says, escorting me into a large, light filled office.

Ransom is sitting behind a big desk on a call, but he smiles at me, and mouths 'one minute'. Colt settles me in the comfortable chair facing the desk, leaving me with a bow and a kiss on the hand. Chuckling to myself, I lock eyes with Ransom, who's also smiling and shaking his head. As he finishes his call, I take a moment to look around his sparse office.

Most of the walls are glass, but I would still expect to see some sort of decoration. Maybe some art or knick knacks. There's none of that. The only thing of a personal nature seems to be the photo frame on his desk. I tilt my head to the side, trying to see the picture, startling when Ransom's hand reaches out, turning it for me. I wrinkle up my nose, giving him a bashful smile, then lean forward.

It's the Knight St. Garage. And standing in front of it, all the guys. This picture must have been taken at least fifteen years ago. They all look so young. But there's no innocence on their faces. Instead, in their gazes, I see lives already hard lived. But there are smiles too, and arms wrapped around each other. They were family, even then.

"That was taken a few years after we opened the garage." Ransom's smiling at the picture as he hangs up, his eyes a million miles away.

"You all look so young."

"We were," he says with a low chuckle. "I was twenty-one. Most of the guys were still officially living at the group home."

"Micah told me a little about how you guys started. Did you always plan on getting into the car business?"

His grin is sharp. "No. But I saw an opportunity and took it." He shrugs, "It turned out ok."

I laugh. "I guess it did."

He stands, moving to sit next to me, easily sliding my chair sideways so we're facing each other. He studies me carefully. "What can I do for you Holly?"

I swallow the moisture pooling in my mouth. Flattening my hands in my lap so I don't betray my nervousness by twisting them, I blurt, "Do you think I'll be able to divorce Brent?"

His mouth firms but a knock on the door stops him from answering. "Mav, come in." He says, not looking away from me.

I turn to smile nervously at Maverick. I haven't spent much time with him. He always seems heavy, somehow, like the weight of the world is solely on his shoulders. He rarely smiles, though when he does, it's stunning.

He sends one of those stunning smiles my way as he pulls Ransom's chair out from behind the desk to join us.

Ransom clears his throat. "I invited Mav here this morning because I thought having his legal perspective would be helpful." He turns to Mav. "She's wondering about divorcing Brent."

Maverick nods, eyes cool. "What steps have you taken so far, Holly?"

Did he know I was going to ask him about the divorce? Why else would we need a legal perspective when we meet? "Well, I went down to legal aid. They helped me draw up papers. But, uh, Brent wouldn't sign them."

Maverick tenses, his jaw tightening. "You went to the prison? By yourself?"

"Yes," I admit, lengthening my spine and squaring my shoulders. "I was trying to finally take control. But it didn't work out that way."

"That could have been dangerous! You shouldn't—"

"Mav," Ransom interrupts calmly. "I arranged it. She was safe."

Maverick's shoulders drop. He blows out a breath. "What exactly did he say?"

No way I'm telling them what he actually said. I know it's not supposed to be a reflection on me, but having someone call you a cum bucket isn't really something I want to share. "Basically, that he would never let me go. That I was his, and he's never going to sign."

"That's not his choice to make." Ransom's words send a chill down my spine, and I'm thankful again that his ice isn't directed at me.

"I don't understand." I say, glancing between the two of them.

"It means that you're entitled to your freedom, whether he wants to sign or not." Maverick smiles, the way a shark would smile at his soon to be dinner. "He's too stupid to realize he can't do anything to keep you."

"So...I can get a divorce?" I ask hopefully.

"Yes, you can. You have a few options, actually."

My smile is wobbly, but comes easier than it did when I walked in here. Maybe it's not as hopeless as I thought. "If you have time, I would very much like to hear them."

"I cleared our schedules for the morning, sweetheart," Ransom murmurs. "We have as much time as you need."

Tears spring to my eyes. "Why?" I ask, my throat tight. "Why are you so ready to help me? I'm just an employee—"

"You're not *just* anything Holly." Maverick says sharply.

"He's right. We would still help you if you were just an employee. But that's not why you're sitting here with us. You're here because my brother's happiness depends on you. That means we'll do anything we need to do to make sure you're safe and happy."

"But...we're not even officially together. I mean, it's all been so fast, with the fire and my injuries..." I trail off, unable to finish the sentence. While it's been fast, yes, it's also been right in a way that's a bit scary. I won't deny it.

Maverick's warm chuckle wraps around me. "Micah's been talking about you for months. Every conversation somehow came back to you. I'd ask him how his latest build was going, and he'd tell me about a part you ordered for him, then spend a few minutes describing your dress and how pretty you were. Every. Single. Time."

I cover my hot cheeks, dropping my head to hide my smile. There's something about having Maverick tell me how Micah feels that settles deep. Micah has told me, but I don't think I was fully able to believe it. Now, it's starting to feel a little more true. I don't know if I'll ever be able to take a man's affection at face value. I did once and regretted it. I guess that lesson embedded itself pretty deep.

"Can I ask...why didn't you go to Micah with this?" Ransom asks.

My eyes fall to the space between our chairs. My feet in cream flats look tiny compared to Ransom's glossy black loafers. "My relationship with Micah feels very...one sided. He's done so much for me. Coming to you feels a little more like I'm fixing my own mistakes, maybe? I'm sorry, that probably doesn't make any sense. I mean, you're his brothers, so I'm not trying that hard, but..." I shrug, feeling ridiculous.

"Is it wrong that he wants to take care of you?" Ransom asks with an arched brow.

I shrink a little under his gaze. "No, it's not wrong," I say, wetting my lips nervously. "But I lived with a man who took care of me. I didn't have to worry about anything, but it came at a heavy cost. I...I've been talking to someone about that. I know not all men are like that, but it feels like I'm on unequal footing."

"For what it's worth," Maverick says quietly, "I haven't seen Micah as alive as he's been in the month with you. The day you were in the fire he was...gutted, but once he knew you were going to be ok...well he seems happy every time I see him."

Ransom sits back in his chair. "What are your intentions towards Micah?"

My eyes widen at the casual way he asks that. Like he's a father talking to his daughter's boyfriend. It never even crossed my mind that we might have this conversation.

"I really want to tell you to mind your own business, but I won't." I shake my head. "He's lucky to have you guys. People who care so much for him." How would my life have been different if I had an older brother, or a dad who cared about me the way these guys do for Micah? Would I have ever married Brent?

"Micah's the best man I know. I want a chance to explore...possibilities with him. But I need to get out from under the cloud of my marriage first." Resisting the urge to squirm, I let the men study me as I wait for their judgment. They seem to have some weird mental chat, then lean forward in their chairs.

"Ok," Maverick says, "Let's go over your options. There are two basic ways to play this. One, you file for divorce and get a judgment. We've got good relationships with lots of judges, so that's easy enough to fast track. The second is to make Brent want to sign."

"Make him want to sign?" I echo.

That predatory smile comes back to Mav's face. "Oh yeah. Declan did a full background on Brent. He's got significant assets; the house, a large investment portfolio and 401K. He made good money during your marriage. Your half of the assets would give you a significant nest egg, somewhere in the neighborhood of $250,000. But if he doesn't want to grant you a divorce, well, you're his wife and can make use of all that as you see fit. You can sell the house, drain the accounts. He'd be left with nearly nothing by the time he gets out."

"But...I don't think my name is on anything. The house or the accounts. He always told me I had nothing."

"You're not on there...yet. But within an hour, all of that can change. Don't worry about the hows, just know that it will be handled."

"He'll never believe me. It wouldn't work."

"You'd have paperwork to show him. But Kade, Ransom and Micah would be happy to pay him another visit instead."

I freeze, moving my eyes to Ransom. For the first time, he looks a little uncomfortable, flashing a glare at Maverick.

"What does he mean 'pay Brent another visit?' When did you visit him?" I ask him.

Ransom meets my eyes. "After he was formally charged. He was hunting for lawyers. He was sure that he'd be proven innocent and released, so Micah, Kade and I all paid him a visit. Explained to him that he was much safer in prison, and that pleading guilty would be his...healthiest option."

I sink back in my chair, stunned. I always wondered why Brent would plead guilty. It wasn't like him at all to just accept defeat. He was always convinced he was smarter than everyone else. And he'd never want to give up control like that.

"And what, you just talked to him, and he agreed to plead guilty?"

Ransom steeples his fingers, resting his elbows on the arms of the chair. "A man like your husband wouldn't just believe us, no. Something must have happened while he was in holding that convinced him our path was smarter."

"Something?" I ask.

Ransom just smiles and shrugs. He's not going to say any more on the subject.

"I was dreading a trial," I whisper. "I would have testified, but..."

"None of us wanted you to have to go through that, but Micah was very insistent, so we handled it. That's the way this works now, Holly. You're family, so we take care of you."

I let the idea that I'm part of their family sink in. Their easy acceptance and defense of me is...confusing. How did these men decide I'm worth taking care of when my own parents wouldn't? They always told me I was flawed, and sinful, that I had no innate worth. But that doesn't seem true. These men, Becca, all of them seem to see value in me.

And maybe, just maybe, I'm starting to see it too.

30

HOLLY

It started small. With a comment on my outfit, and a suggestion to change. Then he started shopping with me. Pretty soon, I wasn't allowed to buy anything without his approval. Brent liked dark colors on me. They were more 'slimming', he said. That applied to nightwear too. He liked me in negligees, with scratchy lace and g-strings.

I hated them.

Hated how they felt, and hated what they represented. I don't like lace. I don't ever want to wear black again. Those negligees meant that my husband was going to demand something from me that I didn't want to give. 'Go be a good girl and put on something pretty' he'd whisper to me.

His whisper against my ear would send a shudder through me. He always smiled, but to this day I don't know if it's because he believed the shudder was from desire, or because he knew I was terrified of him. I'd peck him on the cheek and slowly make my way upstairs, thinking about how I might stop it.

Because the nights I did as he asked made me feel worse somehow. I would feel the tension in my body rising as I carefully hung up my clothes and washed my face. Brent didn't like anyone to think I was attractive, so I rarely wore makeup, only needing a few minutes to remove my mascara.

Then, I would begin my horrible preparations. Removing the lube from the back of the closet where I hid it, using my fingers to apply it, though I was usually so tense it was uncomfortable to insert even my own finger. Then hiding the bottle and pulling on one of the little lacy somethings Brent preferred. He'd want me sitting, waiting, on the edge of the bed for him.

Sometimes, I'd only wait a few minutes. Sometimes it was hours. It was all mind games, never allowing me to relax, forcing me to stare at the bedroom door, anticipating his arrival. I would sit there, anxious, wondering if it wouldn't be better to push the screen out and jump down two stories. Maybe I could finally get away.

Then I have to remind myself of all the times I tried early on, and how painful my punishments were when his police friends brought me back to him.

I would convince myself that this is what wives do: submit. And sometimes it worked. Brent would come in and I'd pretend for a while that his kisses meant he loved me, that if he pulled my hair too hard, or bit me too deeply it was because he was so passionate for me. He'd coax me onto the bed, pulling my panties aside and pushing into me, telling me how good I was, that he owned me, and that he loved me. If I was lucky, he'd come quickly, then roll over and let me clean up.

If I was unlucky, he'd decide I wasn't doing something right and get aggressive, trying to draw a response from me. Tears, screams, anything. And if he was feeling particularly nasty, he'd tighten his fists in my hair and push himself down my throat. Those were the nights that I wished I had provoked a fight, or tried to run. Anything but let him choke me until black spots danced in front of my eyes, then pull out so I can take a gasping breath before doing it again.

Anything but be treated like an object, a thing with no value.

So why, I ask myself, *do I think that I can do this*? As I study my reflection, I can honestly say I like what I see. My blonde hair is tousled, my eyes especially blue, reflecting the light blue of the satin nightgown hugging my curves. I thought it would be fun shopping for it, but the idea of Micah seeing me in it kept me on edge as I tried things on. The idea of what was going to happen tonight sending me into a mix of desire and panic.

He's out there right now, on our rug. Waiting for me. He thinks this is going to be another night of me touching him, exploring him, tasting him. We've done a lot of that. I've learned his body better than I know my own. I've traced every scar with my tongue, swallowed his groans when he comes. Nothing about his body scares me anymore. It's the opposite, actually. The desire, the heat that I thought was fiction, made up to sell romance novels, is actually real. I feel it. My whole body tingling, pulsing as I touch him.

I backed off after the first night. Focusing on feeling him, pleasing him, rather than my own pleasure. And Micah's complete surrender to me, to the process, was heady. He was so welcoming of my touch, wanting it desperately, it made me feel...desirable.

But tonight, it's my turn to surrender.

I exit my room on bare feet, stopping to watch Micah, seated cross-legged on the rug, petting Minnie as she swirls around him, bumping him with her head and presenting her bum for scratches. He's smiling, humming to her as she rubs on him. His head rises suddenly, his body stilling as he sees me.

I resist the urge to rush back to my room for a sweater...or an entire comforter to cover up with. He rises, walking towards me slowly, stopping to pick up his cat before she trips him. Placing her on her cat stand with gentle hands, he turns and prowls towards me, his body pure power. His eyes travel over me, but they lock on my heavy breasts, the nipples pebbled and pressing against the satin. I am suddenly hyper aware of my lack of underwear.

He swallows heavily, licking his lips. "Ah…" He stutters to a stop. *"You naked under there?"*

"Yes," I whisper through suddenly dry lips.

"W…Why?"

"I'm hoping we can try something new tonight." I take a deep breath, exhaling heavily. "I was wondering if you might be willing to…touch me."

Micah makes an odd choking sound, and bends forward, bracing his hands on his thighs. "Willing," he repeats, his voice muffled. "Willing." A low chuckle rolls through him, and just before I turn and run back to my room, he straightens. "Want," he growls, eyes burning with lust, chest heaving. *"Tell me. What do you want? What should I do? What shouldn't I do? What are the rules?"*

My heart's going to pound through my chest wall. "Ah… I'm not ready to have sex. Other than that, there are no rules."

His eyes widen comically. "No…rules?" He chokes out. *"I'm going to need you to be more specific, baby."*

"Specific," I mutter, covering my red cheeks. "I don't understand…just, do what you want?"

His jaw clenches. *"I can't do that. You've given me some details on the shit that Brent did to you. Why would you just…give me control so suddenly? It doesn't make sense."*

Well, hell.

Why couldn't he just be a typical guy and take what was being offered? "It's not that sudden…we've been doing lots. Even my counselor agreed that I could move forward if I wanted to." I say defensively. "Besides, it's not about giving you control," I explain in a whisper. "It's about giving you my trust."

"Trust." He echoes.

"Yes, trust. I trust you to treat me with care...with love. I trust you to make me feel good."

His face softens, his shoulders drop. Stepping into me, he wraps his gentle arms around me, pulling me tight to him. His breath drifts across my head. "Tell...me...stop" he orders, pulling back to scowl at me.

"I'll tell you. If something doesn't feel good, I promise."

"Or...scared," he insists.

"Or if I'm scared."

He seems satisfied with that, leaning down to kiss me softly, before taking my hand, leading me back into my room.

My nerves ratchet up as I lay eyes on my big bed. Being with him on the rug seemed doable, but as he sits me on the edge of the bed and leaves the room, a thousand other nights flash through my mind, setting my heart racing.

He comes back, and must see the panic on my face. *"Just wanted to lock the door. I set it to do-not-disturb, so we don't have to worry about Kade walking in."*

I nod, soaking up his warm smile, then watch as he moves to the bathroom to pull off his shirt and wash his hands. I'm distracted watching him move around the room, repositioning pillows, smoothing comforters.

His expression is rueful as he catches my eyes. "Nervous," he mutters, rubbing the short hair on the top of his head. *"I don't ever want to do anything to hurt you. When you were in charge, it was easier to relax into it."*

His nervousness is chasing mine away. "Brent never cared, Micah. Not even at the beginning. My pleasure was...irrelevant to him. The fact that you're nervous about this makes me feel better about it." I stand, moving to him at the head of the bed, grasping his hand in mine. "We're going to be ok," I whisper. "Tell me where you want me."

"Bed...lay...on...side," he says hoarsely. I follow his instructions, crawling into the bed, settling on my side facing him. I smile at his low groan.

"*I just need to hold you for a while, breathe you in. Then, when we're both feeling it, I'll make you feel so good.*" He hisses in a breath through his teeth. "*My hands are going to be busy on you. That means our communication will be…simple. But baby, the more noise you make, the better. Your words, your moans, all of that is going to help me know what you like, and steer me away from anything you don't. So don't you dare hide your reactions from me.*"

"Even if I'm freaking out a bit?" I ask hesitantly.

"*Especially then.*" He says with his trademark scowl. "*Don't hide your fear from me, just to make me feel better. I see you Holly. You always try to smooth things over, always wanting everyone to be ok. But in this bed, together, you have to give me your truth. Whatever that is. Believe me baby, you letting me do something that hurts you, that would destroy me.*"

"I hadn't really thought about it like that." I admit. "It's a habit, putting what I want aside for someone else."

"*No more. I need you selfish. Demand things of me, woman. Order me the fuck around. Grab my ears and steer me, please. I will fucking worship at your feet if you do.*"

I press my legs together at the image of him, down on his knees, looking up at me. Worshiping me. It's so far from any reality I've ever experienced, it's hard to even imagine it.

But I want it.

Badly.

His slow smile makes my belly clench. His hands move to his waistband, pushing his sweats down, leaving him in black boxer briefs. Still watching me, he slides into the bed until he's lined up with me, our skin separated by millimeters. "Come," he says, voice tight as he pulls me into him, settling my head on his bicep, pulling my thigh over his.

Tucking his nose into my hair, his chest rises and falls with a contented sigh, his big hand stroking up and down my back. Tears fill my eyes as I soak up his warmth and comfort, the simplicity of being held with such love. Because it's radiating between us, lighting up all my shadowed corners. And it's not scary anymore. Not a weapon that can be used against me. It's a gift, delivered into strong waiting hands. Hands that will treasure it, keep it safe. "I love you," I whisper.

His body stills for a moment before a shudder racks through him. I feel the hand on my back clenching the material of my nightgown. His mouth moves to my ear. "Thank... fuck," he says like a prayer. "Love...you...m...my...Holly."

I revel in the feeling of his lips on my eyelids and cheeks, kissing away my tears. I stay cradled in his arms, feeling more connected to him than I've ever felt. Like I finally dropped the walls around me, letting him in. I bury my nose in the warm hollow of his throat, breathing in the hints of sweat and grease from his day at the shop. But underneath those scents is him. The musky, fresh smell that is Micah. I drift, wallowing in the warmth, his hand drifting down my back, skimming lightly, teasing me.

Then his fingers creep under the hem of my nightgown.

My breath catching in my throat, my mouth drying, I anticipate his next touch.

31

HOLLY

My mouth drops open as my focus narrows on those questing fingers, stroking down my thigh, then under the hem, back and forth, moving a little higher each time. His body is relaxed, his mouth still pressing gentle kisses to my face, dancing along my skin but never landing on my mouth.

That's good, because I'm sure I look like a gaping fish right now as I focus on that maddening hand. Languid and slow is not something I was expecting tonight, and I find I'm...in need. Every time he moves higher, my breath stutters in my chest. I catch a whine in my throat when he moves away again. Why is he teasing me?

Finally, that hand pushes higher, taking my nightie with it. The cool air of the room drifts across my exposed bottom. Then his big, calloused hand traces down to cup and shape my cheek, squeezing and stroking. He groans, his body tightening. He reaches down, pulling my leg further over him, parting them and exposing my center. He pulls his chest away from me, and I immediately miss his warmth.

Before I can follow him, his teeth grab the neckline of my nightie and start pulling it down. I pull my top arm out of the thin strap, giving him more room to move. He groans in approval as he rubs his cheeks between my breasts. I have a brief moment of worry, a brief flash of Brent shaming me for the way my heavy breasts would press together, especially after I gained weight, but I forced the memory away. I don't want him in this bed with me.

Besides, based on the noises Micah's making as he tastes me, he has no complaints.

I'm already overloaded with sensation, but when I see his plump lips close over my pebbled nipple, and feel him draw me deep, my brain shuts off. The twin sensations of his fingers stroking closer and closer to my center, and his deep rhythmic pulls on my nipple become my whole world.

"Perfect," he says hoarsely.

The way he's making me feel is perfect. I clutch his head to my chest, lost in sensation, barely aware that he's rolled me onto my back. His big figure looming over my frame startles me, but his warm brown eyes, so unlike Brent's icy blue, keep me from getting lost.

"Ok?" he asks.

"Yes...please don't stop."

His wolfish smile makes my stomach clench. Eyes locked on mine, he slowly pulls my nightgown lower, down my stomach, over my mound, down my legs, and off, pressing worshipful kisses the whole way.

He stops to rub my feet, making me groan. My eyes widen as he sucks and bites at my toes, nervousness about being completely exposed to him forgotten. My legs had naturally closed as he pulled my negligee off, but now, he very deliberately places my feet on either side of his body, as he slowly crawls closer to my core.

I'm panting, watching in anticipation as he runs his hands up my legs, stopping at the top of my thighs, letting his thumbs play on the tender skin at the sides of my groin. "Soft," he murmurs, the reverence in his tone loosening any tension left in my muscles. He lowers to his stomach between my legs, turning to kiss the inside of my knee, up the skin of my thigh. Then moves down to my other knee, and back up.

I push up onto my elbows, not wanting to miss a thing. "Brent never...um."

His eyes sharpen on me, roaring with heat. "Only...me" he says savagely. Rising up over me, he takes my mouth in a blazing kiss full of appreciation. He pulls away, raising me up to tuck a pillow behind me. "Better...view," he says with a wink.

It's an amazing view. His broad, golden shoulders spreading my pale thighs wide. His dark head resting on my leg as he breathes in deeply. I have a moment of shyness, automatically trying to pull my legs together, but his low hiss stops me. His fingers are there suddenly, at my core, spreading me, exposing me to his gaze. And then his mouth is on me, sucking and licking and it's overwhelming and amazing, and too much and not enough.

I'm dimly aware I'm moaning. I can't stop the words from bubbling up as he draws my clit into his mouth and sucks. I rear up, stomach clenching, as I chase something big. "Micah, God, yes."

His sounds of pleasure and encouragement spur me on, and when he gently pushes one, then two fingers inside of me, rubbing and twisting, I detonate.

I thought that riding his belly last week made me feel amazing, but this is so much better. Everything with Micah is better, and it makes me crave it all. Before I can drag him up, his mouth, which had been soothing and gentle as I shuddered through my orgasm, starts pushing me back up that cliff. "It's too much...I...oh," and I'm flying.

My whole body is shuddering, and I feel changed. Like the person I was before is gone. I slipped her skin and freed myself. Or maybe I let Micah free me. I'm dimly aware of him moving up my body, pressing gentle kisses on my sweaty skin on his way up, soothing me. Sweat cooling on my body makes me shiver, but I don't even need to ask before Micah is pulling the comforter over us, wrapping me up in his arms, resting his forehead on mine. "I can smell me on you," I whisper.

"Taste...amazing."

Giving into an insane urge, I flick my tongue over his lips, then dive inside, tasting myself. Micah groans deeply, pulling me closer, pressing against me. I can feel the hard, heavy weight of him against my thigh, and the fire that I thought was banked ignites again. An echo of my orgasm shudders through me.

Pressing against his chest, I push him onto his back, feeling brave and new. I grab the waistband of his boxers. "Off. Now," I demand, and with a quick quirk of his brow, he complies, pushing them off quickly, allowing his erection to slap against his stomach.

I reach out, stroking it firmly the way I know he likes it. I've gotten to know and love this part of Micah, too. No longer fearing the pain it could cause me, knowing that Micah would never hurt me.

Micah's arm is thrown over his face, his throat working. He's expecting me to keep stroking, making him come the way I have in the past, but I have other plans.

Because I'm tired of waiting.

The fear of taking him into my body, of being completely vulnerable with him, is gone. I don't know if it's gone forever, but I want to take advantage of this moment. And with the fear gone, the want, the need rages into its place.

Moving quickly, I toss off the comforter and throw my leg over his stomach, settling him against the weeping entrance to my body. I take a deep breath as I register his size. I researched this too, after the first night I touched him. Even with a man as big as Micah, we'll fit.

I just might have to work at it.

Micah startles, his arms slapping the bed as he rears up. "Holly!" he bellows, chest heaving. His eyes are flying from the V of my body to my eyes and back again. "Sure?" he asks, swallowing.

Pulling him closer, with a hand on the back of his neck, I wait for his arms to wrap around me. "I'm sure. I want to feel you inside me."

"Slow," he says, gripping my hips. "Wait!...p...preggo" He mumbles, making me smile.

"We're good. I have an implant, remember?" I move experimentally, pushing down, taking a little more, and he chokes.

Fascinated by the pained expression on his face, I watch him as I lift up and push down again, loving the way he hisses through his teeth. The muscles and veins of his neck are exposed, his whole body tight. Even the grip of his fingers on my hips is firmer than they've ever been.

Usually he treats me like something delicate, breakable. He's losing a bit of control, and for a woman with my history, that would normally be terrifying. But I've seen him look this way, like he's going to die, and not once, in those other times I touched him, did he ever force me to do anything. I am safe.

I know it at my core.

He lets me set the pace, rising and falling slowly as I take him deeper and deeper, marveling at how slick my passage is, and how easily I'm taking him, despite all my worries. A wave of pride fills me as I realize my body works perfectly, easing the way for him.

No lube required.

Finally, my bum comes to rest on his legs. I've taken him all. Our mouths are pressed against each other as we gasp, sharing air. I take his mouth in a passionate kiss, pouring all my desire, and hope, and happiness into it. Soon it's too much, and I have to move, rocking my hips in an instinctive rhythm. I'm climbing higher and higher, but can't seem to tip over until Micah adjusts our angle and presses against my clit with each stroke.

I shudder and moan through my third orgasm of the night, then lay limp, breath heaving, letting him hold me up. As I calm, I feel him still hard within me. Urging my limp muscles to work, I pull away, kissing away the hint of disappointment on Micah's face.

Unwrapping his arms from around me, I climb off, sitting on the bed beside him. Then slowly, watching his face as I do, I slide down the pillows, spreading and lifting my knees. "Fuck me," I order him, refusing to blush as I use a word always forbidden to me. I'm flying high, feeling so absolutely in the moment that I want to wash away one more bad memory. I want Micah to take control. I want him powering over me.

I see the last threads of his control unraveling as he studies my face and sees nothing but want and need. Then he's over me, lining us up, ready to push home. He spreads his legs, cocking one knee up so my leg rests on top of his, and plants his elbows at my sides.

"It's your turn." I whisper against his lips. "I want to watch you take your pleasure."

A small grin briefly touches his mouth before he pushes into me in one thrust. I gasp at the fullness, rubbing the side of his face reassuringly, showing him I'm okay. He starts a slow push and pull, watching me carefully, so I show him how much I love him. How much I love us together, and how unafraid I am. The last thread of his control breaks. Shifting his arms to cup my shoulders, he speeds up, setting a punishing pace, racing to his finish.

I thought I would just feel, and watch, and enjoy him falling apart, my body spent. Enjoy the fact that Brent is banished. Because he is. The magic of being with Micah, his love and patience, has wiped away seven years of marriage.

Being with him, feeling how good we are together, makes me sure that this is exactly where I'm supposed to be.

But as his strokes speed up, he also changes the angle of his thrust, pressing against me in just the right spot. And I light up all over again, forcing myself to keep my eyes open so I can watch him fall apart too, until our shudders get so strong they force them closed.

Micah's breath is hot and damp against my throat, his grip still tight, like he's afraid I might leave. I tighten my arms and legs around him, loving his weight over me, still in me, turning my head to press gentle kisses against his ear, cheek, corner of his mouth, anywhere I can reach. Our lips connect again and we drift into the simplest, smallest kiss. But it feels monumental to me. Parting our lips I whisper, "I've never done this before," I tell him.

"What...before?" He asks curiously?

"Lay in bed, holding the man I love. It feels..." I frown, unable to put how monumental this moment is to me.

He takes my mouth in another lingering kiss and I feel the heat rising between us again. He pulls back, loving eyes raking over my face with a smile. "Feels...like...everything."

"Yes," I murmur. "Everything." I trace his heavy brows with my fingertip. "Thank you for not giving up on me. For loving me through the fear and doubt. Through the pain."

His eyes are glassy. "Never...stop...I...promise."

Our lips meet again, our connection a living thing, growing with each touch, each kiss, each whispered word. It's a promise.

It's everything.

32

MICAH

I tighten my hands around the steering wheel, imagining they're wrapped around Brent's neck instead. I don't want her anywhere near him, and it's fucking killing me that she's going to go in there. She's been talking about this for weeks, how she wants to march back in there and get her divorce. Prove to him that he's got no power over her. Ultimately, I know she needs to prove it to herself more than anything.

But I still hate it.

That need I have to protect her, shelter her is a raging beast in my chest, louder and stronger now that she's officially mine. Now that we're in that big bed together every night. She's absolutely everything, and it turns out she's also fucking fire in bed, and more than a little bossy. I am her willing slave, and we love every second of it. The last two months have been magic. The only dark spots are Holly's worry over her friend Evie, and still being legally tied to Brent.

Her soft hand covers mine on the wheel. "Are you ok?"

"No, I hate...this. Go home." She smiles, just like she does every time I make an effort to speak longer sentences to her.

I've been working with a speech pathologist, and turns out my case isn't as hopeless as I thought it was. My speech will probably never be anywhere close to normal. My brain damage didn't magically go away, but apparently I can make new neural pathways, whatever the fuck that means.

All I care about is being a better man for Holly. Not that she gives a single shit about how I speak. The way she holds my hand and smiles at me when we're out in public makes me feel like the luckiest man on the planet, knowing she's happy, proud even, to be with me whether I sign or speak.

If I'm honest, I'm going for me. Because I hate taking my hands off her in bed to talk to her. This way, I can have my cake, and eat her too.

Reaching out, she brushes her thumb over my eyebrow. "We'll be in and out of there in no time. Then we'll go home and snuggle up."

I'm lost imagining snuggling up with her, when her words finally penetrate. "We…I'm going…in?"

"Yes," she says with a gentle smile. "I want you with me… but I'm doing all the talking. Your job is to stand off to the side a bit and look scary. Is that ok?"

I rub my hands together gleefully and smile. "I am… scary." I know exactly how to be the menacing guy in the corner. I haven't had to do it in a while, but it'll all come back to me, I have no doubt.

She presses a laughing kiss to my lips, then exits out of the car. A growl slips out of me when she doesn't let me get her door. Her giggles chase the grump away. She's not afraid of me, not even a little bit, and I thank whatever God is up there for that.

Ransom made the same arrangements as last time, so Brent is chained to the table when I walk into the room. The cast is off, but I can see a brace on his leg. The fresh bruising and cuts on his face sends a wave of satisfaction through me. His eyes widen when he recognizes me, his Adam's apple bobbing with his nervousness. I make sure my face shows all the rage in my body when I look at him, all the painful things I want to do to him.

"Why...why are you here? I did what you asked. I've been following the rules." He stammers nervously.

I bare my teeth at him, then move aside to let Holly into the room. She's a whole fucking rainbow in this drab beige room. She looks like a fifties pin up girl. Her calendar would have been on every garage wall in the fucking country, guaranteed.

Her dress is snug on her beautiful curves, emphasizing her small waist and luscious round hips. I watch Brent as she walks in the room, and I see exactly what I knew I would. Lust, obsession, greed. He wants her so fucking bad, and seeing her here, looking so beautiful, is killing him. He masks his reaction, but not well.

Sliding a sneer over his face, he sits back in his chair, eyes trailing over her. "Haven't lost that weight, have you, Hannah? Fucking cow." He smiles meanly at her, waiting for his words to damage her, but she smiles serenely.

I, on the other hand, take a big step closer, baring my teeth at him, satisfied when he shrinks back into the chair.

Holly's shoulder brushes mine as she slides her hair back, exposing her neck. She meets my eyes and gently taps her index finger on the side, tilting her head slightly.

She knows she's got me wrapped around her finger. Not even Brent's presence would stop me from obeying that silent command. I step back, sliding in behind her, letting my hands slide around her waist as I bring my mouth to her neck, pressing a slow, reverent kiss there. Her hand comes up to cup my cheek as I nuzzle her.

"I love you," she says, her voice thick and low.

"Love you...more," I mutter, taking one last taste before letting her go, backing up one step. This is her show. The sooner she gets done, the faster I can get her home and under me.

I almost break character when I see Brent's face. He looks like he just got slapped by a twelve-inch-cock. Holly's tinkling laugh fills the room. "You stupid fuck. As you can see, I traded way up. He worships every inch of my body. So tell me, Brent, why the hell do you think your words mean anything to me?"

I fucking love it when she swears. She's been shaking off the remnants of her past, having fun trying out different swear words. Fuck is one of her favourites. I mean, how can it not be? She's surrounded by a bunch of foul-mouthed guys who use it as a verb, noun and adjective.

Brent's rage ignites as he stands, yanking on the cuffs. He howls as he puts pressure on his knee and he falls back into the chair. "I fucking own you, you cunt. You're my wife. He doesn't have any right to put his fucking hands on you. I fucking taught you better."

Spit is flying as he rages. Holly's still standing well back, watching him with a cocked head. She doesn't seem bothered in the least. She's a whole lot stronger than I am. Because I'm really fucking bothered. I'm ready to destroy him.

He winds down as he realizes that instead of looking hurt and broken by his words, she just looks bored. Lifting her hand, she studies her red manicured fingers. My request. I love watching those red nails trail over my skin, and she's more than happy to oblige.

"You done?" she asks in a bored tone.

He ignites again, but I'm not listening to a word he's saying, because my girl's turned to grin at me. She's fucking having fun. I grin back at her then slide my mean mug back on, moving back two steps to lean on the wall so they're both in profile. She's fucking got this, and I want to watch the show.

Finally he winds down, for the first time looking...lost.

"Well," Holly says, "now that you've finished your little tantrum, let's get down to business, shall we?" She pulls the yellow envelope out from under her arm. "I'm here to present you with two options, Brent. It will be up to you to choose one. Either way will end in divorce. That's non-negotiable. The only choice you have is in how poor I leave you."

Brent laughs in disbelief. "You're crazy. I already told you I'm not signing anything."

"Not signing is one option. Here's how that will go. I'll liquidate every single thing you own. The cars, the house, your investment accounts. Everything. Then, I'll go before a judge and get a divorce judgment."

"You can't fucking do that. I have to sign to divorce you and I'm not doing it." He says smugly. "And you can't fucking touch anything. Your name isn't on anything."

"You're so stupid." She mutters, her lip curling. "Of course I can divorce you. My lawyer already has the paperwork drawn up. As for the rest?" Opening up her envelope, she pulls out a stack of papers, placing most of them down one by one. "The car title, my name on it. House? My name too. Investment accounts? Yep, you guessed it. My name. I have the power to liquidate everything."

Declan's a fucking magician.

For the first time, Brent looks panicked. He drags the paperwork closer, shaking his head in denial. "This...that's not possible. You don't own a fucking thing. I made sure of it."

Holly's chuckle sends blood rushing to my groin. "Oh, Brent, of course I own everything. We're married after all. What loving husband wouldn't want his wife to be able to handle things if he were...incapacitated?" He's staring at her, wide eyed, mouth open dumbly.

She straightens, lengthening her spine until she looks at least five-foot-two. "Are you ready to hear your options now?"

He doesn't say a word, still staring at her in stupefied silence.

"Alright then, option one. You sign the divorce papers I'm holding. Then I liquidate everything; the house, the car, the investments. I put half of that money into a basic savings account for you. The rest is mine. A simple fifty-fifty split. Then, when you get out of here, in twenty-some years, you'll have a bit of money to start over with." She pauses as she studies Brent's face. "You don't like that option, huh? That's ok. Maybe you'll like option two instead. In this option, I sell everything, same as option one. But I keep all the money. Then I file for judgment and divorce you, anyway. You have five minutes to think it over."

As a red faced Brent erupts again, she comes to me, softness over a core of steel, leaning into my body, raising her face to rest her chin on my chest. "Maybe tonight, after snuggles, we invite the guys for takeout?"

Brushing my fingers through her soft waves, we make plans for the rest of the weekend. Plans to eat, plans to spend time with the people we love.

We make plans to live.

Our lives are just starting, and they're so, so good. Looking at Brent over Holly's head, I see realization dawning. He doesn't factor in her world at all anymore. He has zero influence on who she is now, and when she walks out of here today, he'll never see her again. He won't get anything from her. He has no control. No say.

She pushes off my chest with a soft kiss, then moves back to Brent. "Decision time. Are you signing the divorce papers? Or not?"

"I'll sign," he grits out, fists balled on the table.

She nods, unconcerned with his choice, and slaps the divorce papers on the table, followed by a cheap pen. I don't like the way he's looking at her, or the way he's gripping the pen.

"Careful," I warn him. His eyes flash to mine, and he swallows, loosening his grip on the pen. He scrawls his name on all the tabs sticking out of the paper, then drops the pen and papers. I push off the wall, stalking over to pick up all the paperwork, staring at him the whole time. Little pissant can't even look at me. Laughing darkly, I back up to Holly. "Anything else…to say?" I ask her.

"You know what? No," she says, surprise coloring her voice. "I had a whole thing prepared, but…I'm done. With him. With all of it."

I wrap my arm around her. "Home then." As we buzz to alert the guards we're done, I turn my head. "Tell Joker I said…hi." I say with a twisted smile and a wink. I get the satisfaction of watching his face pale as we walk out.

I avoid Holly's questioning eyes until we get into the car, then turn to her. "Ask." I mutter.

"Who is Joker?"

I shift my neck, cracking with tension, then blow out a breath. *"He's someone we trust. He makes sure that Brent doesn't get too…comfortable in there."*

"Comfortable?" she asks with an arched brow.

"Yep," I say shortly, hoping she doesn't push this. I don't really want to tell her that he makes sure Brent lives in fear inside. And pain. The kind of pain he made her suffer through. But I won't keep any secrets from her.

She laughs quietly, reaching up to pull my head down to hers. "I'm not going to ask. I don't want to talk about my ex anymore." Thank fuck.

Her hand stays on my arm the whole drive home. As we pull into the garage, she gasps, looking at her cell.

"What?"

"Evie's coming. She asked when she could come for a visit." Her voice is laced with excitement. I know how badly she's wanted her friend to come. I know someone else who's pretty fucking anxious about it.

"Tell Colt. He...arrange." Knowing him, he'll have the Jet in the air in an hour.

She's texting madly and dancing on her toes as we step into the elevator. "There. He says he'll take care of it." She squeals. "This is so amazing."

I chuckle, loving how expressive she's become. The quiet, timid woman I met on her first day of work has been shed, leaving this vibrant, amazing creature, all mine to love.

Looping an arm around her back, I lift her up and into me. "Glad. She'll be...ok. We...take...care."

Wrapping her arms around me, she smiles contentedly. "I know, love. I never doubted it. Not for a second. Now, how about we have a little...nap?" She says, wrapping her legs around me as I lift her up.

"Hell, yes." I mutter, taking her mouth. I think we'll both need a long satisfying...rest.

Thanks for reading Micah and Holly's story. Want a little more? Grab a bonus epilogue here:
https://dl.bookfunnel.com/keruof12nt
Up next is Colton and Evie's story in *Colton*.
Look for it on Amazon.

ABOUT THE AUTHOR

Jenna lives in Canada with her family, both human and furry. She's a proud adoptive and foster parent, and has a soft spot for people from hard places.

tiktok.com/jennalovesromance
facebook.com/authorjennamyles
instagram.com/authorjennamyles